THE RHINO BATTED ASIDE A CAR BETWEEN US, JUST AS I FRISBEED A MANHOLE COVER INTO HIS NECK.

He flu[illegible] ed, zappec [illegible] hit him tv[illegible] his face. H[illegible] fly experienced combat astronomy.

He chased me around like that while the police got everyone out of the immediate vicinity. Give it up for the NYPD. They might not always like it that they need guys like me to handle guys like the Rhino, but they have their priorities straight.

I led the Rhino in a circle until one of his thick legs plunged into the open manhole and he staggered.

Then I let him have it. Hard. Fast. Maybe I'm not in the Rhino's weight class, but I've torn apart buildings with my bare hands a time or two, and I didn't get the scars on my knuckles in a tragic cheese grating accident. I went to town on him, never stopping, never easing up, and the sound of my fists hitting him resembled something you'd hear played on a snare drum.

Once he was dazed, I picked up the manhole cover and finished him off with half a dozen more whacks to the top of his pointed head, and the Rhino fell over backward, the impact sending a fresh network of fractures running through the road's surface.

I bent the manhole cover more or less back into shape over one knee, nudged the unconscious Rhino's leg out of the manhole, and replaced the cover; my Aunt May taught me to clean up my messes. I checked the Rhino again, and then gave the nearest group of cops a thumbs-up.

That was when the trap sprang.

Also available from Pocket Books

Spider-Man: Down These Mean Streets
Keith R.A. DeCandido

SPIDER-MAN®
The Darkest Hours

Jim Butcher

based on the
Marvel Comic Book

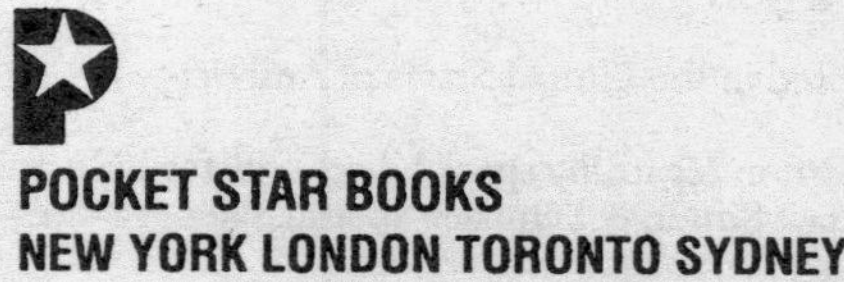

POCKET STAR BOOKS
NEW YORK LONDON TORONTO SYDNEY

An *Original* Publication of POCKET BOOKS

A Pocket Star Book published by
POCKET BOOKS, a division of Simon & Schuster, Inc.
1230 Avenue of the Americas, New York, NY 10020

This book is a work of fiction. Names, characters, places and incidents are products of the author's imagination or are used fictitiously. Any resemblance to actual events or locales or persons, living or dead, is entirely coincidental.

ISBN-13: 978-1-4165-1068-0
ISBN-10: 1-4165-1068-0

This Pocket Star Books paperback edition July 2006

10 9 8 7 6 5 4 3

POCKET STAR BOOKS and colophon are registered trademarks of Simon & Schuster, Inc.

Cover design by John Vairo, Jr; Illustration by Joe Jusko.

Manufactured in the United States of America

For information regarding special discounts for bulk purchases, please contact Simon & Schuster Special Sales at 1-800-456-6798 or business@simonandschuster.com.

Thank you, Stan. Excelsior.

Acknowledgments

A big thank you to Cam "It's Australian for Death" Banks, for giving me the issue that inspired this book. Another big thank you to April, for the most professionally well-timed Christmas present EVER. And one more for Jen Heddle, for the opportunity to play in the Marvel universe.

SPIDER-MAN®

The Darkest Hours

1

My name is Peter Parker and I'm the sort of person who occasionally gets in a little over his head.

"The most important thing," said the man in the dark hood, walking down the hall next to me, "is not to show them any fear. If you hesitate, or look like you don't know what you're doing, even for a second, they'll sense the weakness. They'll eat you alive."

"No fear," I said. "No getting eaten. Check."

"I'm serious. You're outnumbered. They're faster, most of them are stronger, they can run you into the ground, and if you're going to keep it under control, you're going to have to win the battle here." He touched a finger to his forehead. "You get me?"

"Mind war," I said. "Wax on. Wax off."

The man in the dark hood stopped, frowned at me, and said, "You aren't taking this seriously."

"People always think that about me," I said. "I'm not sure why."

"See, that's what I mean," Coach Kyle said. He tucked his hands into the pockets of his workout jacket and shook his head. "You go joking around with them like that, and that's it. You've lost control."

"It's a basketball practice," I said. "Not a prison riot."

Coach Kyle was about six feet tall, with a slender build. Dark skin, and dark hair which apparently hadn't started to go gray, though he had to have been in his late forties. He wore thick glasses with black plastic Marine-issue, birth-control rims. He'd been a Hoosier, starting guard, back in the day. He hadn't made the cut to the pros. "I see," he said with a snort. "You're upset because you were the one who got stuck with running the team."

"Well," I hedged, "I wasn't much for sports when I was in school."

"This was settled at last week's faculty meeting," he told me cheerfully. "If you hadn't been the last one to arrive at *this* meeting, you'd be halfway home by now."

"I know." I sighed.

"Guess you had something more important come up?"

I'd been crawling around about two hundred and fifty berjillion freight-train-sized shipping containers at the piers, looking for the one the mob was using to ship out illegal immigrants for sale on the slave market. Officially speaking, they weren't people, since they hadn't filled out the right paperwork and learned the secret American handshake from the

INS. Unofficially speaking, scum who target people who can't defend themselves incite me to creative outrage. By the time I had the last of them webbed to the side of their slave container in the shape of the word "LOSERS" I'd been five minutes late to the faculty meeting already.

But that's not the kind of thing you can use as an excuse.

"The dog ate my homework," I said instead.

Coach Kyle shook his head, grinning, and we stopped outside the door to the gym. "Look. Your big worry is the tallest kid there. Samuel. Best strong center I ever had, and he could go all the way. Problem is he knows it, and he doesn't play well with others."

"The fiend," I said. "This is a job for Superman."

Coach Kyle sighed. "Peter. Samuel's mom works three jobs to make enough to feed him and his three little brothers and sisters. Their block isn't such a good one. He had an older brother who was a gangbanger—that is, until he got stabbed to death a few years back. That's when Samuel took over as man of the house. Looking out for the little ones."

I sighed, and dialed down my snark projector. "Go on."

"Boy's got a real chance of turning into a top-rate athlete, and if he can make it into a college, he can help out his whole family. Problem is that he's a good kid, at the core."

"That's a problem?"

"Yes. Because if he doesn't get himself under control and make it into a good school, he'll graduate and try to support his family."

I nodded my head, getting it. "And wind up in the same place as his brother."

Coach Kyle nodded. "He's big, tough, and can make good money in a gang. And it isn't as if he's going to have employers kicking down his door to get to him."

"I see." I glanced through the narrow window in the door to the gym. A lot of young people were running and screaming. Shoes squeaked on the floor. Many, many basketballs thudded onto the court in a rhythm that could only have been duplicated by a drunken, clog-dancing centipede. "What do you need me to do?"

"Right now, the kid is his own worst enemy. If he doesn't learn to work with his team, to lead on the court, no university will even look at him."

"But he hasn't realized that yet," I guessed.

Coach Kyle nodded. "I just want you to understand, Peter. Coaching the basketball team isn't just a chore that needs doing. It isn't only a game. The team might be this kid's only chance. Same goes for the others, to a lesser degree. The team keeps them off the streets, out of some of the trouble."

I watched the kids playing and nodded. "I hear you. I'll take it seriously." I met his eyes and said, "Promise."

"Thank you," Coach Kyle said, and offered me

his hand. "To tell you the truth, I was hoping you'd be the one to keep an eye on them for me. I see you with some of the other kids. You do good work."

I traded grips with him and grinned. "Well, I'm so childish myself."

"Heh," he said. "Maybe I should come in with you for a minute. Just to help you get started."

"It's okay," I said. "I can handle it myself. Have fun getting lasered in the eyes."

He tapped his ugly glasses with one finger. "See you next week," he said. Then he headed out.

I sighed and opened the door to the gymnasium. After all, it wasn't like I'd never been outnumbered before. I'd gone up against the Sinister Six versions one through fifty or sixty, and the Sinister Syndicate, and those bozos in the Wrecking Crew, and . . . the X-Men? No, that couldn't be right. I hadn't ever taken on the X-Men and thrashed them, I was sure. But those others, yes. And if I could handle them, surely I could handle a bunch of kids playing basketball.

Which only goes to show that just because I happen to be a fairly sharp scientist, the Amazing Spider-Man, and a snappy dancer, I don't know everything.

2

There's something about gymnasiums. Maybe it's the fluorescent lighting. Maybe it's the acoustics, the way that squeaking shoes echo off the walls, the way thudding basketballs sound on the floor, or rattling against the rim, or the way "bricks" slam into the backboard and make the whole thing shudder. Maybe it's the smell—one part sweat and friction-warmed rubber to many parts disinfectant and floor polish. I'm not sure.

All I know is that every time I walk into a gymnasium, I get hit with a rush of memories from my own days of high school. Some people call that phenomenon "nostalgia." I call it "nausea."

Unless, of course, nostalgia is *supposed* to make you feel abruptly shunned, unpopular, and inadequate—in which case, I suppose that gymnasiums are nostalgic as all get-out for me.

The gym was full of young men in shorts, athletic socks and shoes, T-shirts and tank tops. The color schemes and fabrics employed were slightly different, but other than that they looked pretty much exactly like the b-ball players had when I'd gone to school here. That made me feel pretty nostalgic, too.

I hadn't had a very easy time of it in high school, particularly with the sports-oriented crowd who hung around in the gym. A radioactive spider bite had more than taken care of any physical inadequacies—but my memories of that time in my life weren't about fact. They were about old feelings that still had power.

Fine, so I had one or two lingering issues from high school. Who doesn't?

I also had Coach Kyle's whistle, his clipboard, and his practice schedule, complete with warm-ups, drills, and all the other activities which constituted a training session. Plus, I was an adult now. A teacher. I had the wisdom and experience of age—well, compared to a teenager, anyway. I was the one with the authority, the one who would command respect. I was not a big-brained high school nerd anymore. No one was going to give me a wedgie or a swirlie or stuff me into a locker.

Even if most of them *did* seem to be awfully tall.

I shook my head and grinned at my reaction to all those memories. These days, I'd have to work hard to be sure not to hurt any of them if they tried it, but the emotional reflexes were still there. You can take the nerd out of the school . . .

I stepped out onto the court and blew a short,

loud blast on the whistle and rotated my hand in the air above my head. "Bring it in, guys, right here."

A couple of the kids immediately turned and shuffled over to me. Most of them never even slowed down, being involved in a game of seven-on-one against Samuel.

They probably just hadn't heard the whistle. Yeah, right. No fear, Peter. No fear.

I blew the whistle again, louder, and for as long as I could keep blowing, maybe twenty or thirty seconds of pure, warbling authority. Most of the stragglers came over after ten seconds or so. Samuel, who was big enough and strong enough to dunk, slammed the ball in one more time after everyone else had come over, recovered it, and took a three-point shot for nothing but net. He finally turned to walk over about half a second before I ran out of wind.

"Afternoon, guys," I said. "I'm Mister Parker, and I'm a science teacher, in case you didn't know. I'm going to be standing in for Coach Kyle for a few days, until he's back on the job. The coach has left me a schedule of what he wants you to be doing so—"

"Shoot," said Samuel, with a disgusted exhale. He didn't say "shoot," exactly, but I wanted to give him the benefit of the doubt.

"You have a question, Mister . . ." I checked Kyle's clipboard. "Larkin?"

"Yeah," he said. "Where you played ball?" His expression was sullen and skeptical. The kid was ridiculously tall, and not just for his age. He would have been ridiculously tall at any age.

"I haven't lately," I told him.

"College?" he asked.

"No."

"High school?"

"No," I said.

"Shoot," he didn't say. "You don't know nothing about ball."

I didn't let it rattle me. "Those who can't do, teach," I told him. Then I held up the clipboard. "But I figure Coach Kyle knows what he's doing, so we're just going to stick to his plan, starting with a ten-minute warm-up run and stretching." I tucked the clipboard under my arm and tried to pretend I was a drill sergeant. I blew the whistle once, clapped my hands, and said, "Let's go!"

And they went. Slowly, reluctantly, and Samuel was still standing there glowering at me when the first of his teammates had finished the first lap, but then he shambled off to join them. Good-looking kid, very strong features, skin almost as dark as his eyes, and his voice held authority well. His teammates would look up to him, literally and figuratively.

Once the run was finished, I told Samuel to lead the team through stretching, which he did without batting an eye. He'd done it for Coach Kyle before, I supposed. I could see what the coach meant when he said the kid was a natural leader.

When the stretching was done, Kyle's plan called

for passing drills, and that was when I saw what the coach meant about Samuel's bad attitude.

The team groaned when I said "Drill," and Samuel shook his head. "Screw that. That isn't what the team needs right now." He looked around. "Okay, we'll go half court twice. Starters against me on this end; Darnell, you take the rest to that end and split into four-on-four."

The kids went into motion at once.

Good thing I had that whistle. I blew another blast on it and called, "The coach wants you running passing drills. You are darn well going to run passing drills."

"Hey," Samuel said, "shredded wheat." He shot me a hard, swift pass that should have bounced the ball off the back of my head—but my spider sense, that inexplicable yet extremely cool sixth sense that warns me of danger, alerted me to the incoming basketball. I turned and caught it flat against my right hand, then gripped onto it with the old wall-crawling cling, so that it looked like I had caught it and perfectly palmed it to boot.

Samuel hadn't expected that—but it didn't faze him, either. "You're pretty fast for an old man."

"Thanks," I said, and flicked the ball back at him, making sure I didn't break his ribs with it out of annoyance. "Now line them up and run the drills."

"Screw you, Mister Science," Samuel said. "The team needs real practice."

I frowned at him. "The coach—"

"Ain't here," Samuel said, his tone harsh. "He's off on vacation, ain't he."

"Doesn't matter," I said. "We're running drills. We've got twenty minutes of full-court five-on-five at the end of the day."

The team groaned, and Samuel grinned at me. "Full-court five-on-five? Might as well send everyone else home and let me practice shots. 'Cause that's all that is gonna happen. My way, everybody gets to play."

"You aren't the coach," I said.

He shrugged. "Neither are you."

"I am today."

"Tell you what, Mister Science," Samuel said. "You come out here on the floor with me. We can go half-court one-on-one to five. You get even one past me before I hit five, or if I foul you even once, we'll do it your way. Otherwise you let someone who knows what he's doing run the practice."

I was tempted, but only for a second. Hammering my point through the kid's thick skull wasn't going to do him any good. "We're going to practice," I told him. "If you don't want to practice, that's cool. You can leave whenever you like."

Samuel just stared at me. Then he burst out into a rolling belly laugh, and most of the other kids followed along.

Clearly, the whistle's power was finite. The clipboard's additional failure was sadly disappointing. I was on the verge of trying my luck with pure alpha-male bellowing, when someone behind me cleared her throat, a prim little sound.

I turned to find my professional nemesis standing behind me.

Julie from Administration.

She was fortyish, fake blonde, slender as a reed, and wore a lavender business suit. She had a diamond the size of a baby elephant on her wedding ring, a thick pink clipboard in her hands, and was entirely innocent of original thought.

"Excuse me, Coach Kyle," Julie said without looking up. "I needed you to sign this report."

"I'm not Coach Kyle," I said. "Coach Kyle is a little taller than me. And he's black."

She looked up from the papers on her board and frowned severely. "Coach Kyle coaches the basketball team."

"Hence 'Coach.' Yes."

"Then what are you doing here?"

"He's on a medical leave."

Julie frowned. "I did not see the paperwork for it."

I sighed. "No paperwork? Clearly, Western civilization is on the brink of collapse."

She frowned at me. "What?"

Insulting Julie from Administration is like throwing rocks into the ocean. There's a little ripple, and the ocean never even notices it happened. "I'm standing in for him," I said. "Maybe I can help you."

Behind me, the kids had broken up into two half-court games as soon as my back was turned, just as I told them not to do. Gee, thanks, Julie.

"It's about Mister Larkin," she said. "His immunization record still hasn't been completed, and if he doesn't get his shots we'll have to suspend him until he does. I need you to sign here to show that you've been notified."

"That happens," I allowed, as she offered me the pink clipboard. I signed by the X. "How long does he have to get the shots?"

"Until Monday," she said. "If he doesn't have them Monday morning, he'll have to go into suspension."

I blinked at her. "It's Friday," I said.

"And I'm working late," Julie replied. "Because unlike *some* people who work at this school, I find it important to put in extra effort, instead of calling in sick every six-point-two-nine days. Like some people I could mention."

"Oh," I said, in a tone of sudden revelation. "You're talking about me."

Grrr.

"Yes," she said. "I only hope your attitude doesn't affect Coach Kyle's job performance."

Grrr.

"You missed my point, though," I said as politely as I could. "There's no way to get him into a city clinic before Monday morning. They aren't open before then."

"Well," she said, exasperated, "his parents will just have to convince their family doctor to help."

"Parent," I said. "Single parent, working three jobs to support the family. I promise you, they use the clinic, not a private practitioner."

She sniffed. "Then they should have gotten him to the clinic sooner."

I gritted my teeth. "Have you notified him or his mother?"

"No," she said, as if I was a moron. "I required the signature of one of his teachers before I could run through all the forms, and you're the only one left in the building. You didn't sign for it until just now. Which makes it all your fault, really."

The ironic thing is that Julie is an enormous Spider-Man fangirl.

Deep breaths, Parker. Nice, deep breaths.

"But he didn't know he needed the shots." I blinked. "Still *doesn't* know, in fact."

"Letters were sent to all students' parents last July," she said firmly. "He should have had them before school even started."

"But you're only telling him *today*? When it's already too *late*?"

"It was a low organizational priority," she said. "More pressing matters have kept administration"—which was always Julie plus someone who was going to quit within two weeks—"far too busy to waste time doing Mister Larkin's parents' job."

I rubbed at my forehead. "Look, Julie. If this kid gets suspended, he'll be off the team—and it would make it more difficult for him to be accepted into a university."

Julie gave me a bewildered stare, as though I'd begun speaking in tongues. "University?"

I wondered if I'd get strange looks if I threw myself down and started chewing at the floorboards. "The point is that if he gets suspended over something like this, it's going to be all kinds of bad for him."

She waved a hand. "Well. Perhaps Mr. and Mrs. Larkin will be more careful about following immunization procedures next time," she said, and jerked her clipboard back. She tore off a pink copy of the form I'd signed and said, "This is for Mr. and Mrs. Larkin."

"Julie," I said. "Have a heart here. The kid needs some help."

She sniffed in contempt at the very idea. "I am only following the policy, rules, and law of the New York educational system."

"Right. Just following orders," I said.

"Precisely." She turned on a heel and goose-stepped out of the gymnasium.

My God, the woman was pure evil.

I glanced back at Samuel, who was currently playing four-on-one and winning handily. He wasn't talking smack to them, though. He was focused, intent, moving in his natural element. The kid was a stiff-necked loudmouth, insulting, arrogant, and he reminded me way too much of people who beat me up for lunch money when I'd been in school.

But no one deserved Julie from Administration.

And since Coach Kyle wasn't around to do it, this looked like a job for Spider-Man.

3

"**TALK ABOUT DISASTERS**," I said, as Mary Jane came through the front door of our apartment. "It's like they could smell the high school nerd on my clothes. Mister Science. They called me Mister Science. And shredded wheat. Just did whatever they wanted. And the worst one, this Samuel kid, he challenged me to a round of one-on-one. Told me if I won, they would run the practice my way."

I might have sounded just a bit sulky. My wife got the look she gets when she's trying really hard to keep from laughing at me. "The basketball practice?" she asked.

"Yes." I scowled down at the stack of papers I was grading. "It was like herding manic-obsessive cats. I can't remember the last time I felt so stupid."

"Why didn't you play the kid?" MJ asked. "I mean, you could have beaten him, right?"

"Oh, sure. If I didn't mind the kids finding out that Mister Science has a two-hundred-and-eighty-inch vertical leap." I put my pen down and set the papers aside. "Besides. That isn't what the kid needs. I'm supposed to teach him to be a team player. If the first thing I do is go mano-a-mano with him to prove who's best, it might undermine that."

"Just a bit," Mary Jane conceded. "I thought you were going to go to the faculty meeting early so you wouldn't get saddled with coaching the team."

"I was," I glowered. "Something came up."

"Who could have foreseen *that,*" she said tartly, and walked into our little kitchen and set down the brown grocery bag she was holding. If you'd asked my opinion when I was Samuel's age, I'd have said she looked like a million bucks. Since then, though, there's been inflation, and now I figure she looks like at least a billion. Back then, if you'd asked me to describe her, I would have handed you a laundry list of girl parts. Luscious red hair, bewitching green eyes, flawless pale skin, long and lovely legs—and I would have blushed before I got to other, ah, salient features.

And to be totally honest, I still saw all of that. Somedays more than others, but hey, I'm a man. I sometimes think primitive and politically incorrect thoughts about my wife. I'm allowed. I think it was in the vows somewhere.

But as we grew closer, I saw other things when I looked at her. I saw the woman who was willing to stand beside me through thick and thin, despite a mountain of reasons not to, despite the fact that just being a part of my life sometimes put her in danger. I saw the woman who was willing to spend many nights—far too many nights—alone while I ran around town doing everything a spider can, and leaving her to wonder when I'd be back.

Or even if I'd be back.

I might have been able to juggle compact cars, but I wasn't strong enough to do what she did, to be who she was. She was the one who had faith in me, the one who believed in me, the one who I knew, absolutely *knew,* would always listen, always help, always care. The longer I looked at her, the more beautiful she got, and the more thoroughly I understood how insanely lucky I was to have her beside me.

It was enough to disintegrate my frustration, at least for the moment. Honestly, if a man gets to come home to a woman like that at the end of the day, how bad can things be?

"Sorry, MJ." I sighed. "I ambushed you the second you walked in the door."

She arched a brow and teased, "I'll let it go. This time."

I started helping her with the bag. Not because she needed the help, but because it gave me a great excuse to stand behind her and reach both arms around her to handle the groceries. I liked the way her hair smelled.

She leaned back against me for a second, then gave me a playful nudge with one hip. "You really want to make it up to me? Cook."

I lifted both eyebrows. I cook almost as well as Ben Grimm embroiders, and MJ knew it. "Living dangerously tonight, are we?"

"Statistically speaking, you're bound to make something that tastes good eventually," she said. She took a frozen pizza out of the bag and passed it over her shoulder to me. "Back in a minute, master chef."

"Bork, bork, bork," I confirmed. She slipped off to the bedroom. I flipped the pizza box and went over the instructions. Looked simple enough. I followed the directions carefully while Mary Jane ran the shower.

She came back out in time to see me crouched on the ceiling, trying to get the stupid smoke alarm to shut up. She got that I'm-not-laughing face again and went to the oven to see what she could salvage.

I finally pulled the battery out of the smoke alarm and opened a window. "Hey," I said. "Are you all right?"

"Of course," she said. "Why would you ask that?"

"My husband sense is tingling." I frowned at her, then hit the side of my head with the heel of my hand. "The audition. It was this morning, right?"

She hesitated for a second, and then nodded.

Oh, right, I got it. She'd been bothered by something about it, but I'd been quicker on the draw in the gunfight at the co-dependent corral, and she didn't want to lay it on me when I'd been stressed myself.

Like I said. I'm a lucky guy.

"How'd it go?" I asked her. We got dinner (such as it was), a couple of drinks, and sat down on the couch together.

"That's the problem," she said quietly. "I got the part."

I lifted my eyebrows. "What? That's fantastic! Who'd they cast you as?"

"Lady Macbeth."

"Well of course they did!" I burbled at her. "You've got red hair. Redheads are naturally evil. Did I mention that this was fantastic?"

"It isn't, Pete."

"It isn't?"

"It isn't."

"But I thought you said it was a serious company. That working with them would give you some major street cred for acting."

"Yes."

"Oh," I said. I blew on my slice of pizza. "Why?"

"Because it's showing in Atlantic City."

"Ugh. Jersey."

She rolled her eyes. "The point being that I'm going to have to get over there several times every week."

"No problem," I said. "We can swing the train fare, I'm sure."

"That's just it," Mary Jane said. "I can't trust the train, Peter. Too many things could happen. If it's delayed, if I'm late, if it takes off a couple of minutes early, and I don't show up, that's it: I can kiss my career good-bye. I've got to have a car."

I scratched my head, frowning. "Does it have to be a nice car?"

"It just has to work," she said.

"Well," I said. "It's more expensive, but we might be able to—"

"I bought a car, too."

I looked down at the suddenly too-expensive pizza on my plate. MJ's career as a model had been high-profile, but not necessarily high-paying. I was a part-time science teacher, and the paycheck isn't nearly as glamorous and enormous as everyone thinks. We weren't exactly dirt poor, but it costs a lot of money to own and operate a car in New York City. "Oh."

"It didn't cost very much. It's old, but it goes when you push the pedal."

"That's good," I said. "Um. Maybe you should have talked to me first?"

"There wasn't time," she said apologetically. "I had to get it today because rehearsal starts Monday afternoon, and I still had to take my test and get my license and . . ." She broke off, swallowing, and I swear, she almost started crying. "And I failed the stupid *test,*" she said. "I mean, I thought it would be simple, but I failed it. I've got a chance to finally show people that I can really act, that I'm not some stupid magazine bimbo who can't do anything but look good in a bikini in movies about Lobsterman, and I failed the stupid driver's test."

"Hey," I said quietly, setting dinner aside so that I could put my arms around her. "Come here."

She leaned against me and let out a miserable little sigh. "It was humiliating."

I tightened my arms around her. "But you can take the test again tomorrow, right?"

She nodded. "But Pete, I . . . I got nothing on the test. I mean, nothing. Zero. If there'd been a score lower than zero I would have gotten that, but they stop at zero. It isn't fair. I've lived my whole life in New York. I'm not *supposed* to know how to drive."

I wanted to laugh, but I didn't. "It isn't a big deal," I told her. "Look, I can help you out, you'll take the test tomorrow, get your license, and then we can plan your outfit for the Academy Awards."

"Really?" she said, looking up at me, those devastating green eyes wide and uncertain. "You can help?"

"Trust me," I told her. "I spent years as a full-time underclassman while spending my nights creeping around rooftops and alleys looking for trouble. If there's one thing I know, it's how to pass a test you haven't had much time to study for."

She laughed a little and laid her head against my chest. "Thank you." She shook her head. "I didn't mean to go all neurotic on you."

"See there? You're becoming more like the great actresses by the minute." I kissed her hair. "Anytime."

I heard a low, faint rumbling sound, and glanced out the window. I didn't see anything, but it took only sixty seconds for the sirens to start howling—

police as well as fire department, a dozen of them at least.

"Trouble?" Mary Jane asked quietly.

I grabbed the remote and clicked on the TV. Not a minute later, my regular programming was interrupted by a news broadcast. The news crew camera was still jiggling as the cameraman stumbled out of a van, but I got enough to see what was going on: a panic, hundreds of people running, the bright light and hollow boom of an explosion and clouds of black smoke rising up in the background—Times Square.

"Trouble," Mary Jane said.

"Looks that way," I said. "Sorry."

"Don't be." She looked up and laid a swift kiss against my lips. "All right, tiger. Get a move on." She rose and gave me a wicked little smile. "I'll keep something warm for you."

4

Ah, New York on an autumn evening. Summer's heat had passed by, and let me tell you, there's nothing quite as miserable as webbing around the old town when it's so hot that my suit is soaked with sweat. It clings to and abrades things which ought not be clung to or abraded. My enhanced physique runs a little hotter than your average human being's, too—the price of having muscles that can bench-press more than any two X-Men, and reflexes that make Speedy González look like Aesop's Tortoise.

Autumn, though, is different. Once the sun starts setting and the air cools off, it feels just about perfect. There's usually a brisk wind that somehow smells of wood smoke, a golden scent, somewhere on the far side of eau de New York, that heralds the end of summer. Sometimes, I can stand on one of the many lofty rooftops around town, watching the moon track across the sky, listening to the passage of geese heading down to Florida, and letting the traffic-sounds, the ship-sounds, the plane-sounds of New York provide the musical score. Nights like that have their own kind of delicate beauty, where the whole city feels like one enormous, quietly aware entity, and though the sun was still providing a lingering autumn twilight, tonight was going to be one of those times.

Assuming, of course, that whatever had caused a third column of smoke to start rolling up through the evening air didn't spoil it for me.

I was making pretty good time through Manhattan when that twitchy little sensation of intuition I'd dubbed my "spider sense" (because I was fifteen at the time) let me know that I wasn't alone.

I managed to catch a blur in the corner of my vision, moving along a window ledge on a building parallel to my course, above and behind me, staying in the shadows cast by the buildings in the fading light, and rapidly catching up with me. If I continued in my current line of motion, my pursuer would be in a perfect position to ambush me as I crossed the next street—one of those midair impacts, when I was at the top of a ballistic arch and least able to get out of the way. The Vulture loved those, and so had the various Goblins. If I had a chiropractor, he'd love them too, on account of every one of them would make him money.

Me, I'm not so fond of them.

So at the very last second, just as I would have flung myself into the air, I turned around instead, hit the building my chaser was on with a webline, and hung on. The line stretched and recoiled, flinging me back toward the would-be attacker, and I added all of my own oomph to it and shot at my pursuer like a cannonball.

Whoever it was reacted swiftly. He immediately changed direction, leaping off a ledge and soaring through the air by swinging on some kind of matte black, nonreflective cable to a lower rooftop. He hit the roof rolling, and I had to flick out a strand of webbing to reverse direction again. He might have been fast, but not *that* fast. I hit him around the waist with a flying tackle and pinned him against the roof.

At which point I realized that I had pinned *her* to the roof.

"Well," drawled a languidly amused woman's voice. "This evening is turning out even better than I thought it would."

"Felicia?" I said.

She turned her head enough to let me see the smirk on her mouth and said, "This is hardly a dignified position for a married man. What if some nerdy freelance photographer for the *Bugle* came along and took our picture? Can you imagine the headlines? *Two Swingers Caught in Flagrante Delicto on Roof.*"

"I doubt that the Human Flattop would use that term," I replied. But she had a point. I read somewhere that full-body pins are not a proper greeting for an ex-girlfriend from a married man, so I got off of her in a hurry.

Felicia Hardy rolled over, leaned back on her elbows, and regarded me for a moment from her lounging position. She'd given her Black Cat costume a minor makeover, losing the white puffs at her calves and wrists. Maybe they'd been harder to find since *Cats* closed. She still wore the catsuit, and still filled it out in a way that could cause mass whiplash, but this new suit was made out of some supple, odd-looking black material I'd never seen before, and it managed to give me the impression that it was some kind of body armor. Her hair was shorter than the last time I'd seen her, and she wore a black visor that covered her eyes, until she tipped it down enough to give me a wicked-eyed smile over the visor's rim, and extended her arm up to me. "Give me a hand?"

Part of me was happy to see Felicia again. There aren't a lot of people I'm comfortable fighting beside, but Felicia is one of them. Admittedly, we'd gotten off to a bad start, since she had been a professional burglar at the time, but eventually the bad first impressions became spilt milk under the bridge. She'd reformed—more or less. And she'd helped me out a couple of times when I really needed it.

Plus, she had been hot. Really, really hot. I like to think of myself as a decent guy, most of the time, but what man wouldn't enjoy his work more partnered up with a looker like Felicia?

We became involved during that time, and the romance had been . . . eventful. Tempestuous. On occasion, it had resembled pay-per-view professional wrestling. It had ended amicably, more or less, but

I'd still been worried that she might go back to what she was doing before she met me. Apparently, however, her reform had been sincere, and she was, as far as I knew, on the straight and narrow these days.

I pulled her to her feet. "What are you doing here?"

"I needed to talk to you," she said, rising. She put her hands on the small of her back, winced a little, and stretched again. "Mmmm. I always did like it when you played rough, Spider."

"I could have killed you," I said. "What do you think you're doing, stalking me like that?"

"I was going to knock on your door," she said, "but I saw you leaving. I had to get your attention somehow."

"You know what gets my attention?" I said. "When someone shouts my name and says that they want to talk to me. One time, they even used this magical device called a telephone."

"You don't get it—," she began.

Another enormous crunching, crashing sound from Times Square, only a few hundred yards off, interrupted her.

"No, *you* don't get it," I said, and turned to go. "I don't have time for this right now, Cat. I'm on the clock."

"Wait," she said. "You can't!"

I ground my teeth under the mask and paused, webline in hand. "Five words or less, why not?"

Felicia put her hands on her hips, eyes narrowed, and said, holding up a finger with each word, "It is a trap." She considered and stuck out her thumb, too. "Dummy."

"A trap?" I said. "Whose?"

"That's just it," she said. "I'm not sure."

"You just know it's a trap."

"If you'll give me a second to explain—"

Down the street, a police car tumbled across the road, end over end, bouncing along like a child's toy, lights flashing. It knocked over a fire hydrant, sending a cascade of water into the air, then crashed through the front window of an adult bookstore.

"You've got to admit," she said. "It isn't hard for someone to get a rise out of you if they want to draw you out. That's what Morlun did."

I had been about to swing off, but her words stopped me cold.

Morlun.

Ugh.

Morlun had been . . . bad. A creature, some kind of entity that fed upon the life energy of vessels of totemistic power. That's mystic gobbledygook for superheroes who draw their powers from—or at least compare them to—some kind of animal. Say, for example, your friendly, neighborhood Spider-Man. He was an ultra-ancient being who only looked human, who devoured the life energy of his victims to sustain his own apparent immortality.

Morlun had asked me to dinner, and not as a guest. The invitation had come in the form of a rampage in the fine tradition begun by the Hulk. I sent him a two-fisted RSVP. As brawls go, it had been a long one. Days long. I can't remember anyone who's made me feel more physical pain, offhand. Morlun was strong. Really, really strong. And he took everything I could throw at him without blinking. Or talking. Which cheesed me off. How am I supposed to uphold snappy superhero banter when the other guy won't carry his end of the conversational load?

He almost killed me. God help me, I almost let him. I almost gave up. I'd just been that hurt, that tired—that alone. Morlun showed up in my nightmares for a good long while afterward, temporarily supplanting my subconscious's favorite bogeyman, Norman Osborne.

I came out on top in the end, but only by injecting myself with material from the core of a nuclear reactor, so that when he tried to eat me, Morlun got a big old mouthful of gamma-ray energy instead. After that, Morlun's day went downhill pretty fast.

Here's the kicker, though.

I hadn't told anyone about Morlun.

Not Aunt May.

Not Mary Jane.

Nobody.

As far as I knew, the only one, other than me, who had known what was going on was a guy named Ezekiel. A man who had, somehow, acquired powers remarkably similar to my own, and who had tried to warn me about Morlun—and who had eventually helped me defeat him, nearly at the cost of his own life.

So how had Felicia found out about Morlun?

"Hey," I said. "How did you find out about Morlun?"

"I've turned over a new leaf, remember?" she said. "I'm a security consultant and investigator now. I investigate things, and some of what I turned up indicates that there's someone here to call you out." She slipped off the visor and met my eyes, her expression worried. "The details will take me a while to give you, but the short version is that you're in danger, Peter."

An ambulance siren added its wail to that of the police cars and fire trucks. I could see people running from the area, underneath one of the big flashing signs for the New Amsterdam Theater, where they were performing *The Lion King.*

"No," I said. "They're the ones who are in danger."

"But I already told you—"

"It's a trap, I know. But the longer I stay away from it, the more noise whoever is over there is going to make. I'm going."

"Don't," she said, touching my arm. "Don't be stupid. It's not as if there aren't a couple of other folks around New York who will show up to a disturbance this public."

"No," I said. "I can't let other people do my chores for me. If I wait for the FF to show up, or the Avengers, he'll scamper and do it all again another day." I felt myself getting a little angry, talking about it.

Like I said: I have issues with people who pick on those who can't protect themselves.

"I'm taking this guy down," I said. "Thank you for the warning. But I'm going."

Felicia didn't look happy with me as she jammed the visor back onto her face. "You stiff-necked . . ." She shook her head. "Go on. Go. Be careful."

I nodded once, dove off on my line, and flung myself from building to building down the street. I swung around the last corner, rapidly gathering momentum, and found a scene of pure chaos. Emergency units were trying to cordon off the square. Fires burned. Smoke rolled. Several police cars had been flattened—literally *flattened*—by blows of superhuman strength. Many of the lights were either out or flickering wildly, giving the place that crazed, techno dance club look. Broken glass lay everywhere. Car alarms and fire alarms beeped and wooped and ah-oohgahed. The air stank of burning plastic and motor oil. People shouted, screamed, and ran.

"It's like the mayor's office in an election year," I muttered.

At the center of it all, in the thick plume of black smoke, stood a single, hulking figure. I altered my course, spat a new line from my web shooters, and swung down to give whoever it was a big old double-heeled mule-kick greeting on behalf of the citizens of New York.

Did I mention that I have a tendency to get in over my head?

5

I HOLLERED, "BOOT TO THE HEAD!" as I swung through the black smoke and slammed into Newtonian physics.

Newton. Isaac Newton. You remember him. White wig, apple tree. Played poker with Einstein, Hawking, and Data in an episode of *Star Trek.* You can't really say he discovered the laws of physics, since they'd pretty much been there already, but he was one of the first to actually stop and look at them and get them written down. And while the next several centuries of scientific advancement proved that in certain circumstances he had dropped the ball—*bah-dump-bump-ching!*—he did a good enough job that it took the computer revolution to knock him off his pedestal a bit. Even then, pretty much anywhere on the planet (for example, Times Square), for pretty much everything you might bump into (for example, rampaging bad guys), Newton's material is a darned good rule of thumb.

One of them applied here: For every action, there is an equal and opposite reaction.

I came swooping down and delivered my double-heeled kick all right. Right into the Rhino's bread-basket.

Granted, I'm smarter than most, and I always have something pithy to say, and I can just be a gosh-darned wonderful person when I put my mind to it. But all of that fits into a pretty small package. I'm not big. I'm not heavily built. I weigh about one sixty-five, soaking wet.

The Rhino, now, he's built like a brick gulag. He's huge. Huge tall, huge across, huge through. Not only that, but whatever process was used to ramp up his strength, it mucked about with his cellular makeup somehow, because he weighs on the heavy side of eight hundred pounds. I'm sure some of that can be accounted for by the stupid Rhino hat he wears, but bottom line, he's an enormous gray block of muscle and bone, and even with my oh-so-stylish spider strength, I wasn't really set for this kick. Super strength is all well and good, but if you don't have yourself braced—like if you're swinging on a webline—you're at Sir Isaac's mercy.

But my Aunt May always taught me to make the best of things, so I let him have it.

The kick took the Rhino off guard, even with me shouting and all. Granted, he isn't exactly the shiniest nail in the box, and there were all kinds of bright colors and sounds around to distract him, but still. I think I might have caught him on the inhale, because the kick made his face turn green and threw him fifteen or twenty feet back and smashed him into a storefront.

Of course, the same amount of force came back at me. And since the Rhino weighs four or five or six times as much as me, I got flung a lot farther than fifteen or twenty feet. Then again, I'm the Amazing Spider-Man. Flying around in the air is what I do. So I hit a streetlamp with a webline as I flew by, hung on to be whipped around in a circle twice, arched up into a tumble, and came down in a crouch on top of an abandoned taxi about sixty feet away—where I could see the Rhino, enjoyed a clear field of view around me, and had plenty of room to move.

Felicia is no dummy. If she said that this was a trap, she probably had a good reason to think so.

"Well, well, well," I said. "The Rhino. Again. I thought maybe poachers might have shot you and ground you up to sell as medicine on the Chinese black market by now. They're doing that for all the other rhinos."

The Rhino lumbered back to his feet. Lots and lots of broken glass slid off of his suit and tinkled to the concrete. Rhino wore his usual—the thick gray bodysuit made out of some kind of advanced ballistic materials that I'd heard could blow off armor piercing rounds from antitank guns. I can understand the insecurity. I mean, when your own skin can only handle heavy explosive rounds, you want a little insurance in case some enterprising mugger comes along packing discarding sabot shells.

He had on the hat, too. It was made of the same heavy material, encasing his head in armor and leaving only a comparatively small, square area of his small, square face vulnerable. The horn on it was heavy, tough, and sharp enough that when he put his weight and muscle behind it, he could blow through brick walls like they were linen curtains. All of which is imposing.

But at the end of the day, the hat still looks like a Rhino's head. Good Lord, I keep hoping the NFL will approve a start-up team called "The Rhinos," because then he'll actually look like a comedic team mascot. I wondered if the Chicken could take him.

"Spider-Man," growled the Rhino, presumably after taking a few moments to collect his thought. His consonants were clipped, the vowels guttural, Slavic, though if he really was a Russian, he spoke English pretty well. "We meet again."

"Rhino." I sighed. "You have got to get some better writers for these high-profile events. How are people ever going to take you seriously if you go around spouting that kind of hackneyed dialogue? What you do reflects on me, too, you know. I've got an image to think about."

His face flushed and started turning purple. It's almost too easy to handle this guy. "It will be pleasure to squash you, little bug man," he growled. He seized a mailbox, ripped it up out of the concrete, and threw it at my head.

I moved my head, webbed the mailbox as it went by, and slung it around in a circle, using the elastic strength of the webline to send it back at him twice as hard. The impact made him stagger back a step. "Whoa there, big fella," I told him. "Throwing down with me is one thing. But you do *not* want to tick off the Post Office. They don't goof around."

"I will shut your mouth!" he bellowed. He rolled forward at me, and to give the guy some credit, he moves better than you'd expect from someone who weighs eight hundred pounds. He swung fists the size of plastic milk jugs at me, a quick boxer's combination, jab, jab, cross, but I was fighting my kind of fight and he never touched me. Instead, he pressed harder, throwing heavier blows as he did. I popped him in the kisser a few times, just to keep him honest, and he grew angrier by the second.

Finally, I wound up with my back against an abandoned SUV, and let the Rhino's next punch zoom past my noggin and right through the SUV's door. I hopped around to his rear, and he swung his other hand at me, sinking it into the engine block of another car, and briefly binding his hands.

I popped up in front of him, held up the first two fingers of my right hand in a V shape, poked him in the eyes, and said, "Doink. Nyuk, nyuk, nyuk."

That last bit was too much for him. Something in him snapped and he let out a roar that shook the street beneath me, his anger driving him wild. He flung the cars hard enough to free his hands, sending each of them flying with one arm, inflicting more collateral damage, and charged me with murder in his eyes.

Like I said: He almost makes it too easy.

When you get right down to it, that's how I beat the Rhino every single time. His anger gets the better of him, makes him charge ahead, makes him clumsy, makes him blind to anything but the need to engage in violence. He's stronger than me, grossly so, in fact, and he isn't a bad fighter. If he were to keep his head and play to his own strengths—overwhelming power and endurance—he could take me out pretty quick. That kind of thinking is hard to manage, though, once the rubble starts flying, and he's never learned to control his temper. If he could do it, if he could work out how to force me into close quarters where my agility would be less effective, he'd leave me in bits and pieces. He just can't keep his cool, though, and it's always just a matter of time before he blows his top.

Maybe it's the hat.

I evaded the Rhino's charge, and he kept coming at me. I let him, leading him into the street and as far away from the buildings and storefronts as I could—some of them would still be occupied, and I didn't want the fracas to set them on fire or knock them down. Once the Rhino goes . . . well, rhino, it's possible to turn his own strength against him, but it takes an awful lot of judo to put the man down.

He batted aside a car between us, just as I Frisbeed a manhole cover into his neck. He flung a motorcycle at me with one hand. I ducked, zapped a blob of sticky webbing into his eyes, and hit him twenty or thirty times while he ripped it off of his face. He clipped me with a wild haymaker, and I briefly experienced combat astronomy.

He chased me around like that while the police got everyone out of the immediate vicinity. Give it up for the NYPD. They might not always like it that they need guys like me to handle guys like the Rhino, but they have their priorities straight.

I led the Rhino in a circle until one of his thick legs plunged into the open manhole and he staggered.

Then I let him have it. Hard. Fast. Maybe I'm not in the Rhino's weight class, but I've torn apart buildings with my bare hands a time or two, and I didn't get the scars on my knuckles in a tragic cheese grating accident. I went to town on him, never stopping, never easing up, and the sound of my fists hitting him resembled something you'd hear played on a snare drum.

Once he was dazed, I picked up the manhole cover and finished him off with half a dozen more whacks to the top of his pointed head, and the Rhino fell over backward, the impact sending a fresh network of fractures running through the road's surface.

I bent the manhole cover more or less back into shape over one knee, nudged the unconscious Rhino's leg out of the manhole, and replaced the cover. My Aunt May taught me to clean up my messes. I checked the Rhino again, and then gave the nearest group of cops a thumbs-up.

That was when the trap sprang.

My spider sense is an early warning system hard-wired into my brain. It can somehow distinguish between all sorts of different dangers, warning me of them in time for me to get clear. A few times, my spider sense has become a liability, though. I was so used to its warnings that when I went up against something that didn't trigger it, for whatever reason, it made me feel crippled, almost blind.

When Morlun had come after me, my spider sense did something new—it went into overdrive. Terror, terror so pure and unadulterated that it completely wiped out my ability to reason, had come screaming into my thoughts. It almost felt like my spider sense was screaming "HIDE!" at me, burned in ten-foot letters upon my brain. It had been one of the more terrifying and weird things that had ever happened to me.

It happened again now.

Only worse.

The terror came, my instincts howling in utter dread, and the sudden shock of sensation made me clutch at my head and drop to one knee.

Hide.

Hide!

HIDEHIDEHIDEHIDEHIDE!

"Move, Spidey," I growled to myself. "It's fear. That's all it is. *Get up.*"

I managed to lift my head. I heard myself making small, pained, frightened sounds. Danger. It couldn't be Morlun. It couldn't be. I saw him die. I saw him turn to *dust.*

They came out of the New Amsterdam, where *The Lion King* was rolling onstage. Maybe they'd been watching the fight from the lobby. They came walking toward me, their postures, expressions, motions all totally calm amidst the chaos. Two men. One in a gray Armani suit, the other in Italian leather pants and a silk poet's shirt. Both men were tall and pale. Both had straight, fine black hair and wore expressions of perpetual ennui and disdain.

And both of them bore a strong resemblance to Morlun.

The third was a woman. She wore a designer suit of black silk and had on black riding boots set off by a bloodred cravat. She too was pale, her black-cobweb hair worn up in a Chinese-style bun. She, too, looked a bit like Morlun—especially through the eyes. She had pale eyes, soulless eyes, eyes that neither knew nor cared what it was to be human.

She came over and stopped about five feet from me, her hands on her hips. She tilted her head and stared at me the way one might examine a messy roadkill in an effort to determine what it had been before it was squashed.

"You are he," she said in a low, emotionless voice. "The spider."

"Uh," I said.

I found myself at a loss for words.

She narrowed her eyes, and they flickered with cold, cold anger—and inhuman hate, something that could roll on through a thousand years without ever abating. "You are the one who killed our brother." Her eyes widened then, and a terrible hunger came into them as the two men stepped up to stand on either side of her.

She pointed a finger at me and said, "Kill him."

6

It dimly occurred to me that at this point, if I was Han Solo, faced with a genuine threat to my life, I would officially have moral license to shoot first.

The thought flashed through my mind as swiftly and lightly as a wood chip passing over the surface of a rushing river, but it gave me *something* to grasp toward, and I was able to get my head above the surface of my instinctive terror long enough to grab on to another thought:

If one of them touched me, just *touched* me, I was as good as dead.

Right then. Don't let them touch me.

Tweedle-Loom and Tweedle-Doom stalked forward with a predator's economic grace, but I didn't want to give them time to shift gears when I scampered. I waited until the last second to pop them both in the face with bursts of webbing and jump back out of reach. A quick hop landed me twenty feet above the road on an enormous billboard, and I crawled up it, turning to study them. If they were anything like Morlun, they'd be walking tanks with nearly limitless endurance—but not a lot swifter, on foot, than anyone else.

As it turned out, the boys were apparently a lot like Morlun. They tore off the webbing with about as much distress as I would feel wiping off shaving cream, gave me dirty looks, and continued stalking toward me.

The woman had evidently stood in a different line when they were handing out superpowers. She hit the spot where I'd been standing with one foot and leapt—with grace and élan—up to the top of the sign I was scaling. She crouched there, her head still tilted at that odd angle. "You must know this is pointless," she said dispassionately. "You cannot stop us. You cannot save yourself."

My spider sense was still gibbering at me, but enough of my voice had come back for me to say, "Now let me think. Where have I heard someone like you say something like that before? Hmm."

A cold little smile touched her mouth. "Little Morlun was one. We are three."

Little Morlun? That wasn't encouraging. "I don't suppose it matters to you that I didn't kill him," I told her.

Her lips twitched a little. "He hunted you?"

"Yes."

"He died."

"Yes."

"You saw it. You allowed it."

"I . . ." I swallowed. When it came down to the wire, I'd had him at my mercy. I knew full well that if I'd let him live, he'd only come back another day. I hesitated. And before I could go through with it, Dex, Morlun's demented little attaché, had emptied a Glock into him from ten feet away and blew him to dust.

I'd like to think that if I'd been aware of Dex and his gun I would have stopped him. Part of me is sure I would have. But more honest parts of me aren't so sure.

"I did," I told her quietly.

"Then for his sake, you die."

"What if I'd tried to stop it?"

She smiled a cold little smile, showing me very white teeth. "Then you would die for mine. I am hungry, spider. I will devour you."

"Gosh, that's kinda intimate," I said. "We haven't even been introduced."

She lifted her chin a bit, and then inclined her head to me. "Mortia." She moved a hand in a simple gesture to indicate the other two. "Thanis in the suit. Malos in the silk."

"Spider-Man," I said. "I'm the one standing in the shoes which are going to kick all three of you back to wherever it is weirdos like you come from."

Mortia threw back her head and actually laughed a cold little laugh. "Such defiance." Her eyes widened, showing the whites all the way around. "And it makes you smell sweet."

"Well," I said, "they tell me my deodorant is *strong* enough for a man—"

She flung herself at me in mid-quip. She was fast, as fast as anyone I've ever seen. As fast as me—and my spider sense, already howling at maximum intensity about how much danger I already knew I was in, gave me no warning at all.

I moved, barely ahead of her—and if I hadn't been watching her, ready for it, I would have been too slow. I never thought I'd actually have a reason to be *glad* that that symbiotic maniac Venom had obsessed over me and done his best to make my life a living hell between bursts of attempted arachnocide. My spider sense never registered him, either, and it had forced me to learn how to bob and weave the old-fashioned way, using only five senses.

Her hand flashed out toward me as she passed by, and missed me by less than an inch. I hit the ground moving. Tweedle-Loom threw a television set at me, while Tweedle-Doom went with a classic and flung a rock with such power that the projectile actually went supersonic in a sudden clap of thunder, like a gunshot. I did not oblige either of them by behaving like a good target.

Besides, they were just distractions, and they knew it. For the time being, the woman was the real threat, and she was hot on my trail. She got better air than me, but she didn't have handy-dandy weblines to play with, and I was able to stay ahead of her—barely. I went bouncing around Times Square like a racquetball, playing a lunatic version of tag with the mystery lady while I struggled to come up with a plan. It was harder than usual. Normally, between my reflexes and my spider sense, things just sort of flow by, and it feels like I have all the time in the world to think. That's how I'm able to be all funny and insulting while duking it out with the bad guys. It feels like I've had hours to come up with the material.

This time, my spider sense had ceased to be an asset, and my speed was only just sufficient to stay ahead of the three of them. It took all of my attention to avoid her, plus dodging the occasional portion of landscape her homeys pitched after me—complicated by the fact that if I led them out of Times Square, which the Rhino's efforts had already cleared of most civilians, bystanders would get hurt. Morlun hadn't blinked an eye at the notion of murder, and I didn't think these three would be any more safety-conscious than he was.

It's hard to gauge passing time in circumstances like that, but I gradually got the impression that maybe the reason I couldn't think of a plan of action was that there *wasn't* one. I'd taken Morlun out with the aid of material from the core of a nuclear reactor, and I didn't see one of those around Times Square. The only Plan B I could come up with was for me to keep doing what I was doing until some of the other New York hero types turned on the TV, found out what was going on, and showed up to lend a hand.

Although "hope someone rescues me" was a pathetically flawed Plan B. I mean, I'm supposed to be a superhero. I'm the one *doing* the rescuing.

Thanis took the decision out of my hands. He threw something heavy that hit the car I'd landed on and knocked it cleanly out from under me. I dropped to the ground unsteadily and looked up to find that Mortia had anticipated her brother's action. She was already two-thirds of the way through the pounce that would pin me to the ground and kill me. Thanis's distraction hadn't cost me much, maybe half a second.

It was enough.

As fast as I was, I still wasn't going to be fast enough to get out of her way.

7

ONCE IN A WHILE, Plan B actually works out.

As Mortia came down at me, there was a *phoont* sound of expanding compressed air, and a small, metallic grappling hook flew over my head and hit her right on the end of her upturned nose, trailing a line of fine, black cable. The instant it touched her, there was a flickering of blue-white light, and Mortia's body convulsed, hit by what I assumed was a hefty amount of electricity. She went into an uncontrolled tumble, and I got out of the way in a hurry.

"That's new," I said, hopping to my feet—which I happened to plant ten feet up a handy streetlight, so that I could be sure to keep an eye on Clan Goth.

"I went legitimate," Felicia replied tartly. She landed in a crouch on the streetlight's arm, above me, pushed a button on a small baton, and the cord and grapple reeled swiftly back in. "I never said anything about not finding new toys to play with."

Mortia came to her feet slowly, looking down at the concrete dust clinging to her suit with undisguised annoyance. She traded a look with Thanis and Malos, and then all three of them turned to stare at me.

Absolutely no one moved. The only motion in all of Times Square came from rising smoke and the whirling bulbs on the police cars. The only sound came from a few stubborn car alarms that had survived the fracas (evidently Thanis and Malos found them as annoying as I did), and the harsh clicks and buzzes of transmissions on distant police radios. Nothing happened for a long minute.

What the heck. Every tableau's got to be broken by something.

"What we need," I drawled to the Black Cat, "is a couple of tumbleweeds. Maybe a rattlesnake Foley effect."

"Grow up," she sneered, watching Mortia and her brothers as carefully as I did. "What we need is the Avengers."

"Only because we didn't bring them," I said. "If we had, we wouldn't need them."

"Well, better to have them and not need them than—"

"Do I criticize your equipment list?" I asked. "And, oh. Don't let one of them touch you."

"We aren't dating anymore," she said archly.

I grinned, underneath my mask. "Very funny. Just don't do it."

"Why not?"

"Because once they do, they can track you down. Follow you anywhere. Find you anywhere."

She pursed her lips, the expression made tough to read by the visor, and said, "Got it. We should leave now, then."

I hesitated.

It wasn't a macho thing. I had no idea what Mortia and company might try if I left the fight. In a bid to keep me close enough to kill, Morlun had promptly started brutalizing whoever was handy when I tried to break contact with him for more than a minute or two. That was why I was hesitant to leave.

It wasn't because I didn't want to tuck my webs between my legs and run in front of half of New York and my ex-girlfriend. It wasn't that. At all. Not even a little.

Of course, dying in front of half of New York and my ex-girlfriend didn't sound like much fun, either.

A news chopper came whipping down the street, lower than the level of the buildings; someone was going to get a royal chewing-out from the FAA and whoever else screams and rants about such things. It kicked up a lot of dust and debris in the Square.

Mortia saw it and made a disgusted little noise. "Mortals. So gauche." She glanced at her brothers, then turned to me and said, "We are introduced, Spider. And after all, a multicourse dinner calls for a more . . ."—she gave me an acknowledging nod of the head and another wintry smile—". . . intimate setting. Fear not. We shall be reunited."

"Won't that be ducky," I said.

She flicked her wrist, dismissive. "You and the aperitif may flee, Spider."

"What?" Felicia said, indignant. "*What* did she call me?"

"Come on, bonbon," I told her. "Let's git while the gittin' is good."

Mortia turned to walk away, then paused to consider the fallen Rhino. "Bring the brute," she told her brothers. "He may yet be of use to us."

The two men each took one of the unconscious Rhino's arms, lifted all of him without so much as a grunt of effort, and dragged him along like a giant, armored rag doll in a goofy hat toward the nearest subway entrance.

There was a stir at one of the police control points, and I spat out a breath as I saw the SWAT van roll up. "Come on. Something we have to do."

"What?" Felicia called after me as I swung over to the control point.

I landed on the street next to the police lines. A couple of beat cops stared at me. One of them laid his hand on the baton at his belt. That was actually a pretty good reaction, for me. Usually, the hands go right to the guns.

"Hey, guys," I said. "Who is in charge of this scene?"

"None of your business," one of the cops said. "You ain't the sheriff of this town. You ain't the one that makes the calls."

A spotter had his field glasses focused on the retreating shapes of Mortia and company and was speaking cool instructions into his headset's mike as the SWAT team locked and loaded.

"Guys, you've got to trust me on this one," I told them. "Leave those three alone."

"Look, buddy," the cop said, his face turning red. "You're lucky they aren't getting ready to come after *you*, you freakin' nutball."

"Gosh, officer. Don't be afraid to tell me what you really think."

"Jesus, Frank," the second cop said with a sigh, rolling his eyes. "There's no harm hearing him out."

Frank folded his arms. "He's probably in this with those four, somehow."

The older cop stared at him for a second, blinked his eyes, and, through what looked like a nearly miraculous effort of self-control, did not whack him upside the head. Then he looked at me and said, "Why?"

"Because these people are bad news," I told him. "Big, bad news. They're willing to walk away without a fight, and they don't have any reason to hurt anyone but me, unless you force them to defend themselves. Your men can't stop them. If they try it, they'll die. For nothing."

"But you think you can handle them," he said.

"Not sure. But when I hit them again, I can at least do it someplace without all the civilian bystanders."

He squinted at me for a moment, then looked at the DMZ that had, until recently, been Times

Square. He grunted. "You got anyone on the force will speak for you?"

"Lamont," I said promptly. "Fourteenth Precinct."

His thumb tapped thoughtfully on the handle of his baton. "Sourpuss? Cheap suit? Drinks a lot of coffee?"

"That's him."

The cop grunted. "Sit tight." He stepped a few feet away and spoke into his radio. Maybe five minutes went by, and the SWAT team broke into a measured jog, setting off to pursue the retreating weirdos.

"Ahem," I said. "Time is getting to be a factor, officer."

He glanced back at me, then at SWAT, then went on talking. A moment later, he said, "Check." Then he walked over to the spotter, who was evidently some kind of authority figure with a rear-echelon command style, and passed him the radio.

I couldn't hear the conversation, but it didn't take much more than a minute for the SWAT guy's face to go carefully, professionally blank. He tossed the radio back at the officer, spoke into his headset, and a minute later the SWAT team reappeared. I let out a slow breath in pure relief.

The officer ambled back over to his post, and I said, "Thanks."

He shrugged a shoulder. "I got an auntie I like. She told me you saved her from a mugger. Don't mean I like you."

"Good enough for me," I said. "Thanks anyway."

There might have been the ghost of a smile on his lips. "Stick around. Lamont wants to talk to you. He'll be here in five."

"Anything to help the fine men and women of law enforcement," I said.

It didn't take the whole five minutes for Lamont to get there. He looked like Lamont usually looked: rumpled, tired, grumpy, and tough as old boot leather. His hair was the color of iron. He was a career New York cop who had been unlucky enough to retain his conscience and his concern for the citizens he protected. His hair had gone gray early. His eyes had perpetual bags beneath them, despite the large, steaming Styrofoam coffee cup in his hand. He wore a long black overcoat, his cheap suit and his hair were rumpled, he needed a shave, and his beady eyes glinted with intelligence.

He really didn't like me very much.

"Hey," Lamont said. "Let's walk."

We turned down the street and walked away from the police lines, passing in front of a long row of shops and stores, until we were far enough away to avoid being overheard.

He stopped and squinted at me. "You're doing that just to annoy me."

I shrugged. I was standing with the soles of my feet on a rail of the awning above us, looking at him upside down. "Come on, Lamont. Would I do something like that?"

He grunted and chose to ignore me. "So what happened here?"

I gave him the Cliff's Notes version of the evening's events and their players.

Lamont scratched at his head. "So these weirdos are here for you?"

"Yeah," I said.

"So that sort of makes it your fault, I guess." He sipped his coffee, eyes narrowed. It was as close as I'd ever seen him get to smiling. He nodded at the destruction surrounding us and said, "Where do we send the bill?"

"Call my accountant," I said. "You can reach him at 1–800-In your freaking dreams."

He gave me a bland look, sipped some more coffee, and said, "Judging from the outfit, you wouldn't be good for it anyway."

"Look who's talking."

Lamont stared down at his cup, then up at the bright lights of Times Square. "You say these people are strong. Like the Frankenstein gangster?"

"I took him in a straight fight," I said. "He was from the farm team. These three are major league. Like Rhino, or the Hulk."

"The Hulk, huh."

"Pretty close," I said. "But they don't go in for mass destruction with the same kind of glee."

"So this isn't mass destruction," he said. He coughed as a stray breeze blew some black smoke our way. "That's good."

"Rhino did most of this," I growled. "Probably to get my attention."

"Draw you out in the open, huh."

"Yeah."

Lamont looked around some more, sipped some more coffee, and gave me a shrewd look. "You're in trouble."

I was quiet for a minute, then said, "Maybe. It could get really messy. These things don't care, Lamont. They could kill every man, woman, and child in New York and sip cappuccinos over the corpses."

"Christ." Lamont grunted. His face twisted up abruptly, as if he'd suddenly started sucking on a lemon spiked with jalapeño. "How can I help?"

"You having a stroke, Lamont? Your face is twitching."

"I might be," he said darkly. "Helping out one of the maniacs in tights. I might puke. Maybe on you."

I looked down at him from my upside-down position. "That would be difficult, considering."

"I'd manage. I'm crafty."

"Don't know if there's much you can do," I said. "Except for making sure you aren't putting pressure on the Addams Family. If you start a fight, they'll take you up on it."

"Good plan," Lamont said. "I solve most of my problems by standing around hoping they'll go away."

"If I could give you a better one, I would," I said. "Let me handle this one my way; give me some room to breathe. I'll take the fight to somewhere safe." I glanced at the square. "Well. Safer than *this,* anyway."

Lamont grunted again. "I'll see what I can do. No

promises. And if something like this happens again, all bets are off."

"You try to take these guys down, cops are going to die."

He was stone-still for a moment. Then he murmured, "I know. So you damn well better take them out before it comes to that."

Trust is something precious and fragile. Once it begins to fracture, it isn't ever going to be strong again. Lamont didn't like me, I knew. But I hadn't realized that he trusted me. It was an enormous gesture, especially for him.

"I'll handle it," I told him, voice serious.

He finished the coffee, crushed the cup in a frustrated fist, and then pitched it down into the rest of the wreckage. "Right. Move along, then, citizen. Nothing to see here."

He was right, thank God. There wasn't.

Yet.

8

I FOUND FELICIA WAITING on the same rooftop where I'd tackled her a little while before. Full night had come on, but in New York, that means little. Even up high where we were, there was enough ambient light to see by, easily. In spots, you could read by it. But when night's curtain is drawn over the azure face of the sky, the light takes on a sourceless, nebulous quality. It stretches shadows, gleams on metal and glass, and emphasizes the brooding shapes of gargoyles and statues and carvings on many of New York's architectural wonders. The sounds of the city come up, but lightly, as though they were little more than remembrances of their makers, no louder than the voice of the wind. It's a kind of fairyland, and it always makes me feel as if I am the only real, tangible object in the world. It's beautiful, in its own way, and peaceful.

I figured the next day or three might be real short on peace. So I sat down next to the Black Cat for a minute and soaked it up while I still could.

"Hey," she said after a moment of silence. "You're trembling."

"Am I?"

"Yes."

I shook my head.

She stared at me for a second. Then she took off the visor again. Her eyes were worried. "Peter?"

"I'm all right. It's what happens when I'm scared."

Her silver blonde eyebrows went up. "What?"

"Scared. Frightened. Afraid. Having the wiggins."

"That doesn't sound like you," she said.

I shrugged.

"How bad *are* these people?" she asked quietly.

"They aren't people," I said. "They look like us, but they aren't. I studied Morlun's blood. Their genetics are . . . almost an amalgam of hundreds of different species. Maybe thousands."

"What's so bad about them?"

"They feed on life energy," I said quietly. "The way I hear it, they're from the mystical end of the universe. They devour the life energy of totemic vessels."

"Totemic what?"

"People," I explained, "who have chosen to use an animal as a personal totem. Who, in some sense or fashion, draw power from that association." I pointed at the spider on my chest. "Like Spider-Man." I chewed over an unpleasant thought. "Or like the Black Cat."

She blinked. "Just because of my name? What if

I were . . . I don't know. The Black Diamond or something."

I shrugged. "Don't ask me."

She frowned. "So, this Morlun. He tried to eat you?"

"Nearly did," I said. "He was . . . the Hulk's opening shot was kind of soft, compared to Morlun's. He was strong. Really strong. And he just kept coming. I fought him for about two days, almost nonstop." I glanced at her. "I hit him with everything I had, Felicia. He just kept coming." I shuddered. "Like the Terminator, only relentless. He could follow me everywhere. And every time I tried to bail, he'd start hurting people until I came back."

She grimaced. "How'd you beat him?" she asked quietly.

"I injected myself with radioactive material from a nuclear reactor. When he tried to feed on me, he got that instead. It dazed him, weakened him. I beat Morlun down. He had this little Renfield clone named Dex with him. When Morlun went down, Dex snapped and Wormtongued him."

"He what?"

"Doesn't anyone *read* anymore?" I asked. "Dex killed Morlun."

"Injected yourself with . . ." She shook her head. "That's insane."

"I was getting a little punchy when I came up with it," I said, agreeing.

"Still. They can't be all that tough. They turned

tail and ran once enough people showed up." She frowned. "Right?"

I stared down at the city. "Morlun . . . he was just so old. He'd seen everything. He said he only fed once in a while. That I would have sated him for a century. But the hunt was something that was nearly a ritual with him, something that he had to get right. The only time I got him off me was when I blew up a building with him in it. He came out without a scratch, but his clothes had been incinerated. He called a time-out to go get dressed again, because he knew he had all the time in the world. He knew that I wasn't going to be able to stop him."

"And that's why Mortia stopped?"

"I think that she wants to be able to take her time, when she gets me. She wants to be able to do it right."

Felicia shuddered. "She's insane."

"No. Just inhuman. Though I suppose it amounts to the same thing." I glanced up at her. "Which reminds me. How in the world did you know about Morlun? And about these three?"

"I think that 'know' is probably too strong a word," she said. "Look, I told you I've been working in the private security sector, right?"

"Yeah."

"Well, I've been doing some private investigation on the side. A couple of years ago, I get hired by a man who wants me to find out the exact time of Spider-Man's first appearance in New York, and every time he has appeared in foreign cities."

I blinked. "What?"

She spread her hands. "Exactly. So I play this guy along, trying to find out more about him, why he's asking these questions like he did. I figure he was trying to figure out who Spider-Man really was. Who *you* were. Like, maybe he was looking for puzzle pieces, and he just wanted me to find one of them." She shook her head. "No clue why he'd do that. I tried to find out more about him, but the paper trails and money trails all ran into dead ends. Zip, nothing, like the guy didn't exist. All I got was his first name. Ezekiel."

I blew out a breath. "Wow. Ezekiel. He told me he had hired several investigators to find out pieces of my background. He kept them ignorant of each other so that none of *them* would realize who I was. He was protecting my identity."

Felicia looked even more surprised. "You know this character?"

"I did," I said quietly. "He's dead."

My tone did not convey the sense that further questions along this line were welcome.

Felicia, being Felicia, feared my wrath about as much as she would a bubble bath and a glass of chardonnay. "What did he want?"

I kept my temper and answered as calmly as I could. "To protect me from Morlun," I said. "To hide me in some big expensive life-support unit he built, so that Morlun wouldn't find me and kill me."

"That was nice of him," she said.

"Heh," I said. "He was only doing it so he could

feed me to something *else,* later. Something that had been coming for *him.*" I clenched my teeth on my bitter tone and forced myself to lower my volume. "In the end, he didn't do it. Maybe he really did want to help. Maybe he didn't really know what he wanted. I don't know. Never had the chance to talk to him about it."

Felicia shook her head. "A few months later, I get another job. This time, someone wants to know about the recent appearances in New York of a missing family member named Morlun. Specifically, if he was ever seen in an altercation with the Amazing Spider-Man, and if so where. I dig, and find out that the description I've got matches this loser in a cravat who was seen trying to pound Spider-Man's face in."

"Made you suspicious, eh?"

"I'm always suspicious. You know that."

"True. What did you do?"

She ran her fingers back through her hair and let a cool wind play with the strands, her eyes distant in thought. "I fed them a little good information, a lot of false information, and played them along while I tried to find out everything I could about them." She shook her head. "I thought they belonged to some kind of secret society—like the Hellfire Club or something."

"Ah," I said fondly. "The Hellfire Club. What did you find out?"

"They're loaded," she said. "Seriously rich, managed through all kinds of law firms and accountants and hidden under enough red tape to choke a senator. They referred to themselves as 'The Ancients.' Like I said, it sounded like a club or something."

"The Ancients." I sighed. "You'd think they'd pick something a little less done to death."

"Maybe they had it first," she said. "I did some more digging and I managed to find several references to the Ancients—and eventually a picture of Mortia." She dipped a hand into the suit and drew out a slender PDA. It lit up, made a couple of beeps, and then she held up the visor. "Here. See for yourself."

I put the visor on, and was treated to an infrared display of New York. "Whoa," I said. "Predator-cam."

She touched a button on the side of the visor, and it cleared away to a light-enhanced image of the Big Apple, mostly black and white, the colors all oddly muted. I could see the bad toupee on a passing pedestrian thirty-five stories below. Then, an image appeared in front of me, as if on a projection screen—a newspaper clipping.

"It's from a microfiche archive I found at the University of Oklahoma," she said. "An article from the Dust Bowl era."

I read the article. It detailed the disappearance of a number of individuals from a traveling circus that had been passing through Tulsa, including a snake charmer, a lion tamer who was purported to actually wrestle the beasts, and the self-proclaimed world's greatest equestrian. They had last been seen in the company of a woman who generally matched Mortia's description. The article included an artist's rendering of the suspect as described by witnesses. It wasn't a perfect sketch, but it bore Mortia enough likeness to get the job done. "How did that connect you to the Ancients?"

"The owner of the circus attempted to bring a suit against the company that owned the hotel his people had been in when they disappeared. It was one of the properties owned by the Ancients." She was quiet for a moment. Then she said, "I also found this. A friend of mine got it out of the archives of the Texas Rangers, early fifties." Her PDA beeped again, and I saw another image—this time simply a photograph.

I took it for a photograph of a dry creek bed for a second. Then I made out the shapes in the picture. They were dried, desiccated human remains. Nothing was left except for the skin, stretched drum-tight over bones. Dead faces were locked in silent screams. Hair still clung to scalps, but other than their desiccated condition, there was not a mark on the bodies, as if even the animals and insects had refused to touch them.

"Two men, one woman," Felicia said quietly. "One of the men wore a gold wedding ring with an inscription that matched that of a ring owned by the lion tamer who disappeared from Tulsa."

I swallowed, staring hard at the wasted remains of what had once been human beings. This was what was waiting for me, if the Ancients had their way. This is what they had been doing to people for thousands, maybe tens of thousands of years.

I took the visor off, and the image of the wasted remains was replaced with Felicia's worried face. "Is this what they want to do to . . ."—she swallowed—"to us?"

"Looks that way," I said.

She shook her head. "I got this two days ago, and wanted to get a better look, so I tracked down the contact the Ancients had been using to speak with me, so that I could see him when I called him back with the information. It was an office building in Chicago. Mortia was there with him." She took a deep breath. "That's when the client starts asking me some of the same questions Ezekiel did."

I sat up straight. "What?"

She nodded. "I fed them some false information, and came to warn you, Pete. I told you, these folks were rich. And if Ezekiel can spend enough money to find out who Spider-Man is . . ."

"The Ancients can too," I breathed. "Mary Jane. If they find out about me, they find out about her."

"I'm sorry, Peter," Felicia said. "I didn't realize how serious it was or I'd have contacted you sooner."

"You did good," I said quietly. "Thank you."

She tried a smile. "You want to get home, I suppose? Make sure they aren't there?"

"They aren't," I said. I focused on my spider sense and peered around. "They're . . . on the other side of town somewhere."

She frowned. "How do you know that?"

"Mortia didn't manage to touch me," I said. "But I flicked one of my spider tracers into her pocket."

Felicia blinked at me. Then she said, "Gosh, and here I was going to feel all smug that I'd marked her with an isotope paste I put on the end of my grapple. I can track it from maybe three or four hundred yards out."

"Great minds," I said.

"We always did make a pretty good team."

I grinned at her, beneath the mask. Felicia couldn't see it, but she'd hear it in my voice. "Yeah. We work well together."

"What's the plan?" she asked.

I thought about it for a minute. Then I said, "I'm going to head back to the apartment. I'll know if the tracer gets within half a mile or so. I'll get on the net, see what I can find out about these things."

She nodded. "Let me get in touch with Oliver."

"Who's Oliver?"

"He works with me at the company," she said. "Mostly skip tracing, but he's a demon for research, too. He's good. If anyone can find out more about the Ancients, he can."

I mused. "See what he can get on the Rhino."

She gave me a skeptical look. "The Rhino?"

"He's a mercenary," I said. "Maybe we can find a way to make them default on their payment or something. I've got enough on my plate without fighting him, too."

"Are you kidding?" she teased. "You clean his clock every other week."

"Not that often," I said. "I've got his number,

one-on-one, but that doesn't mean he isn't dangerous. If the Ancients had come after me before he went down, instead of after, I'd look like those poor circus folks right now."

Felicia slipped the visor back on, adjusted its controls, and said, "I'll see what I can do." She got out her baton and said, "We can handle this, Pete. Right?"

"Sure," I said cheerfully. "We're the good guys."

I'm fairly sure the Black Cat didn't believe me.

I'm fairly sure I didn't, either.

9

Mary Jane was in the living room when I came home. She was sitting there with the manual she'd gotten from the DMV, trying to look like she'd been studying. I had seen the lights of the television, though, when I came down the wall from the roof.

She got up from the couch when I came in. She was wearing one of my T-shirts and a pair of my socks. "I saw . . . I was watching it on the news. They said something about the Rhino, but the clips were all of these men throwing things. They were throwing *cars* at you."

I went to her and held her, very gently. "Did they get me from my good side?"

She hugged me back very hard. "The cameramen couldn't even find you. They just kept circling these blurs on slow-motion replay and saying it was you."

"My grade school pictures are like that too," I said. "I fidgeted. I was a fidgeter."

We stood there like that for a long time. Mary Jane shuddered once, then exhaled and leaned against me.

"I don't like this part," she said. "The part where I have to worry about people throwing *cars* at you. Cars, Peter. I must have seen twenty cars crushed up like beer cans." She let out a half-hysterical little laugh. "How much do you want to bet all three of those bullies have a driver's license?"

I just held her. "Well. They can throw whatever they want. They aren't going to hit me, so it doesn't much matter."

She finally looked up at me, and her eyes were clear and steady. "Tell me all of it."

I exhaled slowly, then nodded. I didn't want to scare her, but Mary Jane had earned the right to know what was happening—and bitter experience has taught me that keeping secrets from the ones close to you is just not a great idea, in the long term.

I got a glass of water, stripped out of my tights, and sat down with my wife on the couch. MJ settled herself under one of my arms and pressed against my side, which I liked enough to make it a little difficult to speak coherently, but I persevered. I'm brave like that. I gave her the whole story, starting with Morlun. She knew me well enough that I got the feeling she understood more than just the words I was saying.

"God, Peter," she said. "You never told me about that thing."

"Well. You weren't here at the time." We'd been in a rough patch, one we'd since left behind us. "And when you came back, we had enough on our plates already."

She let out a quiet laugh at the understatement. "I suppose we did." She spread the fingers of one hand out over my chest. "But Peter. I'm sorry I wasn't here for you." She frowned. "No. That's not exactly right. I needed the space. The time to think."

"We both did," I said, nodding.

She looked up at me. "I'm sorry you had to hurt alone."

"I'm over it," I said, quietly. "Started getting better when you came back."

Her eyes searched mine for a long time and then she said, "You aren't over it. You're afraid."

I nodded.

She watched me for a second more. Then she said, a faint smile on her mouth, "But you're not afraid of them. These Ancients."

"Oh, believe me. I'm afraid of them. They are not reasonable people."

She shook her head. "But you're not afraid of what they might do to you. You're afraid of what you might have to do to them."

People rarely expect a beautiful woman to have a brilliant mind. My wife is smarter than almost everyone gives her credit for. She'd just realized something I hadn't consciously admitted to myself yet.

"They play hardball," I said. "They'll kill people without losing a second's sleep. Even if I can beat them, if they walk away, they're going to find someone else to eat. Someone else will suffer instead of me."

She laid one hand over my heart, listening.

"I can't let that happen," I said quietly. "I don't know . . . what other choice I have. I know they can be killed. It might be the only way I can stop them." I looked up at her. "I'm just not a killer, MJ. And I don't want to be one."

"What can I do to help?" she asked quietly.

I shook my head. "Nothing I can think of."

She sat up and said quietly, her voice growing brittle, "But Felicia. She can help you."

I sighed. "MJ . . ."

"She's got all the kung fu and criminal training, after all. Maybe even some actual superpowers, unless she's just been lying about that all along. Plus she's got a costume." She walked away from me, over to the window I'd just come in. "But I'm only your wife. I'm not useful."

"Hey, hey, hey . . . ," I said, trying to keep my voice quiet and calm. "Where did this come from? Felicia and I are over. You know that."

Her shoulders stiffened, as did her voice. "Yes, Peter, I know that."

"Then what gives?" I asked her. "Why are you being like this?"

She turned around, green eyes hard and fierce and wet. "You are *my* husband. And I . . ." The tears fell from her eyes and she said, in a very quiet voice, "And I hate it that I can't be the one to help you."

She looked small and frail. Lost. Vulnerable. If I hadn't gone over to her and held her, I think something in my chest would have broken open. She leaned against me again. Her shoulders shook a little, but she didn't let me see her face when she cried.

"I want to help you," she said. "Instead, here I am crying on you. For the second time today. God, that ticks me off."

"What does?"

"Adding to your burden. Being extra weight."

I kissed her hair. Then I put my hand on her shoulder and lifted her chin with a finger, so that her eyes met mine. "MJ, there's more to it than costumes. You've got to understand that. Maybe you don't throw punches for me or blast people with cosmic rays, but you do more for me than you know. Having you in my life makes me stronger. Better. Don't think that you aren't helping me. Don't think that you're a burden. Not for a second."

She didn't look convinced. But I hugged her again, and she hugged back, a tacit, temporary agreement to disagree. "So," she said. "What's the plan?"

"Research online," I said. "And I'm going to call some people."

"For help?"

I hedged. "For information," I said after a moment. "These three are here because of me. I can't ask someone else to fight my battles for me. But maybe someone will know something about them. How to beat them some way other than . . ."

"Killing them," she said.

"Killing them." I looked at the clock and said, "Okay, tell you what. How about we spend a little while getting you ready for your test, huh?"

She looked up at me, blinking. "Are you kidding?"

"Not even a little," I said. "MJ, this is just another freak of the week. It isn't the first time someone's come gunning for me, and it won't be the last. If we start calling a halt to life every time some psycho with a bone to pick walks into town, we'll be spinning our wheels until we retire."

"I'm going to assume you meant that to sound encouraging," she told me, arching an eyebrow.

"I'm trying," I said, nodding. "Look at it like this. Next week, this is going to be over, and I'll be making wisecracks about it to you while you drop me off at school and tell me how your rehearsal is going. Unless we let the latest set of bozos scare us out of living our life and you don't get the license and don't get your part. So. Give me the manual and we'll get you set for the test. We can even go out to the car and I can coach you a little if you like. You can get to bed early, I'll stay up and research things for a while—it'll be fun."

"Fun," she said, her tone flat—but there was, at least, a flicker of life in her eyes again, something that might eventually grow into a smile.

"Studying is fun," I said.

"Once a nerd," she said, sighing, "always a nerd."

"You want to skip the written and go to the car instead?"

She folded her arms. "What if I do?"

"Give me a minute, and I'll go borrow a crash helmet and make sure my life insurance premium is paid up."

She gave me an arch look.

"Does the car have air bags?" I asked. "Because if it doesn't, I can web us in nice and safe."

Mary Jane rolled her eyes heavenward. "*Now* he gets creative with the webbing."

"This is the car you bought?" I asked her. My voice echoed in the parking garage. The acoustics magnified my skepticism.

"I was kind of in a rush," she said. "And there wasn't much of a selection."

"And this is the car you bought?" I asked. "A lime green and rust red Gremlin?"

"Actually," she said, "it's just a lime-green Gremlin."

I leaned closer and flicked a finger at the car's fender. The rust red paint was, in fact, simply rust.

"I got a really good deal on it," she said.

"No air bags," I noted, walking around the car. "Too old for them."

"It's also all metal," she responded. "Being a really heavy car is really the next best thing."

I snorted. "Well," I said. "You can obviously drive. After a fashion, anyway. You took the car to the test, right?"

She raked some fingers through her hair. "Well. Yes. Though we stopped at the written. I was going to tell them my husband had driven me to the DMV, then went for coffee."

"Mistress of deception, huh?"

"Give me a break. I was working under pressure," she said. "And yes, I can drive. I mean, more or less. I didn't smash into anything on the way home, anyway. But everyone kept honking at me whenever I even came *close.* People in cars can be really rude."

I tried to imagine this scene, and had to keep myself from wincing. "Okay then. Let's get in and start with signals and right-of-way."

"Signals?" she asked. "Right-of-way?"

I couldn't help it. My lips twitched. "I'm not laughing at you," I said. "I'm laughing *with* you."

She gave me a very stern look.

I held up my hands. "All right, all right. I'll be nice. Get in the car, and we'll go one step at a time."

We got in, but she didn't put her key in the ignition. "You're a good man, Peter Parker," she said quietly. "I love you."

I leaned over and kissed her on the cheek.

"You know," she said. "We never made out in a car when we were teenagers."

"We didn't have a car," I pointed out. "Plus we weren't dating."

"All the same," she said. "I feel cheated."

She leaned over, pulled my mouth gently to

hers, and gave me a kiss that rendered me unable to speak and gave me doubts about my ability to walk.

We got to the driving lesson.

Eventually.

10

I CLICKED THE PRINT BUTTON and my printer wheezed to life—though at this point, I doubted the dissertation on magical systems of power that it was currently reproducing would be helpful except maybe in an analytical retrospective, long after the fact. I muttered under my breath, and tried the next batch of Web sites, looking for more information, as I had been since Mary Jane went to bed.

There was a sudden, heavenly aroma, and I looked down to find a cup of hot coffee sitting next to my keyboard.

"Morning," Mary Jane said, leaning over to kiss my head. "I thought you weren't going to stay up all night."

"Marry me," I said, and picked up the coffee.

She was wearing my T-shirt, and I could not, offhand, think of anyone who made it look better. "We'll see," she said playfully. "I'm baking cookies for Mister Liebowitz down the hall for his birthday, so I might get a better offer."

"I always knew you'd leave me for an older man." I sipped the coffee and sighed. Then I glowered at the stack of useless information by the printer.

"How'd it go?" she asked.

I made a growling sound and sipped more coffee.

"Peter," she said, "I know that in your head, you just said something that conveyed actual information. But when it got to your mouth, it grew fur, beat its chest, and started howling at the moon."

"That's right," I said, as if reminded. "You're a girl."

That got me a rather sly look over the shoulder. Doubtless, it was the fresh, steaming coffee that made my face feel warm.

"I take it your research didn't go well?" she said, walking into the kitchen.

"It's this magical crap," I said, waving a hand at the computer. I got up from my chair, grabbed my coffee, and followed her. "It's such hogwash."

"Oh?"

"Yes. It's like we're reverting to the Dark Ages here. Which you're not actually supposed to say anymore, because it's not like it was a global dark age, and to talk about it like the whole world was in a dark age is Eurocentrically biased." I sat at the kitchen table. "And that's pretty much what I learned."

"You're kidding," she said.

"No. Eurocentrically biased. It's actually a phrase."

"You're funny." She opened the refrigerator door. "Seriously, nothing useful? Not even in the Wikipedia?"

"Zip. I mean, there's all kinds of magical creatures on the net, God knows. But how do you tell the difference between something that's pure make-believe, something that's been mistakenly identified as something magical, something that's part of somebody's religious mythos which may or may not have a basis in life, and something that's real?" I shook my head. "The only thing I found that was even close to these Ancients turned out to be an excerpt from a Dungeons and Dragons manual. Though I did run across a couple of things that led me to some interesting thoughts."

Mary Jane continued on, making breakfast and listening. I wasn't sure how she did that. Heck, I had to turn off the television or radio to be able to focus on a phone call. "Like what?" she asked.

"Well. These Ancients might have superpowers and such, but they still have the same demands as any other predator. They have to eat, right? And they're thousands and thousands of years old."

She nodded, then frowned. "But I thought that the super-powered types only started showing up kind of recently. I mean, fighting Nazis in World War Two, that kind of thing."

I shrugged. "Maybe. But maybe not, too. I mean, most of the super-powered folks who have shown up are mutants. I've heard some theories that it was nuclear weapons testing that triggered an explosion—"

"So to speak," Mary Jane injected.

"—in the mutant population, but that doesn't make much sense to me. I mean, the planet gets more solar radiation in a day than every nuke that's ever gone off. It doesn't make sense that a fractional increase due to nuclear weapons tests would trigger the emergence of superpowers."

"Worked for the Hulk," she pointed out.

"Special case," I said. "But I think that maybe what we're seeing—the rise in the mutant population—might be as much about the *total* population rising as it is about a sudden evolutionary change. We've got about six billion people on the planet right now. Two thousand years ago, the estimate is that there might have been three hundred million. If the occurrence of powered mutants is just a matter of genetic mathematics, maybe it just seems like there's a lot more mutants running around these days. I mean, they do tend to be kind of eye-catching."

She was making omelets. She assembled them as quickly and precisely as if her hands were being run by someone else's head while she carried on the conversation with me. "And you think that explains how these things ate before? By feeding on the occasional mutant with some kind of totemistic power?"

"Potentially," I said. "Even a reduced population

might be able to sustain the Ancients. They only eat once in a while, sort of like a boa constrictor. Felicia thinks the last time Mortia ate was in the forties. Morlun told me that feeding on me would fill him up for a century or more."

"Tastes great," Mary Jane said. "More filling. I agree."

I coughed. "Thank you," I said. "But, ahem, getting our minds out of the gutter, think about it for a minute. How would people have described someone with, say, Wolverine's gifts, back when? He'd have been called a werewolf or a demon or something. Charles Xavier would have been considered a sorcerer or a wizard of some kind. Colossus would have been thought to be some kind of gargoyle or maybe a fairy tale earth-creature, like a troll."

She lifted her eyebrows. "So, you're saying that maybe a lot of folklore and mythology might be based on the emergence of mutants, back when. Like if . . . say, Paul Bunyan was actually a mutant who could turn into a giant."

See what I mean about brains? My girl ain't slow. "Exactly. Ezekiel told me that the African spider-god Anansi was originally a tribesman who had acquired spiderlike powers. Sort of the original Spider-Man. That he got himself involved with gods and was elevated to godhood."

"Actual gods?" Mary Jane asked, her tone skeptical.

"Hey," I said. "I ate hot dogs with Loki a few

months ago. And I saw Thor flying down Wall Street last week."

She laughed. "Good point. You aiming for a promotion?"

"Not if I can help it," I said. "But think about it. Say, for example, something really odd happened and I joined up with the Avengers. All of a sudden, I'm running around with a new crowd, gone from home a lot, hanging around with Thor, all that kind of thing. If it was two thousand years ago, it sure would look like I'd been accepted by beings with incredible powers, whisked off to their world and welcomed into their ranks."

She nodded. Then asked me, "Would that be so odd? For you to join a team like that?"

"Captain America doesn't think I'd be a team player," I told her. "We've talked about it in the past. And there was that whole thing where I wanted to join the Fantastic Four, but when they found out I was looking for a salary they got all skeptical about me."

"You thought the FF *paid*?" Mary Jane asked.

"I was about sixteen," I said. "I thought a lot of stupid things."

She smiled, shook her head, and started dishing up the omelets. "Eat up, Mister Parker. Get some food in you."

I took the plate from her and set it on the table. "Anyway. I didn't make a sterling first impression on the superhero community. And I've had all that bad press, courtesy of the *Bugle.* So there's always been a little distance between me and Cap and most of the other team players."

"It just seems . . ." She paused, toying with her fork. "You know. If you were part of a team, it might be safer."

"It might," I said. "But on the other hand, the Avengers are pretty upscale when it comes to villainy. They take on alien empires, aggressive nations, super-dimensional evil entities, that kind of thing. I mostly do muggers. Guys robbing a grocery. Car thieves. You know—here, New York, with real people. There's no friendly neighborhood Thunder God."

"Did you call them up, at least?" she asked.

"Answering service," I said. "Who knows where they are this week. I left a message on their bulletin board system, but I don't know if they'll get in touch anytime soon since, you know. They mostly don't know who I am." I paused. "The secret identity thing probably hasn't helped endear me to my fellow good guys, thinking about it."

"What about Reed Richards?" she asked.

"Called Mister Fantastic's lab at six A.M.," I said. "He'd been there for an hour already. He said he'd see what he could find out, but he didn't sound optimistic. And he has to take Franklin to the dentist later. He said he'd get word to me by this afternoon, but . . ."

"But he's a scientist," she said. "Like you. He doesn't like the whole magic thing, either."

"It isn't that he doesn't *like* it. It's that he likes things to make *sense*. Science makes sense. Some of it can be pretty complex, but it makes sense if you know what you're dealing with. It's solid, reliable."

"Predictable?"

"Well," I said. "Yes."

"You don't like things you can't predict," Mary Jane said. "Things you can't control. You don't know the magical stuff, and it doesn't seem to lend itself to being predicted or controlled—so you don't like it."

"So now I'm a control freak?" I asked.

She looked at me for a second. Then she said, "Peter. You've spent your entire adult life fighting crime, protecting people from bad guys of every description and otherwise putting yourself in danger for someone else's sake—while wearing brightly colored tights with a big black spider on the chest. I think it's safe to say you have issues."

"With great power . . . ," I began.

She held up a hand and said, "I agree, God knows. But an abstract principle isn't why you do it. You do it because of what a robber did to Uncle Ben. You could have controlled that if you were there, but you weren't and you didn't. So now you've got to control every bad guy you possibly can. Be there for everyone you possibly can. That's control freaky. Constructively so."

I frowned down at my eggs. "I haven't really thought of it that way before."

"That's right," she said, deadpan. "You're a man."

I glanced up at her and smiled. "I'm glad you remembered."

She blushed a little. She does it much more prettily than I do. MJ leaned across our little table and kissed my nose. "Eat your breakfast, tiger."

The door to our little apartment opened, and Felicia stepped in, dressed in a dark gray business suit-skirt that showed an intriguing amount of leg. She wore horn-rimmed glasses and had her silver blonde hair pulled back into a bun. "Pete, we're screwed. Hi, MJ."

I was still in my shorts, and MJ hadn't gotten dressed yet, either. I sat there with a bite of omelet halfway to my mouth. "Oh. Uh, Felicia, hey."

Mary Jane gave Felicia a glance and murmured to me, "Was the door unlocked?"

"No." I sighed.

Felicia closed the door behind her and peered out the peephole "Sorry. I didn't want to stand around in your hallway and get spotted." She looked back at us and gave me an appreciative glance. "Well, hello there."

Mary Jane gave Felicia the very calm look that comes to people's faces only seconds before they load a deer rifle and go looking for a bell tower. She stood up, and I stood up with her, taking her arm firmly. "Uh, Felicia, give us a second to get dressed, okay?"

"You bet," Felicia said. She tilted her head, sniffing. "Mmmm. That omelet smells good. Are you guys going to eat that?"

"Why don't you have mine," Mary Jane said sweetly.

"Come on," I said, and walked Mary Jane out of

the room. We got into the bedroom and shut the door.

"Are you *sure* she isn't evil anymore?" Mary Jane asked.

"Felicia wasn't ever really evil. Just . . . evil-tolerant. And really, really indifferent to property rights."

Mary Jane scowled. "But if she was evil," she said, "you could beat her up and leave her hanging upside down from a streetlight outside the police station. And I would like that."

I tried hard not to laugh and kissed her cheek, then put the uniform on under a gray sweat suit and stuffed my mask into a pocket. Mary Jane went with jeans and a T-shirt, in which she looked genuine and gorgeous.

"She's not that bad," I said as we dressed. "You know that."

"Maybe," she admitted.

"I think maybe you're having a bad day," I said. "I think that she's mostly a convenient target."

"Of course you'd say that," she snapped. Then she forced herself to stop, the harshness in her voice easing, barely. "Because you're insightful and sensitive. And because you're probably right."

"Yeah," I said. "That's hardly fair to you."

She lifted her hand in a gesture of appeasement. "Peter, I do my best to be rational and reasonable about everything I can. But I think maybe I'm running low on rationality where Felicia is concerned."

"Why?" I asked.

"Because she gets to help you when I can't," Mary Jane said. "Because you used to date her. Because she doesn't respect such banal conventions as marriage and probably wouldn't hesitate to rip off her clothes and make eyes at you, given half an excuse."

"MJ. She wouldn't do that."

"Oh? Then why is she dressed like some kind of corporate prostitute?"

I sat down next to my wife, put my hands on her shoulders, and said, "She wouldn't do that. And it wouldn't matter if she did. I'm with you, Red."

"I know," she said, frustrated. "I know. It's just . . ."

"It's a tough time, and between the two of us there isn't enough sanity to cover everything."

She sighed. "Exactly."

"No sweat. I've got it covered," I said. "I'll take care of business, release the pressure, Felicia will probably go back to her glamorous life in private security, and everything will be like it usually is—which is good."

She covered one of my hands with hers and said, "It is pretty good, isn't it."

"I always thought so."

She took a deep breath and nodded. "All right. I'll . . . somehow avoid clawing her eyes out. I can't promise you anything more than that."

"I'll take it," I said. I kissed her again, and we went back into the living room.

Felicia hadn't eaten anyone's omelet. She was,

however, giving the fridge an enthusiastic rummaging, setting things haphazardly on the counter by the sink as she did.

Mary Jane paused, and her cheek twitched a couple of times. Then she took a deep breath, clenched her hands into fists, and sat down at the table without launching even a verbal assault. She began eating her omelet in small, precise bites while Felicia continued foraging in the refrigerator.

Felicia eventually decided on the leftover pizza and popped it in the microwave while I sat back down.

"All right," I said to Felicia. "What did you find out about Gothy McGoth and her brothers?"

"That we're in trouble."

"Gosh. Really."

She stuck out her tongue at me. "Mortia is connected, and in a major way. She controls at least half a dozen corporations, two of them Fortune 500 companies. She's visited the White House twice in the last five years and has more money than Oprah—*none* of which can be found in documented record or proved in a court of law."

I frowned. "How'd you find out, then?"

"Let's just say that I know some very intelligent and socially awkward men with a certain facility for the electronic transfer of information." She checked the pizza with her fingers, licked a blob of tomato sauce from them, and sent it for another spin cycle in the microwave. "The point is that these people have money, employees, and enormous resources. And bad things can happen to people who start sniffing around. Several investigators looking into their business turned up dead in really smooth professional hits. They looked like accidents."

"How do you know they were murders, then?"

"Because the Foreigner said so."

Mary Jane frowned at me. "The Foreigner?"

"Professional assassin," I said quietly. "He killed Ned Leeds. Hired a mutant named Sabretooth to kill Felicia."

Felicia smiled, and it made her eyes twinkle. "He can *cook*—oh my goodness! And his wine cellar is to die for."

Mary Jane blinked. "You dated him? Before or after he tried to kill you?"

"After, of course," Felicia said with a wicked little smile. "It made things . . . very interesting."

Mary Jane's fork clicked a bit loudly on her plate for a moment as she cut the omelet into smaller pieces with its edge.

"I'm out of the business," Felicia said, "but we keep in touch. I went skiing with him in South Africa last summer. Even the Foreigner's information on Mortia was very sketchy, but it gave me places to start looking." She took a bite of pizza. "And our best move is to blow town."

"What?" I asked.

"I picked up four plane tickets for London, and from there we can cover our tracks and get elsewhere. I can have new identities set up within the day."

Mary Jane blinked at Felicia and then at me.

I finished my omelet's last bite, swallowed, and set my fork down. "Four?"

"You, me, Aunt May, and MJ," Felicia said. "We have to get all of you out together."

"Why do you say that?"

"This is a no-win, Peter," Felicia said, her tone growing serious. "Without more knowledge, you can't take those three on. And if we start nosing around to get that knowledge, one of their managers is going to notice it and correct the problem."

"And hit men are supposed to be scarier to me than the Ancients?" I asked.

She finished the first piece of pizza with a grimace. "I guess you cooked, eh?"

"Stop trying to dodge the question," I said.

She looked down for a moment, her expression uncertain. Then she glanced at Mary Jane. "The Ancients are rich. One person has already found out about Peter's alter ego by spending a lot of money and using his brain. If they're willing to expend the money and manpower, it's only a matter of time before the Ancients know, too." Then she glanced at me. "And then you won't be the only one in danger."

My stomach felt cold and quivery, and my eyes went to Mary Jane.

Her eyes were wide with fear, too. "Aunt May," she said quietly.

Aunt May was out of town at the moment. Her friend Anna had won two tickets on an Alaskan cruise liner in a contest on the radio, and they were off doing cruise-liner things for the next few days. The brochure had said something about glaciers and whales.

It occurred to me that there really wouldn't be anywhere for Aunt May to run or anyplace to hide, trapped out on a ship like that.

"The people they send won't be obsessive, melodramatic maniacs like your usual crowd, Pete," Felicia continued, her voice calm and very serious. "They'll use strangers, cold men, with years of skill, patience, and no interest whatsoever in anything but concluding their business and taking their money to the bank. They'll find you, stalk you, and kill you, and it won't mean any more to them than balancing their checkbook."

"All the more reason to take care of it right now," I said quietly.

"No," Felicia replied. "All the more reason to run right now. For the moment, the Ancients don't know any more about you than you do about them. If Peter Parker and his family vanish now, you'll be able to hide—to bide your time until we can figure out more about the Ancients or else get some help in taking them down."

"I'm not—," I began.

"Whereas if you wait," Felicia said, running right over me, "if you keep going the way you are, they'll find out who you are, probably within a few days. Then it's too late. Then they'll use their resources to keep track of you and everyone you care about, and you won't have the option of running anymore. You won't be able to get out of sight long enough to come up with a new identity."

Silence fell.

I've been afraid of bad guys before. That wasn't anything new. The people I care about have been put in danger before. That wasn't new, either. But this time was different. This time a choice I had to make would determine whether or not they'd be in danger. If I stood my ground, the Ancients would use them to get me out in the open, and the only way I could keep them absolutely safe was to hide them—or else to get eaten, in which case my loved ones would no longer be of value or interest to the Ancients.

But it would mean vanishing, maybe for a while. It would mean leaving behind a lifetime there, in our town, our home. New York can be dirty and ugly and rude and difficult and dangerous, but it is by thunder my home, and I would not allow anyone to just rip it away.

Bold words. But I wondered if I'd ever be able to look at myself in a mirror again if MJ or Aunt May got hurt because of my stubbornness.

I looked up at Mary Jane, searching for answers.

My wife met my gaze and lifted her chin with her eyes slightly narrowed, a peculiarly pugnacious look on her lovely face.

I felt my lips pull away from my teeth in a fierce grin.

Felicia looked back and forth between us and

drew a small packet consisting of airline tickets held in a rubber band from her jacket pocket. She tossed it negligently in the trash can. "Yeah," she sighed. "I was afraid you'd see it like that."

11

FELICIA ACCOMPANIED ME to the libraries, plural. The New York Public Library system is enormous, and it took most of the morning to get through the three different branches I wanted to visit. By the time I was finished hunting through the stacks of books, Felicia looked like she might simply explode from pure nerves.

"What's wrong?" I asked her. "Bibliophobic?"

"Never met a bibble I didn't like," she replied. "It's just that I haven't ever actually come to a library for the books before."

I blinked at her. "Why else would you be here?"

She gestured around us. We were down in the basement of this one, and it was nearly deserted, and quiet. "Look around, Peter. Lots and lots of long rows of books, lots of dim little crannies—not a lot of people." She tipped the rather frumpy horn-rimmed glasses down. "Imagine the possibilities."

"I'm imagining books getting damaged," I told

her, half-amused. "And after that, I seem to remember that libraries occasionally carry rare books, and sometimes important documents or pieces of art."

"Why, Peter. I'm shocked that you would suggest such a thing." She sighed. "Besides, that isn't a terribly good market. It's difficult to move any of the take. It's all too identifiable. You've got to go to a foreign market to get decent money and it adds in several more middlemen who . . ." She gave me a brilliant smile. "Should I go on?"

"Please don't," I said.

"What are you looking for down here, anyway?"

"Stories," I said. "Folklore, specifically Native American folklore. There were powerful totemic images all through their society and their religious beliefs. Especially with regards to their shamans."

"What's a shaman?"

"It's like a wizard or a holy man," I said. "They were often the healers and advisers of a tribe. They communicated with the spirit world, negotiated with spirits for the benefit of the tribe. There was a lot of lore about them taking on the shape of various animals." I shrugged. "Maybe they really did. Or at least, maybe they could do some extraordinary things—like mutants."

Felicia nodded. "You think the Ancients did some feeding on them."

"I think it's worth investigating. It's possible that if anyone encountered them and survived it, it would make one heck of a good story. There's a chance that it passed into their folklore."

Felicia frowned. "Like . . . like if there was a real-live Pecos Bill who was a mutant who could control tornados? And he was used as the source of the myth? Something like that?"

Felicia isn't exactly a moron herself.

"Just like that," I said. Then I jabbed my finger down on the page. "Aha!"

"Do people really say that?" she asked. But she came around the table and sat down in the chair next to me. "What did you find?"

"This is the third mention I've found of a tribal shaman being pursued by a wendigo. It's a Native American manitou—a spirit creature. It's a kind of punishment that happens to people who resort to cannibalism to survive. They're possessed by the wendigo and transformed into a creature of endless hunger, doomed to haunt the earth forever, looking for victims to devour."

"Sounds like our Ancients all right," Felicia said. "Except that from what you've said, they eat energy, not flesh. And they aren't human. And they only eat once every several years. So it really sounds nothing like them."

I shook my head. "But the details of the story don't necessarily have to be accurate. Think about it. One of the Ancients gets hungry. It comes into a tribe, looking like one of them, to pursue its victim. Then, it and the victim go hunting, or gathering herbs or what have you. The Ancient attacks and leaves a dried husk behind. Later, concerned relatives and friends find the ruined corpse, which is nothing but bones and skin, as if the meat had been sucked out of it. And the new tribesman, the Ancient, has vanished." I shrugged. "Why not assume that the stranger had been a wendigo? Give me some time and I could probably make a case for the original Grendel of folklore being something similar."

"Ah," Felicia said, though she didn't look confident in my hypothesis. "So. Does it say how to kill a wendigo?"

"It's got a heart of ice," I replied. "The traditional way to kill it is to melt the ice."

"We could get Mortia a nice card," Felicia suggested. "Some roses, some chocolate, maybe a Yanni CD and a bottle of Chianti . . ."

"Very funny," I said. "Look, each of these stories is different. In the first two, the wendigo destroys the shaman it hunted. In the last one, though, the shaman had a twin brother, who was a great hunter. The two of them overcame the wendigo."

"I know one set of twin brothers," Felicia admitted. "Though admittedly, I'm not sure if they could take on an Ancient, even though they were definitely in great shape." She frowned. "Come to think of it, I'm not even sure I remember their names."

I snorted. "It wasn't that they were twins," I said. "It's that there were *two* of them fighting it."

"What makes you say that?"

"Comparative data," I said. "You notice how quick Mortia and her goons vanished after you showed up?"

Felicia blinked. "I . . . suppose they did."

"Mmmm. And there were police nearby, choppers coming in close. I think that it posed some kind of threat to them."

Felicia laughed. "Are you kidding? I'll be the first one to tell you how fantastic I am, but I'm not stupid, Pete. I couldn't last a round with any of them, let alone all three. I don't think I made them nervous. I don't think the cops made them nervous."

"Maybe," I said. "But *something* did."

"They didn't look nervous," she said.

"Maybe it was only a marginal threat," I said. "Maybe that was enough to make them cautious."

"Why would they do that?"

"It's the nature of predators," I said. "No matter how hungry one of them gets, there are some things they won't do. If the prey is too dangerous, a predator will look for an easier target if possible. They know that if they're wounded in the course of bringing down the prey, it will render them unable to continue hunting effectively. They don't take chances if they can help it."

Felicia frowned and nodded. "Throw the fact that they're immortal into the mix, too. If you had eternity to lose as the price of a mistake, you wouldn't take any chances, either."

"Right," I said. "So we know they've got a weakness. They don't want to face more than one target at a time."

"Good," Felicia said. "Now. How does that help us? Specifically."

"Working on it," I said. "Let me get back to you.

What did you find out about the Rhino and his money? Any way we could nab it, get him to part company with the Ancients?"

"Not a prayer," she said. "The money trail looks like an Escher drawing. It could take months to sort it out."

"Mmmm," I said. "Anything more?"

"Quite a bit, actually. The Foreigner gave me a copy of his own file on the Rhino."

"And?"

"Aleksei Mikhailovich Sytsevich," she began.

"Gesundheit."

"Immigrated to the States from the Soviet Union, back when they had one. He'd come over to get a job that would pay enough for him to bring the rest of his family—the usual American dream. But since he didn't have much in the way of education, he couldn't get a job that would offer him enough money."

I grunted.

"He was big and tough, though. He wound up working as an enforcer for the mob. Someone—the Foreigner isn't sure who—offered him a chance to participate in an experiment. The one where they grafted the armored hide to his skin."

"Did they give him that hat, too?"

"Yes."

"The fiends."

"Stop interrupting," Felicia said. "Later, he went through another experiment that enhanced his strength as well, enabling him to go toe-to-toe with the Incredible Hulk. He lost, but he made the Hulk work for it."

"Engh," I said. "Well, it's too bad we couldn't subtract him, but he won't affect the equation too badly."

Felicia gave me a pointed look. "Equation? Peter. He's fought the *Hulk.*"

"So what?" I said. "*I've* fought the Hulk. The Hulk's personality being what it is, pretty much *everybody* has fought the Hulk."

Felicia leaned over and peered at my face.

"What you doing?" I asked her.

"Seeing if your eyes have turned green." She smiled at me. "The Rhino's had a lot of work with various villains, and has a reputation as an extremely tenacious mercenary. As long as no one sends him after the Hulk, apparently."

"Or me," I said.

She patted my hand. "Or you."

I scowled at her. "Why are you giving me a hard time about this?"

She shrugged. "Maybe it's my background. As mercenaries go, the Rhino isn't all that bad a guy."

"Not all that bad? He wrecks things left and right! Factories, buildings, vehicles—"

"And," Felicia said, "in the midst of all that destruction, he's never actually killed anyone. That says something about him, Pete."

"Even if he hasn't killed anyone, he's still breaking the law. He destroys property, steals money and valuables, and in general makes a profit off of his victims' losses."

Felicia removed her glasses and stared hard at me for a second. Then she said, her voice very quiet, "The way I used to do."

I frowned at that, and fell silent.

"I know you've got a lot of contempt for him," she said in that same quiet voice. "But I've been where he's standing—and I got into it purely for the profit, not to take care of my family, the way he did. He started off with better intentions than I ever had, and he's ended up in a much worse position. It's a bad place to be, Peter. I feel sorry for him."

"I don't," I said quietly.

"And what's the difference, Pete?" she asked. There was no malice in the question. "What's the difference between him and me? What's the difference between him and *you,* for that matter? I mean, I don't know if anyone ever explained this, but vigilantism isn't exactly smiled upon by the law in this town, and you do it every day."

Which was true, and really inconvenient to this debate. "So what? You think I should drop the mask, go to the police academy, and get a badge? Right. Like they'd ever let me do that."

She shook her head. "I just think you should think of him as a human being, not some kind of dangerous wild animal. Speaking of which," she said, "didn't it ever strike you as odd that the Ancients hired the bloody *Rhino*? A goon chock-full of totemic life energy?"

I blinked.

It hadn't.

"I'm not saying you should pull your punches," she continued. "I'm not saying we should give him a hug and sign him up for group therapy. I'm just saying that he's a human being with strengths and flaws, just like anyone else—and that he's in way over his head. He's in as much danger as you are and he probably doesn't even realize it."

I shut the book a little harder than was strictly necessary. "He hurts people for money."

"You hurt people for *free*!" she said tartly. "That just means he has better business sense than you."

"I fight criminals," I said. "Not bank guards and security personnel."

"One man's security guard is another man's hired thug," she said. "And when you get right down to it, men like the Rhino spend far more time pounding on other criminals than they do on law enforcement."

I stacked the books up to return to the shelves. Most people probably don't make enormous booming noises when stacking books. But I think they would if they had the proportionate strength of a spider and the proportionate patience of the crowd control guys on Jerry Springer. "So what are you saying? There's no difference between the good guy and the bad guy?"

Felicia arched an eyebrow at me. "They're both guys. Aren't they?"

"Yeah. One of them a violent criminal, and the other someone who *protects* people from violent criminals."

"My point, Peter," she said, "is that when you get down to it, there's very little difference between a wolf in the fold and the sheepdog who protects them."

"Like hell there isn't," I said. "The sheepdog doesn't eat *sheep*. Which is a really sorry metaphor to use for New Yorkers in the first place. Your average New Yorker is about as sheeplike as a Cape buffalo."

"Not everyone has a heart like yours, Parker," she snarled, her voice ringing out among the stacks. "Not everyone is as *good* as you. As noble. Not everyone *sees* the difference between right and wrong—and once upon a time you didn't, either, or you wouldn't be who you are." She folded her arms and brought her voice under control with some difficulty. "And I'd still be doing jobs on jewelers and vaults and . . ."—she gestured around us, wearily—"libraries."

True enough. Once upon a time, I hadn't seen the difference between right and wrong, and Uncle Ben died for it.

I sighed. "Look, there's nothing else to be gained here. You want to go?"

She nodded. "Yeah. Another library?"

"No," I said. "I have another stop to make."

12

Coach Kyle had been right. It wasn't a great neighborhood.

The Larkins' apartment building was well coated with graffiti and neglect. There wasn't a visible streetlight that hadn't been broken. The windows on the lower floors were all barred and covered in boards. There weren't a lot of cars around, and the ones that were looked far too expensive for anyone living there—except for one old Oldsmobile, which had been put on blocks and stripped to a skeleton of its former self.

Most tellingly, on a Saturday afternoon, there was almost no one in sight. I saw one gray-haired woman walking down the street with a hard expression and a purposeful stride. Several young men in gang colors sat on or around one of the expensive cars while a big radio boomed. Other than that, nothing. No pedestrians headed for a corner grocery store. No one taking out the trash or walking to the mailbox. No children out playing in the pleasant weather.

I'd filled Felicia in on Samuel, and she had listened to the whole thing without comment until we got where we were going. "You take me to the nicest places," she said. "Which building?"

"The one with those friendly-looking young men with the radio."

"I thought you'd say that," Felicia said.

We approached the building and got flat-eyed stares from the young men. They sat with the grips of handguns poking up out of their waistbands or outlined against their loose shirts. None of them were older than nineteen. One couldn't have been fifteen.

"Hey," said one of the larger young men, his tone belligerent. "White bread. Where you think you're going?"

I gestured with a hand without slowing down, as if it had been a polite inquiry instead of a challenge. "Visiting a friend."

The kid came to his feet with an aggressive little bounce and planted himself directly in my way. "I don't know you. Maybe you better just turn around." He looked past me to Felicia. "You're pretty stupid, coming down here with a piece like that. Where do you think you are, man?"

I stopped and looked around, then scratched my head. "Isn't this Sesame Street? I'm sure Mister Snuffalupagus is around here somewhere."

The kid in front of me got mad and got right in

my face, eye to eye. The young men with him let out an ugly, growling sound as a whole. "You trying to start something, man? You gonna get a cap, you keep this up."

It was annoying. If I'd been wearing the mask, I could have taken these kids' guns away and scared them off. Peter Parker, part-time science teacher, however, couldn't beat up gangs single-handed. And if anything started, Felicia was sure to pitch in. She could handle herself as well as anyone I knew, but this wasn't the time or the place to look for a fight.

I lifted my hands and said, "Sorry, man, just joking with you. I'm here to see Samuel Larkin."

"What do you care?"

"I'm his basketball coach," I said.

That drew a round of quiet laughs. "Sure you are." He shook his head. "Time you're leaving."

"No," I said quietly. "I need to see Samuel Larkin."

The young man pulled up his shirt and put his hand on the grip of a semiautomatic stuck in his waistband. "I ain't gonna tell you again."

I met his gaze in silence, and didn't move. He expected me to, I could tell, and as the seconds ticked by he started to get nervous. He had his hand on a gun, all of his friends had guns, and I would have had to be insane not to be afraid. He had expected me to back off, or produce a gun of my own, or attack him—*anything,* really, but stand there calmly. The basic tactics of bullies hadn't changed since I was in school—cause fear and control people with it. Granted, they hadn't carried around the handguns quite so obviously. And if one of them had backed down back then, it probably would have meant a little bit of embarrassment. Depending on how hard-core this gang was, backing off could cost this kid his leadership—which could well mean his life, or at least everything he thought was of value in it.

I lowered my voice so that only he could hear it. "Don't," I said quietly. "Please."

He swallowed. Then his shoulder tensed to draw the gun.

"George," bellowed a deep voice from above us. "What you think you doing to my coach?"

I looked up and found Samuel's scowling face looking down from a window on the fourth floor.

George, presumably, looked away from me and put his hands on his hips to scowl up at Samuel. "I don't know no George."

Samuel rolled his eyes. "Oh, yeah. G. You just G now, huh. George got too many letters."

"You got a big mouth," George said, scowling.

Samuel barked out a laugh. "G, you always been a funny guy." Then he looked at me and said, "Hey, Coach Parker."

"Mr. Larkin," I replied, nodding. "Got a minute to talk?"

"Buzz you in," he said. "Don't be too hard on my man G. Nobody ever gave him a hug or a puppy or anything like that, so he grew up with a bad attitude."

I nodded to him and walked to the door.

Behind me, George stepped in front of Felicia and said, "Now you, girl. You're fine. Maybe you should stay here and hang with me. Me and my crew will keep you safe from the bad element."

Felicia took off the glasses and smiled at him. Not a pretty smile. It was a slightly unsettling kind of smile, very Lecter-like. "I *am* the bad element," she said, toothily. "The question you should be asking is, Who is going to keep you and your crew safe from *me*?"

George let out a laugh, but it sort of died a strangled death a second or two in.

Felicia kept smiling and took a step closer to him.

George took a wary step back from her.

"That's good, G," she told him. "That's smart. Smart men are sexy."

The door buzzed, and I opened it for Felicia. She sauntered through, giving George a dazzling smile on the way, and vanished into the building.

I nodded to George, pointed a finger at my temple, and spun it in a little circle.

"Yeah," George said, shaking his head as the door closed. "Crazy white people."

The elevator was out, so we took the stairs up to the fourth floor, then found the Larkins' apartment. I knocked. It took Samuel a minute to get to the door. He opened it, stepped out, and closed it behind him, so that we didn't get to see the apartment.

"Mister Science," he said. He looked from me to

Felicia. "I really wasn't expecting to see this kind of thing until college recruiters started showing up."

Felicia asked me, sweetly, "How hard is it to play basketball without kneecaps?"

I put a hand on her arm and said to Samuel, "Thanks for stepping in with those guys down there."

He shrugged. "You get killed here, there's gonna be a lot of trouble for people I know. It ain't 'cause I like you, Mister Science."

"Yeah. I can tell what a public enemy you are," I said. "I came by to see if you'd had any luck with getting the shots set up."

"Oh sure," he said. "Soon as my driver gets back with the limo, he gonna take me to my private doctor. Doc's on vacation in Fiji, but I got my personal jet waiting to pick me up."

I gave him a flat look for a minute. Then I said, "I'm serious."

"Then you're stupid," he replied, his tone frank and not bitter. He stared at me for a second and then said, "Shoot." (Which he didn't say, again.) "You really think that I was gonna get to a doctor?"

"I think you really want to," I said. "I thought maybe there'd be something I could do to help you."

"And you came down *here*? And with your woman, too. And you face off with G." He shook his head. "You gotta be brave or stupid or crazy, Mister Science."

"I am not his woman," Felicia said, tartly.

"And my name is Parker," I said, putting a restraining hand on Felicia's arm again. "Look, Samuel, if there's something I can do to help you, I want to do it."

"Like what?" the big young man said. "You gonna get my father back to New York, back with my mom, maybe? So he can work a job, so my mom got time to get us taken care of? Maybe you can make her arthritis disappear." He shook his head. "That ain't gonna happen."

"I know that," I said.

"You even know any doctors?" he asked.

"Um. Not the medical doctor kind," I said. I didn't think Doctors Octavius, Conners, Osborne, or Banner would have the most recent inoculations sitting around ready to go. Reed Richards might, or might know someone, but I didn't like the idea of asking him for his help for something so . . . normal. Mister Fantastic's time is pretty well eaten up by cosmic devices and mad Latverian dictators and threats to the entire universe.

"What use are you then, huh? Part-time science teacher gonna save us urban kids. You're a bad joke, man."

Felicia's hands clenched, the way they did when she wore the gloves with the built-in claws.

"Easy," I said to her. "Samuel. Look. If you don't want my help, you can tell me that. You don't have to keep trying to insult Ms. Hardy and me so that I'll get mad and walk away."

Samuel fell quiet for a long minute, and the door to his apartment opened. A little girl, maybe four or five years old, came out. She was cuter than a whole jar of buttons, with little pink bows in her hair, blue overalls, and a pink T-shirt.

"Samm'l," she wheezed, rubbing at her eyes. "Chris'fer keeps kicking me."

Samuel glanced at us once, suddenly nervous, and turned to kneel down and speak to the little girl, picking her up as he did. "Did you tell him to stop that?"

"Yeah, but he's sleepin'."

"Oh," Samuel said, and his voice was warm and gentle. "Well, he doesn't mean to do that. You know that, right?"

"He won't stop."

"Uh-huh," he said. "How 'bout I put you in my bed for your nap."

She frowned. "And Peter Rabbit?"

He snorted. "Okay. And Peter Rabbit. But only once."

The little girl smiled at him. " 'Kay."

Samuel kissed her on the head and set her back down. "Go on. I'll be right there."

The little girl nodded, gave me and Felicia a shy little glance, then fled inside.

Samuel stood up slowly and shut the door after her. Then he turned to face us, clearly uncomfortable. "My little brother does a lot of running around in his sleep," he explained. "They share a bed. Hard on her sometimes."

"She's a beautiful child," I said.

Samuel glanced back at the door and smiled.

"Yeah, she . . ." He was quiet for a moment, and the smile faded. "She's a sweetheart."

"Okay," I said. "You want to stop with the insults now?"

He rolled one shoulder in a shrug. "I guess you mean well, at least. You shouldn't have come down here, though. Dangerous." He looked up at Felicia and gave her a nod that somehow conveyed an apology. "Especially for you, Ms. Hardy. But there's nothing much you can do."

"Samuel," I said. "Maybe I can talk to someone. I might be able to—"

"I don't want you to," Samuel said, his tone hardening. "I don't want your help. Your charity. I'll do it on my own."

"Even if it means suspension," I said.

He shrugged. "Shoot. Good as I am, the college boys aren't even gonna look at that. Once they see me, that's that."

"They're going to have a hard time seeing you if you get suspended. I checked regulations. You aren't going to be eligible to play for the rest of this season."

He shrugged. "So I arrange something else. I don't need your help, Mister Science."

I exhaled heavily. "Everyone needs help sometime."

"Not me," he said. "Nice of you to come by, but it ain't helping me any. Best if you just go."

"You sure?" I asked him. "It could mean a lot, in the long run. Making sure you're on the team."

"My life. I'll handle it." He shrugged. "I can't do ball, I'll do something else. My mom can't do it alone no more."

"G and his buddies seem to like you," I noted.

"Grew up together here," Samuel said, nodding. "I don't like what they do, but . . . people gotta live."

I stood there for a moment, feeling stupid and awkward. Then I nodded to him and said, "Your call, then." I pulled a scrap of paper out of my note-book and wrote down my number. "But here's my number. In case you change your mind."

"I won't," he said, making no move to take the paper I offered.

"In case," I said. "Keep your options open."

He glowered for a moment and shook his head. Then he took the paper and said, "Just to get rid of you."

We headed for the nearest subway station, Felicia watching me steadily the whole time.

"Sometimes I don't know how you do that," she said.

"Do what?"

"Think about other people. You're up to your neck in trouble, but you're worried about some loudmouthed prima donna. Going out of your way to see him."

"I have to," I said.

"Why?"

"The same reason I won't leave town."

"Which is?"

"If I let my fear of the Ancients force me to abandon my life, if I run away from everything I think is important, they've already killed me. If I hadn't come here, then this time next week, I'd feel pretty bad about leaving Samuel in the lurch without even trying to help."

"If you're alive in a week," she pointed out.

"Right," I said. "I'm planning on its happening. That's one of the things that's helped me survive this long."

Felicia shook her head. "He seems like a pretty good kid, once you get past the attitude."

"Yeah," I said.

"You're going to do everything you can to help him, aren't you."

"Yes I am."

"Even though you're up to your tights in alligators already," she said, her voice amused.

"When am I *not*?"

She laughed, and we walked in companionable silence for a while. I stopped at the entrance to the subway.

She tilted her head at me. "What is it?"

"I hate this mystic stuff," I said, frustrated. "Way too nebulous. I've got nothing but speculation. Theories. Hot air. I've got the next best thing to nothing when it comes to empirical data. What I need is someone who's actually been around the Ancients, who knows them."

"Seems to me that they don't like to go public. I doubt anyone close enough to have seen them in action survived to talk about it."

"But without some kind of information, I'm at a dead end. There's no record, no evidence of—"

Suddenly an idea hit me, and I had to sit there frowning furiously until my brain ran the numbers.

"What is it?" she asked.

"There *is* evidence," I said. "Or there might be."

"What?"

"Renfield Dex," I said.

"Who?"

"He was Morlun's little buddy. Human. Took care of details for him. He was there when Morlun died." I shivered. "Morlun hadn't treated him well. When I beat Morlun down, Dex took a gun off an unconscious guard and emptied the whole thing into Morlun's chest."

Felicia's eyes widened. "There were two people there when Morlun died," she said. "Dex and you."

"Yeah."

"Then I guess we need to talk to Dex." She frowned. "What's the rest of his name? Where is he?"

"I don't know," I said. "But when the cops got to the reactor, they found the gun in the aftermath. I'm sure they lifted prints from it. If we can get the prints, maybe we can identify him. The police should have them on file, even if the weapon went back to its owner."

"Wouldn't they have done that already?"

"I doubt it," I said. "That kind of thing could take a lot of man-hours, and it isn't as though they'd found a murder weapon. What was left of Morlun when they got there couldn't have filled a thermos. The only crimes had been in trespassing and the assault on the guard."

She narrowed her eyes in thought. "That would put it a pretty good way down their priority list, wouldn't it. But they don't exactly leave the evidence room open to the public," she said.

"Felicia," I said. "I'm sure that if anyone can find a way to get them, it's you."

She beamed at me. "It's sweet of you to say that. Even if it makes the air smell just a little bit like hypocrisy, O great defender of the law."

I glowered at her. "Don't start with me."

She smiled, pleased to have needled me. "What are you going to do?"

"What I should have done last night," I said. "I was just hoping to avoid it, because every time I go there, I get the crap beat out of me by something, or shipped off to some funky dimension to get the crap beat out of me, or my astral self gets projected away from my body so that I'm getting the crap beaten out of me in two dimensions at once. It's bad. It's always bad. Every time it happens I swear to myself that I'm never going down Bleecker Street ever again."

"Ohhh," Felicia said. "Him."

"Time's a-wasting," I said.

She nodded, rising. "I'll call the office, and we'll see what we can do about finding Dex. Quick description, please?"

"White male, twenty-five to thirty-five, about

five-eight, straight brown hair, one of those shaggy goatees, hazel eyes. Real thin face, long nose."

She nodded. "Got it."

I put a hand on her shoulder. "Watch your back," I said.

"Always," she said, smiling. She touched my hand lightly and then vanished into the subway.

I slipped into an empty alley, put on my mask, and set off to visit Doctor Stephen Strange, Sorcerer Supreme.

13

I headed over to Strange's place on Bleecker Street. It's easy to find from above. All I have to do is look for the funky round window with its oddly shaped panes. I didn't go in through the window, though. You don't just sidle into a sorcerer's place through the windows or the vents. Guys like Strange tend to protect themselves against that sort of thing. It's safest to go in through the front door.

I had my hand raised to knock when Wong opened the door and gave me a small bow. "Spider-Man."

Wong is tall for a native Tibetan and can look me right in the eye. He had a little piece of tissue paper stuck to a spot where he'd nicked himself shaving, on the top of his head. He wore trousers and a shirt of green silk with black embroidery, accented with threads the color of polished bronze. His expression was what it usually was—serene. To me at least.

Wong's poker face was so good, it nearly qualified as a superpower.

"Wong," I said. "You busted up my groove."

"Did I?"

"Big time. I was going to do the Bugs Bunny routine on the Doc. I brought a carrot and everything."

Wong nodded, his expression serious. "My soul is impoverished by the sin of . . . busting up your groove? Additionally, I mourn my master's disappointment in being unable to properly experience your doubtlessly flawless impersonation of a cartoon rabbit."

I looked at him for a second. "Nobody likes a wiseass, Wong."

Wong's mouth twitched at one corner, though he came nowhere close to actually smiling. "My master is expecting you. Please come in. May I take your . . . carrot?"

I'd picked it up from a vendor at a street market on the way. "No thanks," I said. I pulled up my mask enough to bunch over my nose. I swear, one of these days I'm going to get a mask that leaves my mouth free. I crunched into the carrot because it was good for me. And because I hadn't had lunch.

Wong watched me soberly, then nodded and led me to the doctor's office.

It was a big room, the size of a large study, packed full of books, scrolls, tablets, and oddities, all in neat order, all terribly well organized and clean, all set around an enormous mahogany desk. Though the ceilings were high and arched, the lighting there was always subdued, and lent it a cavelike mien. There was a fire crackling in a fireplace, and the air smelled of incense and cinnamon.

Stephen Strange sat behind the desk. He's a tall, slender man. He's got a neatly trimmed mustache and dark hair, with those perfect silver streaks at the temples that some men seem lucky enough to develop. He looks like an extremely fit man in his mid-thirties, though he's got to be older than that, judging from the sheepskin he keeps on the wall behind him. Neurology. He was wearing a very normal-looking outfit, especially for him: a pale blue golf shirt and khakis. I was much more used to the electric blue tunic and Shakespearean tights, plus the big red disco cloak.

"Spider-Man, master," Wong said in calm, formal tones.

"Thank you, Wong," Strange said. He had a resonant voice. "Our guest has not had lunch. Do you think you could find something appropriate?"

"Eminently so, master."

"Thank you," he said, and Wong departed. Strange leaned his elbows on his desk and made a steeple of his fingers. "Good day to you, Spider-Man. I thought you'd be by today."

"Saw me coming with the old mystical Eye of Agamotto, eh, Doc?"

He moved one finger, pointing at a flat-screen plasma TV on the wall beside his desk. "On the Channel Seven news." He moved his hand and picked up a copy of that day's *Bugle.* There was a picture of the wreckage in Times Square next to the headline

SPIDER-MAN RUNS WILD IN TIMES SQUARE

"You may not be the most subtle man in New York."

I pointed at the newspaper with my partly gnawed carrot. "That wasn't my fault."

"Of course it wasn't." Strange sighed. "Ignorance is part of the tragedy of the human condition. It is in the nature of man to fear what he does not know or cannot control. The average human being is no more comfortable in contemplation of his inner being than he is contemplating magic itself."

"You sound like Ezekiel," I said. "He was always trying to tell me my powers had come from some kind of mystic spider-god entity."

"Are you so sure they did not?"

"I was bitten by a radioactive spider. Period."

Strange smiled at me. "And who is to say that said spider was not the theoretical entity's choice as emissary? One does not necessarily preclude the other."

I looked at him. Then I sat down without being asked. "I was pretty sure I was done dealing with all this mystical muckety-muck."

Strange nodded. "Indeed, you are. The onus of that entire business has been appeased, the obligations completed, the balance restored, the necessities observed."

I tilted my head, like a dog who has suddenly heard a new sound.

"Your account ledger is cleared," he clarified. "That particular business is done."

"Well, it ain't, Doc. I take it you've heard of beings calling themselves the Ancients?"

Strange shrugged his shoulders. "Many claim such a sobriquet. Few deserve it."

"Morlun," I said. "Mortia. Thanis. Malos."

Strange hissed. "Ah. *Them.*"

"Them," I said. "Morlun tried to eat me. He wound up dead. Now his siblings are looking to return the compliment."

Strange lifted his eyebrows. "You defeated Morlun?"

"Yeah. With freaking radioactive material not unlike the radioactive freaking spider that gave me my freaking powers," I retorted. "No freaking mystical juju at all."

"Interesting," he mused. "Then their motive is not a factor of mystic balance, but one far older and more primal."

"Yeah," I said. "Payback. I need your help."

"Help?"

"Aid. Assistance. Advice."

Strange stared at me for a moment. Then he closed his eyes, settled back in his chair, and murmured, "Absolutely not."

Which made me blink. "What?"

"I cannot interfere in what passes between you and the Ancients."

"Why *not*?" I demanded.

He leaned back in his chair, frowning, his expression genuinely disturbed. "You understand, of course, that all forces in the universe act in balance. In a harmony of sorts."

"That's kind of Newtonian, but let's assume that you know what you're talking about," I said.

"Thank you," he said, his voice serious. "The powers at my command are part and parcel of that balance. I am not free to simply employ them on a whim without serious consequences resulting—and in fact, it would be dangerous to do so around one of the Ancients you face."

"Oh," I said. "I guess they deserve the name?"

"Indeed. They are older than mountains, older than the seas. Since life first graced this sphere, and since that life called out to the mystic realms, echoing in harmony and sympathy, these beings, these Ancients, have been there to feed upon it."

"Really, you could have said, 'Yes, they're old,' and it would have been enough."

"My apologies," Strange said. "I occasionally forget the limitations of your attention span."

"Thank you."

"Yes. They are old."

"And you can't do anything to them?"

Strange frowned. "It is a complex issue, and does not lend itself to monosyllabic explanation."

I cupped my hands to either side of my head. "Okay. These are my listening ears. I've got my listening ears on."

"Let me know if you experience any discomfort,"

Strange said, his voice dryly amused. Then he made a steeple of his fingers. "What you call 'magic' is a complex weaving of natural forces—life energy, elemental power, cosmic energies. And, like more familiar physical forces such as thermal energy, electricity, or gravity, they abide by a set of governing laws. They do not simply obey the whims of those who employ them. They have limitations and foibles. Do you understand that much?"

"Yes," I said brightly. "And I didn't get a nosebleed or anything."

"The nature of my access to these powers determines how I might employ them," he said. "I cannot simply randomly choose anything in my repertoire to counter any given situation, just as you could not expect to mix random chemicals and attain the desired results."

"So far, so good," I said.

He nodded. "The Ancients are predators, as you are doubtless aware. And while they are not a particularly pleasant part of the natural world, they are, nonetheless, a part of it. My powers are meant to defend and protect that world from those who would attempt to damage or destroy it. Were I to turn my powers against the Ancients it would be"—he actually turned a little green—"an abuse of that which is entrusted to me. A corruption of the energies in my charge. A most abominable blasphemy of the primal forces of our world."

"And what? The magic wand police would give you a ticket?"

"You speak lightly," Strange said. "But you are well aware of the evils that can be wrought with the abuse of power. Were I to turn the energies with which I work against the Ancients, the repercussions could be severe."

"Why?" I asked.

"Because of what and who the Ancients are. They are some of the eldest predators upon this sphere, creatures of enormous mystic strength—though they do not refine and utilize that energy in the way I do. It is, however, consciously focused by their force of will to give them enormous resilience, strength, and speed."

"Yeah. They're magically malicious. I figured that part out already."

"Their formidable physical attributes are minor compared to the enormous potential that dwells within them. Should I wield my powers directly against them, the results could be catastrophic."

"Uh-huh," I said, lowering my hands. "When you say 'severe,' and 'catastrophic,' you mean. . ."

"The end of all life upon this sphere."

"Right." I took a deep breath. "Couldn't you at least give me some more information about them? Anything would help."

"My personal knowledge of them is limited. And even were I to employ my arts to learn more, I would be constrained to tell you nothing."

"What? Why?"

"Knowledge is power—a fact with which I suspect you are intimately familiar. If I used my power to gain knowledge, and then shared that knowledge with you to affect the outcome of this situation, it would be as disruptive as if I had done so myself. It would upset certain critical natural balances and as a result, the eldritch portals would open in order to create a redressing of the forces so unbalanced."

"Which would be . . . ?" I asked.

"A series of confrontations like those you experienced a few months ago—beginning with Morlun and continuing through Morwen's incursion and confrontation with Loki, your battle with Shathra, all of which culminated in Dormmamu's attempted destruction of this reality on your birthday. You would again be a critical variable in the equation. It would expose both you and uncounted innocents to enormous peril. And so I must do nothing. Even having this conversation at all is potentially dangerous."

I shuddered. Then I slumped in my chair. My head suddenly felt really heavy on my neck. What was the point? For crying out loud, it had been nothing short of a miracle that I had survived Morlun, much less the rest of that mess. I wasn't asking Strange to make them go poof. I just wanted him to help me. Just a little.

Strange spoke quietly, and his voice was strained with regret and compassion. "I am sorry that I cannot aid you in this battle, as you have so often aided me in mine. It is unjust. Unfair."

"Since when has life been fair?" I asked.

Strange smiled. "In the long view, I think it might be worse if life *was* fair, and each of us received everything he deserved. My mistakes would have earned me torments to disturb the dreams of Dante himself."

"Amen," I said quietly, having pulled some epic blunders of my own.

"I wish you luck in your struggle," Strange said. He rose and offered me his hand. "But you should know that I believe you have the necessary potential to overcome this foe. Do not lose heart. There is more strength in you than even you know. I am truly sorry that I cannot do more."

I thought about just storming out, but Aunt May didn't raise me to be rude. Besides, if Strange said he couldn't help, he couldn't help, period. He might be weird, wordy, and unsettling, but he's not a coward or a liar. If he could have helped me, he would have. I believed that.

"S'okay, Doc." I shook his hand, and he walked me to the door of his office. "I never got the chance to thank you for that birthday present."

Strange inclined his head, a solemn gesture. "It was my pleasure and honor to be able to bestow it. Even so, it in no way lessens my gratitude and obligation to you for times gone by."

"Don't worry about me. I'm used to going it alone."

"Which is the problem," he said.

I stopped, blinked, and looked up at him. "Hey. Did you just—"

Strange smiled, very slightly, and quietly shut the door in my face.

Strange said he couldn't share information, but had he just tried to slip me something? If he was going to do that, why not just come out and say it? Why the heck does everything have to be so confusing when he's involved?

Freaking sorcerers. Freaking mystic mucketymucks.

Wong entered the room on nearly soundless feet, carrying a paper lunch bag. I turned to face him.

"I have always found," Wong said, "that the master quite often is able to say something important without ever coming anywhere near it in conversation. I would humbly suggest that you consider his words singly, collectively and most carefully."

"Why does it always have to be twenty questions with him?"

"Because he is the master. Did your talk go well?"

I grunted. "Not really. I was hoping for a little good luck this time around."

Wong bowed his head, then offered me the lunch bag. "I regret that the outcome of your visit did not please you. I hope that ham on wheat will satisfy."

I accepted the bag as we walked to the door. "It's my favorite."

"Really? Then one might say that you found a little good luck after all."

I blinked at him. "Wait. Wong, did you just—"

Wong bowed politely and shut the door in my face.

I looked at the door.

I looked at the lunch bag.

"Their weakness is ham on wheat?" I asked the door.

The door was almost as informative as Strange and Wong.

"This is why I don't like messing around in this magic stuff!" I hollered at Strange's mansion.

People on the sidewalks stopped to stare at me.

I scowled. "I swear, one of these days I'm going to snap and throw a garbage truck through that stupid window." I shook my head, muttered some things I'd never say around Aunt May, and opened the lunch bag.

Ham-on-wheat sandwiches, two of them, in plastic bags.

An apple.

And a black-lacquered square box as wide as my hand, maybe half an inch thick.

Interesting.

It reminded me of a jewelry case. I opened it. Inside were three small, black stones, along with a folded piece of paper that looked like a page torn from a book.

I read over it.

Very interesting.

For the first time that day, I felt something almost like real hope.

I closed the lunch bag, tied it to my belt with a bit of webbing, and swung for home.

14

"LET ME GET THIS STRAIGHT," Mary Jane said as she sat down across the kitchen table from me. "You went to ask for Doctor Strange's help, and he gave you magic beans?"

"Well. He didn't give them to me. Wong did."

"Wong did."

"And they aren't beans. They're rocks."

"Magic rocks. And he told you they would help?"

"No," I said.

"Wong did?"

"No," I said. "Wong gave me lunch. And rocks. And this. But he didn't tell me anything." I slid her the piece of paper Wong had packed in the lunch bag while I munched on the sandwiches.

The ham was that expensive honey-baked kind that Aunt May can only afford once a year, for Christmas, and it was delicious. The bread was wheat bread, sure enough, but homemade and fresh, and Wong had made it with a splash of Italian dressing and had somehow found a fresh-grown tomato, not one of those Styrofoam imitation tomatoes my grocery store sells. It was good.

Maybe I should think about asking Wong for cooking lessons. If only he wasn't such a wiseacre.

"Alhambran agates," Mary Jane read. "Long used to detain the most savage nonmortal corporeal beings. Touched to the flesh of a willing or insensible entity, they resonate with a static pocket dimension from which there is no simple means of egress." She frowned. "Static pocket dimension?"

"A tiny reality where not much happens, and where time doesn't progress at the same rate as everywhere else," I said. "It's like a combination prison cell and deep freeze."

"But magic," she said.

"Well. There are some quantum theories that indicate that something like this *could* be possible, but . . ."

She reached for one of the stones. "So you just touch the Ancient with the magic rock and poof?"

I caught her wrist gently before she could touch it. "I'm not sure exactly what they will and won't do," I said. "But they're evidently powerful and dangerous. I think it's best not to take any chances."

She blinked and drew her hand back. "Oh."

"Here's the thing," I said. "They have to want to go. Or else they've got to be unconscious. Otherwise, the rock doesn't work."

"Oh," Mary Jane said. "Well. That's doable,

right? I mean, you can just punch their lights out and stick a rock in their ear. Can't you?"

I grunted. "I blew up a building with Morlun in it. Gas explosion. His clothes got flash-burned and he walked out of it naked as a jaybird and without so much as a bruise. It barely mussed his hair. And I put him through brick walls, smashed him with a telephone pole to the noggin, threw him off the roof of a thirty-story building—nothing."

Mary Jane folded her arms. "So, the magic rocks aren't going to help after all?"

"Not unless I can devise a way to knock out the Ancients," I said through a mouthful of sandwich. "Or else talk them into doing it willingly."

"I see," she said quietly.

One of those tense silences fell.

"How did the test go?" I asked her.

"Hmmm?" She shook her head a little and gave me a false laugh. "Don't worry about it. It's not really important."

"Sure it is," I said quietly.

She frowned at the table for a minute. "I passed the written," she said.

"Uh-oh."

She rolled her eyes and waved her hands in frustration. "It's so *stupid.* I got to the driving test and panicked. I couldn't remember anything I was supposed to remember. I mean, in the traffic and everything, and I was worried and it turned into one huge blur. I couldn't get my breath."

"Ah," I said. "What happened?"

"I just tried to figure out what to do by watching the professionals. I mean, I figured they knew what they were doing, right?"

"The professionals?" I asked.

She nodded. "Cabbies."

I choked. I couldn't help it. I bowed my head and tried to cough as if something had gone down the wrong way, to strangle my laughter before it could hurt her feelings. I looked up at her after a moment, with my face turning red from the effort of holding it in.

She sighed and shook her head with a small, rueful smile. "Go ahead."

I laughed.

"I just don't understand it," she said, when I recovered. "Locking up like that. It isn't as though it's particularly *difficult.*"

"The driving test, you mean?" I said.

"Yes."

I thought about it. "You say you were short of breath?"

"Yes."

"It sounds like a panic attack," I said. "They happen."

Mary Jane's mouth twisted in distaste. "Really? I used to make fun of the models who said they had them before a show. I never thought they might be real." She shook her head. "Maybe I should just check myself into a funny farm."

"Might be a little extreme this early in the game," I said. "I mean, we're talking about a reaction to psychological pressure—of which you have had plenty lately. You'd be crazy if you *didn't* have a twitch or two."

I didn't mention anything specific. No need to bring up the ugly details. Her abduction and imprisonment following her apparent death. Our split. Our happy reunion, but always with homicidal madmen, with or without costumes, prancing in and out of the wings. All the while, dashing around the world on planes, trains, and automobiles (admittedly, someone else did the driving) to appear in shows, to be photographed in exotic places, attending openings and soirees and all the other duties expected of a celebrity.

Mix in some pain, some trauma, some terror. Blend well. All of that would be more than enough to rattle anyone's cage.

"Then why do I feel like such a wimp?" she asked.

"I don't know," I said. "Sometimes I feel kinda wimpy myself. Look, MJ, this isn't a big deal. If we have to, I'll drive you down until you can pass the test."

She frowned and then shook her head. "No. I'll do it myself. I'll pass it Monday morning. If you can deal with immortal, unstoppable monsters, I can handle the DMV."

"Easy there, Superchick. If you're working up an archenemy, you don't want to start with the DMV. Go with someone a little easier to deal with. Doctor Doom, Magneto."

She smiled at me—more because I'd gone to the effort to make the joke than because it was funny. She glanced at the stones. "I'm not sure I like this Strange person," she said.

"The doc's okay," I said. "I get the feeling he's doing everything he can. He's got limits."

"I don't care about limits," Mary Jane said, her tone practical. "I care about you. He isn't doing well by you, and you're what matters to me."

I slipped my hand from her wrist, and twined her warm fingers in mine. "I think you might not be totally objective."

"Why would I want to be?" she asked. She leaned down and pressed a soft, warm kiss to my hand.

I pushed my food aside, and went around the table to kiss my wife. She returned the kiss with an ardent sigh, her arms sliding around my neck, holding on as tightly as she could.

She was afraid.

So was I.

So the kiss became our whole world. She became my whole world. I let her warmth, her desire, her love wash over me, and gave it back in kind. Words would have been a waste of sensation. So I picked her up and carried her toward our bedroom, where the fear, for a while, couldn't touch us.

I hadn't really planned on falling asleep, but I'd pulled an all-nighter after a fairly strenuous round with the Rhino and a follow-up game of Dodge the Ancient, so once I had relaxed body and mind, it was apparently inevitable. I woke to the sound of voices speaking quietly in the living room.

I got out of bed and suited up, put some jeans and a sweatshirt over my colors, and walked into the living room.

"There's nothing going on," Felicia was saying. "Even you must have that one figured out by now."

"Believe me, sweetie," MJ said in a poisonously friendly voice, "I do not regard you as a threat."

I thought about maybe putting on the mask and going out the window. Nothing I could possibly say or not say, do or not do, would let me avoid a fight. Although it didn't seem very heroic to go running and hiding like that. On the other hand, it didn't seem prudent to go rushing into the conversation, either. So I stayed put for the moment, listening.

"A threat? Now why would I be a threat to you?" Felicia asked. "Just because I can actually do something to help Peter—other than waving pom-poms and baking him cookies, that is."

If the barb scored on MJ, I couldn't tell it from her voice—which meant that it probably had. "Ah, yes, your job skills. I can't count how many times I've wished I knew how to steal cars or sneak around in an outfit from Strippers 'R' Us. It would be so helpful to Peter, in his day-to-day life, if only I could unzip my top a little farther down past my belly button."

Felicia let out a catty little laugh. "That's pretty bold, coming from the girlfriend of Lobsterman. Have I mentioned, by the way, how much I admired your acting in that fine film? I think the scene in the pink bikini was probably the most moving, though it must have been a cold day on the set. Did they get you an acting coach to tell you how to scream in terror, or did they just shove head shots of you on a bad hair day into your face?"

"It was traumatic," MJ said. "Thank goodness there was someone who wanted to share his life with me to help me recover. Does your husband comfort you after a hard day at work, Felicia?"

"If I ever find anyone I can put up with," Felicia said, "at least I'll make up my mind when I marry him, not bounce back and forth like an airy little Ping-Pong ball."

At which point, good sense departed, and I'd heard enough.

I pushed open the bedroom door, and said, in a very quiet, very even voice, "Felicia. That's my wife."

Felicia pressed her lips together before she could say whatever hasty response had come to her mouth. She folded her arms and turned away from MJ and me, stalking stiff-spined to the window.

"MJ," I said in the same quiet voice. "That's my friend. And yours. You know that."

Mary Jane's face flickered with anger, but then she closed her eyes and shook her head once, and nodded to me. "I just . . ."

"We're all tense. This isn't the right way to handle it," I said quietly. "You're both better people than that. I need you to call a cease-fire. Please."

Felicia rolled her eyes at my reflection in the window. She was back in the Black Cat outfit again, though she'd slung a gauzy peasant skirt and a leather jacket, both dark blue, over it, and it would pass for a clubbing outfit to the casual eye. "Fine," she said. "MJ?"

"Yes," Mary Jane said in a measured tone. "There's no reason we can't be civil."

"Thank you," I said with exaggerated patience. Which was probably asking for trouble, but ye gods and little fishes, they were supposed to be adults.

"Are my leftovers in the fridge?" I asked my wife.

"Yes. Go ahead and eat," Mary Jane said.

I grunted and did, getting what remained of Wong's Shangri-la-level sandwiches out of the fridge. I took them to the table with a glass of milk and asked Felicia, "Did you get the prints?"

"Yes," Felicia said calmly.

"Do I want to know how?" I asked.

"Does it matter?"

I chewed on my sandwich. "It matters to me, I guess."

"Because I might have broken the law?"

"Yes."

"Ah," Felicia said. "You mean, the way the Rhino breaks the law. I mean, that's what you said made him a bad guy. How he broke the law all the time."

"What I said—"

"I mean, logically speaking, if you would have busted him for doing something illegal, I should expect you to treat me the same way. If I tell you that I broke all kinds of laws getting the prints, are you going to take me in, Peter?"

Mary Jane said nothing, but her lips compressed and her eyes narrowed.

"No," I said. "Don't be ridiculous."

"Ah," Felicia said. "Well. You'll be pleased to know that I broke no laws whatsoever."

That surprised me a bit. I guess it showed on my face, because Felicia laughed. "All I had to do was contact Lamont. I told him what it was about and that I was working with you and he was happy to let me get a copy."

I blinked. "He was? Why?"

Felicia fluttered her eyelashes. "I asked him in person."

I snorted and shook my head. "You're shameless."

"Why, thank you," Felicia said. "I'm told you had some success this afternoon? MJ said something about magic rocks."

"That remains to be seen. I don't see how they're going to be of any help to us—at least not yet." I explained the rocks and showed her the page describing them. "Were you able to turn anything up from the prints?"

"Too soon," she said. "Oliver's good, but it will take several hours, at least, to start comparing them to all the databases."

I nodded. "All right," I said. "Meanwhile, we need more information. I think we should head out and tail these creeps around a little, find out what they're up to, where they're staying."

She nodded firmly. "Way ahead of you. I think we should—"

My spider sense began to stir, a slow tingling that rippled lightly over my spine and scalp.

Mary Jane sat up straight, her eyes widening as she saw my face. "Peter?"

"My spider tracer," I said quietly. "It's close."

"What should—"

"Shhhhh," I said, trying to focus on the sensation. There. The electronic signal the tracer emitted resonated off of whatever it was that made my spider sense work. It was south of us, and coming closer, fast.

Just then, Felicia's jacket beeped. She reached in, grabbed her visors, and put them on for a moment. Then she let out a quiet curse. "My tracking paint," she said. "Closer than three hundred meters." She looked up with suddenly wide eyes. "Peter, we need to go *now.*"

My spider sense quivered oddly, and I began to feel the first stirrings of the primal dread the Ancients caused in me.

"It's too late," I murmured. "They're here."

15

NO TIME. NO TIME. Think fast, Spidey.

"Mary Jane," I said. "I want you to grab the credit cards, any cash we have, and a change of clothes. Now, move."

My wife nodded and hurried to the bedroom.

"Felicia," I said. "Get her out of here."

Felicia had never been much of a fan of tanning beds, but she looked especially pale about now. "Right. Where?"

"Aunt May's. Then we—"

Mary Jane emerged from the bedroom in a flowered dress and a fleece coat. She carried a nylon backpack in either hand. "That was fast," I told her.

"I thought it might be smart to have a traveling kit ready for emergencies," she said. "This one's mine. This one's yours. Cash, two credit cards we haven't used, medicine, a first aid kid, a blanket, some dried food, clothes."

I felt a surge of sudden pride. "That was pretty good thinking," I said.

"It never hurts to plan ahead."

I kissed her on the mouth. "All right. Felicia's going to get you to the car, and then you're both going to scoot to Aunt May's."

"What?" Mary Jane protested. "I'm not going to—"

"Be used against me," I interrupted. "You're going with her."

"Peter . . ."

"Don't worry about me, MJ. I'll just bounce around insulting them for a while and then run away." I pulled off my street clothes, put on the mask, and the whole time the sense of panic in me continued to rise. "This can't be a discussion right now. They're getting closer. Go."

She swallowed, nodded, then said to Felicia, "We should use the stairs."

Felicia detached the flimsy skirt, produced that grappling baton from a sleeve, and opened the window with a grin. "Stairs?"

"Oh my," Mary Jane said.

"Don't worry, MJ," Felicia said with a feline smile. "It won't be like with Peter, but I'll get you there." Her head tilted to one side as she presumably looked at something in the visor. "They're within a hundred meters already."

I checked in with my spider sense. "Yes. Mortia's almost directly below us. They're at the front of the building."

"They came in fast," Felicia said. "Come here,

MJ." She produced a strap of nylon webbing, clipped one end to a ring at the waist of her bodysuit, and flipped it around Mary Jane. "I thought you said they had to touch you to track you down."

"They do," I said. "They must have found us some other way."

"Like what?"

"If I knew, I'd have been making sure it didn't work," I said. "Tick tock, Cat."

"Don't get your webs in a knot," she advised me. She ran the strap around Mary Jane and secured it to something on her own outfit with a muted click. "Okay, MJ. We go out the window on three. Hold on tight."

"Wait," Mary Jane said. "Do I have my car keys?" She fumbled a set of keys out of her pocket and clenched a plastic tag on the key chain in her teeth. Then she nodded, donned her backpack, and she and Felicia went out the window on the slender cable extending from the Black Cat's baton.

I went out behind them, part of my attention on Felicia and MJ as they descended at a controlled pace that Felicia couldn't possibly have managed on upper body strength alone. It was hard to tell in the near-dark, but I was betting that there was some kind of rock-climbing-type harness built into the suit. Felicia guided them down in long, smooth rappels, obviously being careful. That would be for my sake, I knew. Given a choice, Felicia generally likes to do things in the most insanely dangerous fashion she thinks she can survive.

I hit the building above us with a webline, let it stretch, and used the snap to get some more air and throw myself out into the autumn air, nailing the building's corner with another webline to swing around. I sailed clear across the street in front of our apartment, stopped on the building across the street, and froze in a shadow halfway up while my spider sense clubbed me with what had become an almost familiar amount of brainstem-level terror.

There was the usual foot traffic for that time of night, a cool autumn evening, and there were several people moving down the sidewalks while city traffic prowled by at a relaxed pace in the wake of rush hour. Couldn't the Ancients have waited until midnight? At least then, there wouldn't have been quite so many people around. Rude, these psychotic life-eating monsters. Very rude.

Mortia stood on the sidewalk outside my apartment building, wearing the same outfit as the day before, plus a long evening coat. She was staring thoughtfully at the building. The Rhino stood behind her in, I kid you not, a khaki trench coat you could have made a tent out of and a broad-brimmed fedora. He had a gym bag in one hand—it doubtless held the stupid hat.

My spider sense quivered, and I glanced down. Malos was on the sidewalk immediately below me, walking slowly down the length of the building like a pacing mountain lion, gazing thoughtfully up at lit windows. Down the block, Thanis was doing the same thing on the other side of the street from Mortia and the Rhino, neither of whom was headed into my building.

I sucked in a breath. So. They had a general idea where I was, but didn't know exactly where. That meant that they hadn't found out about Peter Parker, at least not yet, which in turn meant that they wouldn't know about Mary Jane—or Aunt May's place. Good. With that off my mind, I would be free to worry about myself—something which is really quite useful when one is in combat.

In fact, given that they were still searching, there was really nothing to be gained from a fight, except possibly getting tagged and tracked down. Not only that, but there were way too many people around who could get hurt. I decided to sidle out and run.

Which is when I got an object lesson in how important it is for prey to stay downwind of predators.

Hey, whaddya want from me? I lived my whole life in New York City. The only time I worried about the wind was during games at Yankee Stadium and in fights with real stinkers like Vermin and the Lizard.

Mortia suddenly tensed and then whirled, eyes intently scanning up and down the street—and then tracking up to me. I was hidden in deep shadow, invisible. *Invisible,* for crying out loud. There aren't many people on the whole planet who can sneak around better than me, and I know invisible when I do it.

I guess nobody told Mortia that, though. She bared her teeth in a very slow, very white smile, and as she did, both Thanis and Malos froze in their tracks and looked up at me as well.

The Rhino continued to look around, evidently bored. It took him a second to notice Mortia, and then he squinted upward and around, expression puzzled.

I dove off my perch just as Malos ripped a steel wastebasket off of the sidewalk and chucked it at me. I hit a flagpole sticking out from the building three stories up, flung myself up, flicked a web-strand at Mortia's feet in midair with one hand while sending out a zipline down the street and hurling myself forward with the other. Thanis leapt at me as I did, and I had to contort and twist in midair to alter my trajectory and avoid him.

I hit the sidewalk rolling, then hopped up over a mailbox and landed on its other side, with Thanis coming hard behind me. I reached out and seized the parking meters on either side of me and ripped them from the concrete, one in each hand as Thanis approached.

I caught him on the end of one of the four-foot lengths of metal, the broken concrete jabbing into his belly, and planted the actual meter on the ground beneath me. This had the effect of slamming him in the breadbasket pretty hard, as well as keeping him physically away from me, sending him flying over my head, his flailing fingers missing me by an inch or more.

It was harder without my spider sense working at full power, but I assumed the worst—that Malos was already closing in—and bounded to one side, then up onto the wall, then into a double backflip that carried me all the way to the roof of an old Chevy sedan parked on the street.

My fears had been well founded. Malos missed catching me in a simple tackle by a fraction of a second, but the flip carried me straight over his head and behind him. He whirled around to face me, expression furious. I played "Shave and a Haircut" on his noggin with alternating blows of the parking meters. I put a lot of extra oomph into the "six bits" part, and the meters exploded in mounds of silver coins when I did. Malos was driven back several steps by the impact, and his knees looked a little wobbly for a second.

But just for a second. Then he gave his head a shake, speared me with an annoyed glance, and started in again.

By that time, Mortia had torn her foot loose from where I'd webbed it to the sidewalk, and she was coming after me at a sprint. Wow, she was quick. And if she'd gotten out of my webbing that fast, she wasn't exactly as dainty as a schoolmarm in the muscle department, either.

Fighting all of them in the open was a losing proposition. Sooner or later Mortia and her brothers would be almost certain to inflict harm on the citizenry—and I had no illusions about outmaneuvering Mortia this time. If this went on too long or I got unlucky, she'd at least get to tag me. Once that happened, I could run, but not hide.

So, I needed somewhere to fight that would leave me with enough room to move around, while simultaneously being hostile to long lines of sight *and* relatively free of bystanders. New York being what it was—packed with people—unpopulated spaces tend to be the kinds of places no one wants to hang around in: places that are dangerous or unsettling to linger in, places where bad people do bad things.

So I headed for the nearest parking garage.

I leapt onto an awning, bounced on it to gain speed, and whirled around a traffic light to get airborne. I took a long, long swing and flipped myself into a helplessly ballistic arch with Mortia only a few leaps behind me. I was making an easy target of myself, and she went for the opening, coming after me.

Excellent. I flipped in midair, gave her some webbing in the face with one hand, stuck a line to a passing garbage truck with the other, then joined the two, and watched the truck jerk her off-course and begin dragging her down the street.

It looked painful. Also cool.

I landed in a backward roll, flipped up into the air, and used a webline to whirl in a couple of big circles around a streetlight before throwing myself up onto the garage's roof. A little ostentatious, maybe, but this way Malos and Thanis would be certain to spot me. They looked like the types who might not exercise their brain cells very often.

Malos showed up first, by climbing up the side of the parking garage. He wasn't sticking to the wall or anything amazing and stylish like that. Instead, he just made a claw shape with his fingers and sank their tips several inches into the concrete, like it was so much soft clay. He went up hand over hand very nearly as fast as I could have done it. He flipped himself up the last five or six feet and landed on his feet with credible grace. His silk shirt was torn in a couple of places where my follow-through with the meters had wreaked havoc, and both his shirt and his long black hair were covered with dust.

"You got dust all over that pretty shirt," I told him in a cheery tone. "And your hair, too. And look, there are security cameras. Everyone is going to see you all mussed and disheveled."

"Oh dear," he said in a very low, velvety-soft voice, and walked toward me in no great hurry. "However will I survive?"

Then he turned to a dark green Volvo and picked it up.

They might be the safest cars in the world, but when they're thrown from an eight-story parking garage, I really doubt that their Swedish engineering does very much to soften the blow. So I simply hopped off the roof, popped the garage with a webline, and swung back in on the sixth level, out of Malos's sight, and hoped that he wouldn't waste the effort to throw the car.

A distinct lack of crashing crunches told me I'd been right, and I breathed a little sigh of relief—right up until Thanis stepped out of the shadows of a stairway in his expensive Italian suit and threw a haymaker at me.

I didn't sense him coming until the very last second. I got a little lucky. If he'd just reached out to touch me with his near hand, it probably would have been fast enough to land. He'd gone for the whole enchilada, though, and I had time to get my head out of his way. I danced to one side with Thanis breathing down my neck and dodged another pair of quick blows. He was good at throwing them, but I was better at getting out of their way. I could keep this guy from laying a glove on me, if I was careful, and if he didn't get any help—and if he didn't realize that I had no intention of hitting him back.

But he figured that part out—and within a few seconds, to boot—and the shape of the fight altered. It's like that in hand-to-hand combat. If you can simply discard the notion of protecting yourself from counterattack, it's a whole heck of a lot easier to get through an opponent's defenses with a focused, concentrated offensive, and it was suddenly everything I could do to keep him off me—until I ducked under a sledgehammer blow aimed at my neck. Thanis's fist hit the wall behind me, and shook loose a fire extinguisher from its mount on the wall.

I caught it on the way down and hollered, "Batter up!"

I swung with both hands and hit him. I didn't hold *anything* back. I don't do that very often, but for Morlun and his kin, I cared enough to send the very best.

There was a sound halfway between the ringing

of a gong and the thump of a watermelon hitting the sidewalk, and Thanis left the garage by way of having his head line-drived through a section of concrete wall.

Without pausing, I cleared the pin from the firing mechanism of the extinguisher and sent a cloud of white chemicals billowing out behind me—right into the face of Malos, who had emerged from the stairway in pursuit. He came through blind and aggressive. My second swing of the extinguisher lifted him from his feet and into the concrete roof above me, sending a web-work of cracks about twenty feet across it, and leaving the extinguisher bent into the shape of a boomerang.

"G'day, mate!" I shouted in a cheesy Australian accent, and whipped the extinguisher at him in a sidearm throw. The impact slammed his head back into the front grille of an old Impala, driving his skull into the body of the car up to his ears. "Spider-Man! That's Australian for 'Headache!' "

The ground started to shake in rhythm, and the Rhino came pounding up the car ramp at a modest pace of thirty or forty miles an hour. He'd ditched the coat, the broad-brimmed hat, and his bag, and he had the silly rhino-head hat on. The fashion slave. He doesn't corner well, and he had to windmill his arms to keep his balance as he bent his course around the ramp. Then he saw me, bellowed, and came my way, picking up speed fast.

Figures. Someone I can actually punch finally shows up and it's already time to leave.

I charged him right back.

He wasn't expecting that, but after a fraction of a second of surprise, he simply lowered his horn and came at me faster, letting out a bellow as he did.

I waited until the last second, then bounded straight up and over him, and clung to the ceiling. As he passed, I tagged his broad gray butt with a webline, then sent another web at Malos, who was just then regaining his feet. And since it had already worked once, I merely joined the lines together.

The Ancient looked down as the webbing plastered itself to his silk and the belt area of his leather pants. Then he tracked the line of the web-strand back to the thundering Rhino.

He closed his eyes in irritation and sighed. "Oh, bother."

I gave him a cheerful, upside-down wave from where I crouched on the ceiling.

The Rhino tried to brake, but he had too much momentum going. He went out through the wall.

The line stretched a little, so that there was a Looney Tune instant of motionlessness, and then it snapped back like a bungee cord and dragged Malos out of the garage after the plummeting Rhino.

"Sometimes I amaze even myself," I said in a cheerful voice. Then I hurried to the far side of the garage and beat a hasty retreat. I'd delayed the Ancients long enough for Felicia to get MJ out of there, so there was no point in staying. It was time to fade out and fight another day.

Except that in the middle of fading, I saw Mortia running down the street back toward me, running on *top* of the power lines as if they were as wide as a city sidewalk. She spotted me, bounced like a diver on a board, flipped through the air, and landed at a bounding run. I saw that she was wearing one of those tiny headsets some cell phones have, and she was speaking into it as she pursued me.

Maybe thirty seconds later, the Rhino caught up to us and joined her. He's a lot lighter on his feet than you'd think—he can top out at better than a hundred miles an hour, even if he can't change course much while he does so. Mortia looked like something out of Japanese anime, streaking along in a bounding run that would have run me down in about ten seconds flat on level ground.

I could use that speed against them, to keep them separated from Malos and Thanis.

So I poured it on, zipping down the street, using every trick I knew to move as fast as I possibly could. I didn't have an infinite amount of webbing, and I was burning through it fast, using its elasticity to maintain my momentum and add speed, while taking a lot of turns to prevent the Rhino from getting enough momentum to catch up.

Mortia came after me the way the Lizard always chased me—fast and nimble, bounding over cars and passersby, her feet hardly touching the ground. She leapt to sprint along window ledges occasionally, when traffic on the street was too high-volume.

The Rhino lumbered along the road in the middle of the right-hand lane, passing cars and at one point shouldering aside a cabby who had tried to change lanes and was crowding him. The cab flew into the side of a building.

I made sure to keep the pace down just enough that they seemed to be catching up with me, always gaining a little ground, and as a result they never slowed. We left the other two Ancients to trail along blocks behind us—because while they were super-strong, they just didn't have the raw speed necessary to keep up with Mortia and the Rhino. I started changing the pace as we pulled away, hopping over a block this way, then doubling back and heading three blocks the other way, until I was sure Malos and Thanis were nowhere in the immediate area.

I went by Shea Stadium on long, slingshot-style weblines, zoomed over a line of docks filled with small commercial fishing vessels and largish pleasure boats, and came down in the hangars on the eastern end of La Guardia. Ongoing renovations had several of the enormous buildings gutted and under repair, separated from the rest of the place by those orange construction fences, so there wouldn't be many people around. It was nice and dark there, plenty of three-dimensional space to play in, and not many people.

I swung over the fence and landed on a little open space between acres of yawning buildings, bounced up onto the side of one of the hangars, and made myself scarce and sneaky in the abundant shadows.

Mortia came down practically in the same spot my feet had landed in and froze, her stance a marvel of liquid tension, her eyes open wide. The Rhino wasn't far behind her. He had to jump over the fence to get to her, maybe a seventy-five-foot hop, and nothing his enhanced muscles couldn't handle. He landed on the concrete beside her. The impact sent several cracks running through it, and it took the Rhino a few steps to arrest his momentum.

Mortia gave him another contemptuous look. Then she turned in a slow, slow circle, looking for me. But I'd kept downwind this time.

"You're quite clever," Mortia called out, turning in a slow circle. "But then, the spiders always are. Separating me from my brothers this way is an excellent tactic."

I wanted to make a comment about family therapy, but I kept my mouth shut.

"I should also like to thank you for your gifts," she said. She reached into a pocket and held up my spider tracer between two fingers. "My people tell me that this is some sort of tracking device. They say it was built quite cleverly, but out of unremarkable parts. Which told us that you were not a being of substantial material wealth. But then, spiders rarely are."

She held up the cravat next. "This potion upon my clothes, on the other hand, is quite expensive and quite rare. Even governmental military bodies do not use it; its availability and use is restricted to private security firms. And there can only be so many lovely young white-haired women with access to it."

True enough. Gulp.

"We *will* find you, spider. You will fall. It can be no other way. Once we learn your name, there will be no place for you to hide. There will be no way to protect those you love. But if you come forth and face me now, that need not happen. I do not know who your loved ones are, nor do I care. My business is with you. I have no interest in them, except in how I might use them to attain you. Come forth and we will depart, our business done. Deny me, and I will destroy them along with you."

For a minute I was tempted to deal with her. Anything I could do to keep the conflict between just myself and the bad guys was something that appealed to me. My fights had spilled over onto innocents far too many times. But I wasn't sure I could trust Mortia. If she really was here on a vengeance kick, she might well choose to take someone close from me, just as I had taken family from her.

Either way, the smart thing to do was to pull a swift fade, break contact, and let them flounder around looking for me. Definitely, that was the smart thing to do.

But no one threatens my family.

It took me maybe a second and a half to hit a scaffold on the opposite hangar, a heavy rig loaded with heavy steel structural support beams. I gave the scaffold a hard pull, and brought the entire stack of metal struts down onto Mortia and the Rhino, burying them in at least a ton of metal.

They weren't under it for long. The mess wasn't done settling before the Rhino started slapping struts away like they were so many drinking straws. Though Mortia did not seem to be the same kind of powerhouse as her brothers, she wasn't a wimp, either, and was able, with visible effort, to begin freeing herself from the tangled steel.

While she was doing that, I swung down at the Rhino and shouted, "Boot to the head!" as I kicked him there.

The Rhino flew into another stack of building materials—heavy-duty rebar and lumber. He came surging out of them with a bellow of anger and charged me, swinging. I let him do it like he always did it, barely dodging him—only this time I danced over toward Mortia, and just as she came to her feet, one of the Rhino's furious swings struck her squarely and slammed her back into the mound of twisted metal.

"Great hook! Thanks for the assist, big guy," I said in a cheery tone. Then I popped him in the face with a glob of webbing, goosed him, and ran.

But not far.

I doubled back to the far side of the hangars, nipped up to the roof, found a place where I'd be neither scented nor seen, and waited to see what happened.

The Rhino ripped the webbing off his face and bellowed in frustration. He spun around looking for me, and naturally did not spot me.

Mortia sat up, her hair mussed. She might be tough as nails, but when the Rhino tags you, you know it, and I don't care who you are. Where Mortia hit the thicket of support struts, they had been mashed into a definite indentation. It matched her outline exactly. Her cold eyes locked onto the Rhino. "Well?"

"He is gone," the Rhino replied. He let out a frustrated growl and then turned to Mortia to offer her a hand up. "My apologies, ma'am. It was not my intention to strike you."

The Rhino could be polite?

"I told you not to commit yourself against him until I signaled you," Mortia said, rising. "You disobeyed me."

"Da," he growled, frustration evident in his voice. "I lost my temper. He makes me angry."

"You allow him to do so," she said in that same cold tone. "You are a fool."

The Rhino looked like he couldn't decide whether to be angry or chagrined. "One day, he will not be lucky. One day, I will strike him, once, and it will all be over."

Mortia looked at him for a moment and then said, "No. I do not think that will happen."

The Rhino glanced at her, a question on his face.

"You have just become more liability than asset," she said, quite calmly. And then, in a motion so fast even I barely saw it, her hand shot out and clenched over the Rhino's face, her nails somehow digging into his superhumanly durable flesh. There was a flash of sickly greenish light beneath her fingers.

The Rhino screamed. Not a war bellow, not a cry of rage, not a shout of challenge. He screamed like a man in utter agony, screamed without dignity or any kind of self-control, and his superhumanly powerful lungs made it *loud,* loud enough to shake the ground and the shipping containers around him. His body bent into an agonized arch, and if Mortia hadn't been holding him up with one arm, he would not have remained standing.

Instead, she whirled with him, eyes burning with the cold light one might associate with a hungry python, and drove his skull into the same debris she had struck. "Pathetic little vessel. You are worthless, incapable of even simple destruction. Be grateful that your life will at last have *some* sort of purpose."

The Rhino screamed again. Weaker.

I watched it in pure horror.

She was killing him.

The Rhino was no friend. But he was a long-term enemy, and in some ways that's close to the same thing. I've butted heads with him, metaphorically speaking, since my earliest days in costume. And Felicia was right about one thing: The Rhino wasn't a killer. So much so, in fact, that one time, when the Sinister Somethingorother had me dead to rights, the Rhino had refused to participate in killing me with his fellow villains and had, in fact, argued against it. Sure, he hated my guts. Sure, he wanted to beat me down once and for all, prove that he was better than me, stronger than me.

But he wasn't a killer.

The Rhino was one of the bad guys, but there were worse bad guys out there.

Like the one murdering him in front of my eyes.

That unholy light poured up through her fingers, showing the outlines of oddly shaped bones that belonged to something else, something other, a creature who did not feel, did not fear, did not care. Who only hungered.

Aleksei was still a human being. There was no way I would leave a human being, *any* human being, no matter his sins, in the hands of a creature like that.

I couldn't make a fight of it; the wonder twins would be coming along any minute. So I took a cheap shot. I got to my feet, dove toward Mortia, and shot a webline at the wall of the hangar behind me. As the line stretched, it slowed me, and I stuck a second line to Mortia's rear. The first line snapped me back, and as the second line stretched, I gave it a sudden hard pull with all the power I could summon. The resulting combination of tension and strength ripped her away from the Rhino, sent her tumbling cravat-over-teakettle into the evening air, and flung her over the hangar and out of sight. She let out a wailing, alien howl of rage as she went, one that blended in with the roar of a jet lifting off.

I landed on the ground near the Rhino and said, "Right. Never say I've never done anything nice for you."

The Rhino didn't reply. Or move.

I hopped over and checked on him. He was alive, at least, and he let out a soft, agonized moan. There was blood on his face, trickles of it coming from the marks Mortia's nails had left there. The skin was horribly dry and cracked, flakes coming off as he moaned again, as if his face had been left out in the desert sun for several days.

He was barely conscious, even with his enhanced resilience. If I left him there, he was as good as dead.

"For crying out loud," I complained. "I haven't got enough to do?"

Mortia screamed again. It sounded like she was a lot farther away this time, maybe all the way to the edge of the inlet. A second later, I heard another brassy, weird-sounding call from the opposite direction. Thanis and Malos were closing in.

"No good deed goes unpunished," I muttered. Then I bent down and slung the Rhino over my shoulder. The extra eight hundred pounds was going to make web-slinging difficult, but I couldn't just leave the loser there to die.

So I got moving again, if more slowly, this time carrying an unconscious foe, avoiding the incoming Ancients, and making my way back to MJ and Felicia.

I hopped over and checked on him. He was alive, at least, as he let out a soft, agonized moan. There was blood on his face, trickles of it running from the mouth. [illegible] I left there. His skin was horribly dry and cracked, flakes coming off as he moved, again, as if his face had been left out in the desert sun for several days.

He was barely conscious, [illegible] his unnatural resilience. If I left him there, he was as good as dead.

"For crying out loud," I complained. "I haven't got enough to do?"

Merda shrieked again. It sounded like she was a lot farther away this time, maybe all the way to the edge of the mist. A second later I heard another banshee-like sound/call from the opposite direction. Tlaloc and Malor were closing in.

"No good deed goes unpunished," I muttered. Then I bent down and slung the Rune over my shoulder. The extra eight hundred pounds was going to make web-slinging difficult, but I couldn't just leave the [illegible] to die.

So I got moving again, if more slowly this time, carrying an [illegible], avoiding the incoming [illegible], and making my way back to Mal and Red [illegible] tion.

16

When I tapped on the glass, Felicia opened the window of Aunt May's apartment. She looked at me. Then at the Rhino, wrapped in webbing from the shoulders down and strapped onto my back like a hyperthyroid papoose, the horn on his silly hat wobbling as his head bobbed in the relaxation of the senseless.

Then she looked at me again, blinked, and said, "You're kidding."

"Just open the window the rest of the way and stand back," I told her.

"I hope Aunt May is insured," she said, but she did it.

I climbed in with the Rhino on my back. I wasn't worried about hurting him if I banged him into something. I was more worried about the something. So I brought him in as carefully as I could and laid him out on the kitchen floor.

Aunt May's apartment is somewhat spartan, for

an elderly lady. When she moved out of the house I grew up in, the one she had shared with Uncle Ben, she put many of her belongings in storage, rather than attempting to stuff them into her little apartment. She still has some of her furniture—a table, chairs for it, her rocker, her couch. She replaced their double bed with a single one; there's a small guest room where she put the double, for when Mary Jane and I visit. She keeps a couple of bookshelves filled with everything from *Popular Science* (which I'm still half-sure she only subscribes to so that I'll have something to read when I visit) to romance novels to history books. She has a few small shelves, a few knickknacks, and that's about it.

Mary Jane came in and hugged me tight, then stared at the man on the floor. "Oh, God. What happened to his face?"

The Rhino looked bad. No worse than he had when I had picked him up, but no better, either.

"Mortia did it to him," I said. "She decided he wasn't useful anymore and started feeding on him."

Felicia regarded the Rhino with a cool, distant expression. "He's dead, then?"

"Not yet," I said.

"Are you insane?" Felicia asked quietly.

Mary Jane gave her a sharp glance.

"If Mortia did this to him," Felicia explained, "she touched him. If she touched him, she can follow him, find him, as long as he is alive. Which means—"

"She can find us here," Mary Jane breathed. She looked at me. "Peter?"

"No names," I said quietly. "He's out, but he'll be coming to anytime now. He doesn't need to know any names."

"This is massively stupid," Felicia snapped. "You're going to get yourself killed. And me with you."

"She was going to kill him," I said. "What else could I have done?"

"You could have *let* her kill him," Felicia said.

I was glad that I had my mask on, because I wasn't sure I could have kept the anger I felt off of my face. "What happened to treating him like a human being? To his not being all that bad a person?"

"He might not be Charles Manson, but he chose which side to play for." She folded her arms. "It isn't a pleasant thought, not for anyone, but he knows there are risks in this kind of life. You should have let her have him. If nothing else, then she might not have been quite so hot and bothered about coming after *you*."

"So I guess he's not a person after all," I said, and I didn't keep the bitterness out of my words. "Is that it?"

"It isn't about that," she said. "It's about you putting your life at risk. If I had to choose between the two of you, it would be you. Without a second thought. All I was saying is that I wanted you to show a little respect for him. I never wanted you to throw your life away trying to save him."

"He isn't worth that?"

"Worth *you*?" Felicia asked, her voice tired. "No. You can't save everyone. This time around, you'll be lucky to save yourself. Don't throw your life away on some boy scout scruple you can't survive."

Mary Jane stood to one side of the kitchen, motionless, almost invisible, listening, her wide green eyes on me.

I forced myself to take a slow breath. Then I asked, "What do you think I should do?"

"Put him on a train. A plane. Throw him on a truck. Anything, but get him out of here until we can learn more about the Ancients. Once we get up close with these things, once they've touched us, we only have one chance to put them away. If you keep the Rhino here, they'll find us. Maybe in the next few minutes. Certainly soon. So you use him to lead them off and buy us more time."

"That would be the same thing as murdering him myself," I said quietly.

Felicia shook her head, frustration evident on her face. "You didn't ask him to come back to New York. You didn't force the Rhino to get involved with the Ancients. You didn't make them turn on him. He did that all on his own."

"Should that matter?" I asked.

"If your places were reversed," she said, "he'd do the same to you. In a heartbeat."

I looked down at the Rhino, maimed and helpless on Aunt May's kitchen floor.

What Felicia said was probably true. But . . .

maybe not, too. The Rhino could have done nothing while Doc Ock and his buddies finished me. He'd opposed them. They hadn't worked up to a fight or anything, but he'd said something, at least.

If our positions were reversed, would he have stood by and done nothing? Would he have let me die to save his own life?

Probably.

But . . .

But in the end, that didn't matter. Regardless of what the Rhino might or might not have done, it did not change who I was. It did not change the choice I had to make. It did not change the responsibility I would bear in making that choice. It did not change what was right and what was wrong.

"Earlier," I said quietly, "you asked me the difference between people like the Rhino and people like me." I looked at the man, then slowly nodded. "Maybe it starts right here. I'm not letting them have him. I'm not letting them have *anyone.*"

"Gosh, that's noble," Felicia said, her voice tart. "Maybe MJ can put it on your tombstone."

"Felicia," Mary Jane said, stepping up beside me, putting a hand on my shoulder. "You know he's right. If you could stop thinking about yourself for a minute, you'd realize that."

"Hey, Mrs. Cleaver. When I want your opinion, I'll read it in your entrails," Felicia snapped.

MJ's eyes narrowed. "Excuse me?"

"*Enough,*" I growled, loud and harsh enough that

even MJ looked a little surprised. I turned to Felicia and said, "This is what I'm doing."

The Black Cat stared at me for a long moment, and then demanded, something almost like a plea in her voice, "For him? Why?"

"It doesn't matter who he is. I won't leave him to Mortia."

She got in my face, quietly furious, spitting each word. "This. Is. Suicide."

"Look, I get it that you're afraid—"

"Don't you patronize me," she hissed. "I'm not afraid of anything and you know it."

"I'm not saying you're a coward. There's no reason to feel ashamed of being afraid."

She jabbed a finger into my chest. "I am *not* afraid. I am also *not* going to commit suicide for some lowbrow thug too stupid to be careful who he works for."

I pulled the mask off, and met her eyes. "I'm not asking you to do it with me," I said quietly.

Her eyes narrowed, searching mine. Then they became hooded and unreadable, her voice calm. "Good," she said. "Then I don't need to tell you no." She spun on a heel and walked quietly to the door. "I'll call you if I find out anything else. Good-bye."

She slammed the door on the way out.

I flinched a little at the sound of it.

My head pounded in a dull, steady rhythm. My brush with the Ancients had left my spider sense screaming, and the headache was, I began to understand, some kind of natural aftereffect of having the gain on my extra sense turned up to eleven, some sort of psychic hangover. My mouth felt fuzzy. More than anything, I wanted to crawl into a dark hole for a while and rest.

I've noticed that you rarely get a chance to do any dark-hole-crawling when you seem to need it most.

Mary Jane's fingers touched my chin and gently turned my face toward hers.

"Why did you provoke her?" she asked, her manner very serious.

"Provoke her?" I said. "I don't know what—"

She rolled her eyes. "Oh, please. Don't try to deny it. I know you too well."

I felt my mouth turn up into a tired smile. "Well. Maybe a little."

She gave me a small, strained smile and slid her arms around me. "You're pushing her away. Trying to protect her."

I held MJ for a moment, closing my eyes. "Maybe."

"You're a good man," she whispered, her arms tightening. "Which makes me think that she must be right about how dangerous it will be to protect him."

"Maybe," I said.

"What's the real plan, then?"

"The Jolly Gray Giant here should wake up sometime soon. I hope. When he does, I'll tell him about the danger and send him on his way."

Mary Jane was quiet for a moment. Then she said, "How is that different from putting him on a train?"

"Because I'm not going to use him as a lure. I don't think Mortia will chase him down until she's concluded her business with me. He deserves to know what he's up against, and needs time to recover and prepare for it, in case I don't . . ."

I didn't finish the sentence. Mary Jane's arms tightened around me. We stood that way for a minute.

Then I said, "All right. The webs will hold him, but not for long. So I need to be here with him when he wakes up, so I can start talking right away. If he panics, he'll rip out of the webs in a few seconds, and God only knows what will get wrecked. So if he freaks, I'll pitch him out the window."

She nodded, biting her lip thoughtfully. Then she turned the kitchen lights out.

I frowned at her quizzically.

"I don't have a mask," she explained. "I'd rather not be someone he recognizes, generally speaking."

I gave her a small smile and put my mask back on, leaving my nose and mouth uncovered. It hit me that I was starving, so I opened Aunt May's fridge to rustle up something.

"How long will it take them to find us?" Mary Jane asked.

"Technically, they could have been right behind me. But you don't live for thousands of years by taking unnecessary risks. They'll come in carefully, quietly, checking out the area. With any luck, Sleeping Beauty here will wake up in the next few minutes. We'll let him go on his way, which ought to confuse them, at least. Then you and I will slip out and make them start looking for me all over again."

Mary Jane nodded slowly. "But you still don't know how to beat them."

"No."

"Do you know how to find out?"

"No."

"Then what good is running going to do?" she asked. "Ultimately, it's just a delaying tactic."

"So's exercise and controlling your cholesterol," I said, and it came out more frustrated than I meant it to. "I don't know how to deal with freaking magical, Spider-Man-eating monster people." I lost control of my voice completely and found myself shouting. "I'm scared, all right? I can't think! *I don't know!*"

"But you'd risk drawing them here, to both of us, for this man?"

I was quiet for a moment, staring at the inside of the fridge. Then I said, "I couldn't just leave him."

Mary Jane's voice turned warmer. "No. You couldn't."

"If it comes to a fight, I'm not going to stay around here. I don't want them to grab you."

She was silent. I assumed she nodded.

"I'll try to lead them off somewhere where it will minimize the damage. And . . ."

And what, Pete? Bounce around until you get tired, while they don't? Then miss a step. Then die.

"Here's a thought," Mary Jane said.

"Hmmm?"

"Maybe the doctor didn't mean those stones for the Ancients."

I frowned and blinked at her. "Huh?"

"Maybe he meant them for us." She shrugged. "I'm just saying. If it's some sort of timeless prison—maybe he meant us to use them to go there for shelter. Maybe he'd come and get us out."

"Maybe," I said quietly. "But . . . maybe he wouldn't. Or couldn't."

"Did he say that?"

I frowned. "He said that he believed I had what I needed to defeat this foe."

"Oh." She thought about it for a moment, and then said, "He's a difficult man to pin down."

I grunted. Aunt May's fridge was largely bare. Of course. She had been planning to leave for a week on Anna's prize cruise. She wouldn't have left anything in the fridge that would go bad. The freezer had TV dinners, but with any luck we'd be gone from here long before they could be done. So I made do with some microwave popcorn.

As the scent filled the room, the Rhino let out a groan.

I looked up sharply at Mary Jane and nodded toward the bedroom. She swallowed and went there in silence.

Popcorn rattled in the microwave. The Rhino muttered something I didn't understand, in what sounded like Russian. His head tossed left and right. Then he snorted and tried to lift his head.

"Take it easy there, big fella," I told him. The microwave beeped, and I took the popcorn out. "Yes, you're tied up. Yes, I'm Spider-Man. No, I'm not going to hurt you, or even turn you over to the cops. And to prove it, I'll split some popcorn with you if you give me two minutes to talk to you without you going berserkergang on me."

"Spider-Man," the Rhino spat. I could dimly see him bare his teeth in the shadowy kitchen. His basso voice rolled out the thick, half-swallowed consonants of his accent. "You think this is funny, I bet."

"No," I said. "Ow, hot popcorn. Augh, that steam, right when you open the bag? Anyway, I don't think it's funny. I think it's really scary. I think that both of us have bigger problems to worry about than one another."

The Rhino growled, a sound full of suspicion and not much in the way of intellect. "Then why am I bound?"

"What do you remember?" I asked.

"Mortia. She touched me and . . ." He shuddered. Eight hundred pounds of shuddering Rhino is a lot. The plates rattled in the cupboard.

"How are you feeling?" I asked.

"I . . . hurt." There was a note of almost childish surprise in his tone. The Rhino did not often get hurt. Heck, he wasn't even showing any bruises from the massive walloping I'd given him not twenty-four hours before. My knuckles, on the other hand, were still swollen. "Heat, on my face. Headache."

"Mortia and her brothers are extremely bad news," I said. "They feed on life energy like yours and mine."

"They eat super-powered people?" Rhino asked.

"Close enough," I said. "They had a brother who came to eat me several months ago. He got a case of the deads."

"So they came to even the score," said the Rhino. I had to give the big guy credit. Not much in the way of brains, but he understood the meaner things in life.

"Exactly. They hired you to draw me out. Then stood around doing nothing, by the way, when I beat the stuffing out of you."

The Rhino growled, and for some reason it was a much more threatening sound in Aunt May's kitchen than in Times Square.

"The point is," I said quickly, "they didn't exactly give you any backup. And when you inconvenienced Mortia, she decided to kill you."

The Rhino was silent for a second, and then he said, "You stopped her?"

"Yeah."

"Why?" he demanded.

"Despite what you may have read in the *Bugle,* I am one of the good guys. I don't let people get eaten on my watch."

"But I am your enemy," he said.

"Sorta, sure," I agreed. "But Mortia and her brothers are bad news in a big and scary way. You and I have had our disagreements. I imagine we'll keep on having them. But if they get the chance, those three will kill us. Both of us. And they'll barely remember it a few days from now."

His mouth spread into a sneer. "And what do you want? For me to fight beside you?"

"No," I said. "I want you gone. Out of here, somewhere safe. This is going to be nasty, and no one sane is going to want any part of it. Get yourself clear until you have a chance to recover. I think they're coming after me first, but if they get past me, you'll be on your own."

"Da. Am always on my own," the Rhino said, a glower in his tone. "But what do you really want?"

"Nothing. I pulled your big gray butt out of the fire because you once did something similar for me. I just want you to get up and get away from me as fast as you can manage it. The way I see it, that'll balance the scales between us."

His voice became even more suspicious. "This is some trick."

"No trick," I said.

"Prove it," he said. "Untie me."

I haven't spent all this time as a human spider without learning to tie some outstandingly groovy knots. I leaned down, gave the webbing around him several sharp tugs, and the whole thing slithered away from him.

The Rhino sat up slowly, a little unsteadily, as if shocked that I had actually untied him. "Now, the blindfold."

"Uh?" I said. "There's no blindfold, big guy. I mean, it's a little dim in here, but . . ."

I saw him lift his fingers to his face. He drew his hands away after a single touch, and spat out something in Russian that probably should not be said in front of Russian children.

I turned and flicked on the kitchen lights.

The Rhino's ruined face looked awful, but not as bad as his eyes. They had gone entirely white, as if cataracts had entirely occluded them in the few seconds Mortia had touched him.

Holy Moley. This put a nice big old hole in the "get everyone away from Peter so he can fight the battle without them getting hurt or in the way" plan. There was no way I could send him out on his own like this—helpless, utterly unable to defend himself.

"Bozhe moi," the Rhino said, staring sightlessly. "I am blind."

17

THE RHINO SAT ON THE KITCHEN FLOOR munching microwave popcorn while I tried to figure out what would go wrong next. He went through the bag fast, though he didn't seem to hurry, and asked, "Is there perhaps water?"

The simple question startled me. I mean, of all the people I'd ever have thought I'd be talking to in Aunt May's kitchen, the Rhino was about third to last on the list. And the question was just so . . . normal. He ate popcorn. It made him thirsty. The Rhino was pretty much supposed to be all about bellowing and smashing—not being beaten, blind, and conversational.

I got him a glass of water and said, "Hold out your hand."

He did. I put the glass in it. He gave me a grave nod, making the silly rhino horn bob, and said, "Thank you."

The Rhino. Saying thank you. Excuse me while I boggle.

At this rate, I was going to have to reboot my brain before it locked up entirely and went into meltdown. A thought struck me. The Rhino was blind. There was no reason I had to keep wearing the mask.

I took it off and stared at it for a minute. It was just a piece of cloth, but it had done more to protect me—and the people I cared about—than any number of locks or security systems over the years. I'd thrown it away several times. I'd always picked it up again. Looking at it now, it just seemed a little worn and in need of a ménage à trois with a washer and a sewing machine.

I looked at the Rhino. I could count the number of times I'd seen him without looking through the mask on the fingers of one hand—and never from this close, this clearly. He finished the water and set the glass carefully to one side. I had half-assumed he would smash it in his fist when finished. Perhaps follow that by chewing up the pieces and swallowing. It was the sort of recreational activity I had expected from him: *I am the Rhino. My favorite movie is* Rocky IV *and my turn-ons include exotic haberdashery and rubble.*

"I assume," he said instead, "that we are in your secret headquarters."

"Secret headquarters," I said.

"Da," he said. "The armory and lab where you design your weaponry. The bulletproof, stealth-technology super costumes. All the equipment you have used over the years. The cloaking technology that hides all of it."

I nearly burst out into a laugh, but kept it from happening. "Ah. That headquarters."

"Mysterio once said it was the only way you could counter his illusion technology so completely. With access to advanced equipment for the design of countermeasures, like that of Mister Fantastic."

"Mysterio thinks a whole lot of himself," I said.

The Rhino snorted. "Da."

Wait.

I had just agreed with the Rhino on something.

I wondered if my brain would explode out of my ears or just sort of flow out of my nostrils in steaming gobs.

"I presume," the Rhino said, "your security measures are monitoring me."

Why not?

"Every single one," I said. "I'd prefer it if you didn't give me a reason to use them."

At that, he tensed a little, and his jaw clenched. "You think you can frighten me?"

"No," I replied. Normally I would have added something like: *You're obviously too stupid to be afraid of anything.* It would have been funny, but maybe not entirely accurate. Whatever else his faults, the Rhino was tough-minded, and no coward.

Besides. I didn't need to be a telepath to realize that he was scared. Who wouldn't be, in his position, blinded and captured by a bitter foe? But all I said was: "You've never had a problem with fear. There wouldn't be any point to trying to scare you now."

He grunted. We were both guys, so to me, the grunt sounded like, *Good, because I'm willing to fight you, blind and helpless and doomed, rather than let you think you frighten me.*

It was the kind of grunt I might have used myself, were things reversed.

"I am ready to go," he said.

"What?" I asked.

"Go," he said, tensing again. "You said you intended to set me free. Do you mean to go back on your word?"

"No," I said, tiredly. "But that was before I knew about your eyes."

The Rhino shifted his weight warily. More dishes rattled. "You did this to me?"

"No, bonehead," I replied, mildly annoyed. "But I'm not going to send you out there blind. God only knows what you might blunder into and smash." I shook my head, my voice trailing off. "Besides. When the Ancients came for you, you wouldn't have a prayer."

"Then I am your prisoner?" he asked.

"No. You're free to go." I paused for a second. If I just put my teeth together and kept them that way, the Rhino would be out of my hair. It would be simple, practical, and easy.

Who am I kidding? I've never really been all that good at simple, practical, easy things. Things like baking frozen pizzas and abandoning enemies to their gruesome fate.

"You don't have to leave," I said. "If you need some more time to get back on your feet, you can stay." I paused. "So long as you give me your word that you and I have a cease-fire until Mortia and company are dealt with."

The Rhino tilted his head, sharply, blank eyes staring at nothing. "My word? You would trust this?"

"Yeah," I said, and realized, as I did, that I meant it.

The Rhino was quiet for a long moment. Then he nodded and said, "Until they are dealt with and for twenty-four hours after."

Because he didn't want me pitching him into the pokey if we managed to survive. Understandable. "No rampaging while you're here, and you leave town peacefully after. Deal?"

He nodded. "Done."

I picked up his glass and got him some more water, and a glass of my own. Then I gave him his glass, clinked mine against it, and we drank in silence.

Suddenly, rap music with a lot of bass and someone chanting "Unh, unh, unh-unh yeeeeaaaaah" blared through the room.

"What is that?" I asked.

The Rhino tossed off the rest of the water, set the glass aside, and said, "Is me." He fumbled a bit at the rhinoceros hat, then patted his legs and chest before saying, "Ah," and ripping open a panel in the gray-armored suit I had never seen before. The sound of Velcro tearing scratched through the room, and the music got louder as the Rhino produced a little cell phone from the hidden pocket. It looked grotesquely tiny for his enormous, blunt hands. He put it to his ear and said, "Da."

His jaw clenched.

He held the phone out in my general direction. "For you."

Well. That couldn't be good.

I took the phone and put it to my ear. "Da," I said in my best growling Russian accent. "Ivan's Pizza Shack. Ivan take your order."

There was a moment of puzzled silence, and then Mortia's cool, quiet voice asked, "Is this the spider?"

"If it isn't," I said, "he's going to be upset when he finds me running around in his tighty-whities."

"Your kind," she said, "are irritating in the extreme."

"Oh gosh," I said. "Now I'm going to blush, you sweet talker. We can go on like this, but I should warn you that your credit card will be billed at two ninety-nine per minute."

Mortia's voice got colder. "Spider. I grow weary of you. Listen well, for I will not repeat myself, nor make this offer again."

I let my tone get harder. "Speak."

"The Metro Used Auto Center in Flushing. Twenty minutes before dawn."

"Why?"

"Because it is more convenient to meet you there

than to expend resources upon my optional initiative."

My stomach fluttered and felt cold. "Which is?"

"Look out the window to your left."

I froze for a second. Then I turned my head, just enough to see out the window.

Mortia crouched on a four-inch-wide windowpane across the street, on a level with Aunt May's place, balanced easily on her heels. She had a phone to her ear, and the wind blew her hair and coat around her in a fashion every bit as chilling and unsettling as Venom on a good day. She stared at me, at my partial profile, with the emotionless patience of a shark waiting for a bleeding seal to weaken.

It was scary.

I turned sharply away before she could see any more of my face.

"Meet me there," she said. "If you do not, I will kill you where you stand."

"You think you'd get away with—"

"Whether you escape or die," she continued, "my staff will detonate the explosive charges currently planted on the building in order to cover our tracks. There are, at present, nearly fourteen hundred people in your building. Including one hundred and twenty-six children."

At which point, the fear vanished, replaced by raw anger.

"And if I meet you?" I asked.

"Then I will withdraw my staff and the threat to the innocent."

"How do I know you won't blow up the building anyway?" I said.

"I have no interest in the residents. Only in you. You have five seconds to decide."

"I don't need *one,*" I snarled. "I was planning on pounding you to scrap in any case. See you there." Then I hung up on her, turning enough to watch her indirectly.

Her eyes glittered, a weird and somehow insectoid sight, and then she leapt from the ledge in a flicker of black cloth and white teeth, and was gone.

I leaned down and put the phone back into the Rhino's hand. "What does she want?" he asked.

"A beating," I said.

Tough words.

But the bottom line was that in all probability, I'd be dead by the time the sun rose once more.

18

I WENT INTO THE BEDROOM and shut the door behind me. Mary Jane took one look at my face and went pale.

"Peter?" she whispered.

I sat down slowly on the bed while she hovered over me.

"The thing is," I heard myself say, "you've got to feel the traffic around you. You've got to have your eyes watching other people, making sure some idiot isn't about to turn in front of you. The laws, the lights, changing lanes, all of that really isn't hard at all. Most people can drive while they're half asleep and stand a reasonable chance of arriving safely anyway. You just have to keep an eye out for the idiots. It's the idiots that mess up an otherwise decent system of transportation. As long as you know you've got your eye on any potential morons, it's a lot easier to feel confident about the rest of it."

She shook her head, lips pressed tightly together.

"It's like listening to music. You know it when something starts going wrong. You know how it's supposed to sound, and when you hear that first difference, that's when you know you've got to look sharp. Or like science. You know what's supposed to be in a given environment, and when something changes, you can see it, see what caused it. It's the same on the road. You listen for the change in music. You watch for the active variable. That's really all there is to driving, MJ."

She sat down with me. "Peter. You're scaring me."

"I just . . . I just don't want you thinking that this driving test is something big or complicated. It's simple. Sometimes the simple things aren't easy. But it isn't anything that's going to stop you for long. You'll beat it."

She took my face in both hands and made me look at her. "What happened?"

I told her about the Rhino's blindness and Mortia's phone call.

"So. I guess we'll have this finished by dawn," I said.

We sat together in silence for a minute.

"I have to go," I said. "If I don't . . ."

Mary Jane gave me a quiet smile. Then murmured, "Yet do I fear thy nature; it is too full o' the milk of human kindness to catch the nearest way."

"What's that mean in English?" I asked her.

She kissed me. "That I love you."

We held hands for a while. Then she said, "Can you win?"

"Not that it matters," I said. "But I think so. If I could figure out how."

"You always do," she said.

"Yeah," I said, without really meaning it. "Maybe something will come to me."

"Well," she said quietly, "you'll need some dinner. And to get some sleep, if you can."

Sleep. Right.

"Come on," she said. "You'd better introduce me to our guest."

"MJ . . . ," I said.

"He's our guest, Peter. Didn't you invite him to stay? Offer your protection to him? Didn't he agree to a truce?"

"Yes," I said. "But . . ."

"Then he's probably hungry, too. I'll see what I can put together." She stood up to leave.

I touched her wrist and said, "Just, uh. Be careful of him. All right? Don't go within reach of him. I'll move him to the couch."

"Where is he now?" she asked.

"Um. The kitchen floor."

"Oh, *Peter,* for goodness' sake."

"I'll move him," I said. "As long as you promise to be careful."

"All right," she said.

"Oh," I said. "One more thing . . ."

"I am curious," said the Rhino as he sat on most of Aunt May's couch, with a cup of hot tea. The Rhino hat occupied the leftover space beside him.

He held the cup between two fingers and stirred very carefully as Mary Jane sat the sugar bowl back on the coffee table. "What kind of salary does a high-profile superhero's majordomo require?"

"Never as much as I'd like," Mary Jane responded. "But the hours aren't bad and there are decent benefits." She walked back toward the kitchen and rolled her eyes at me. I gave her a thumbs-up, while she plundered the freezer. Aunt May had a bunch of frozen hamburgers left over from the big end-of-summer cookout we'd had, and some pasta, and some tomato paste, and Mary Jane set about making something out of it.

"Benefits," the Rhino said. "Never have gotten anything like that. That is a problem, working as an independent contractor."

I had a cup of tea, too, but I wasn't sipping. Still too weird seeing the freaking Rhino on Aunt May's couch. Sipping tea. "I like that phone," I said. "Great speaker."

"Da, is also MP3 player," the Rhino said, pleased. "When I first get into this business, tried to carry radio with me, but I had no pockets in the suit. I lose or break half a dozen radios, then cell phones, and one day think to myself, Rhino, what kind of idiot designs suit with no pockets?"

Mary Jane turned her head away and bit down on a wooden spoon to keep from laughing.

"Yeah," I said, glowering at her. "Idiot."

I was going to design pockets into my costume.

Eventually. It wasn't like I didn't have better things to be doing with my time.

"Got to be practical in this business," I said.

"Exactly," the Rhino said. "Is business. Lot of people cannot accept this."

I was quiet for a minute. Then I asked, "Why'd you get into it?" The Cat had told me why he'd gotten his start already. I wanted to hear what he had to say.

The Rhino sipped his tea for a moment. Then he said, "The money. I had other ideas, back then. I was younger. Very naïve. Stupid." There was more than a little bitterness in his voice.

"When you're young it isn't necessarily stupidity," I said. "It only means that there's a lot you haven't learned."

He shook off what looked like bad memories and resumed speaking in a neutral, conversational voice. "No, this I admit: I was stupid. Made stupid, young-man mistakes. After getting the strength enhancement and that first job against the Hulk, I had to find work. If you believe this, I had planned to enter professional wrestling. To become a wrestling star and make money." He let out a rumbling chortle. "Of course, I am stupid, but not *this* stupid. I realize in time what a disaster it could be and ask myself, Rhino, what kind of moron gets superpowers and sets out to enter professional wrestling?"

"Hah hah," I chortled with him. "Hah hah, yeah. Heh."

Mary Jane's face turned bright red, and she had one hand firmly covering her mouth as she stood over the stove.

"Of course," the Rhino continued, "you know what happened next. The armored suit began to bond to my skin, and I could not take the costume off." He shook his head. "There I was, young man, big, strong, plenty of money, stuck in a gray suit I could not remove. Do you have any idea how difficult it is to pick up girls when you have been stuck in armored suit for six months?"

I thought about it and shuddered. In *that* suit? "Ugh."

"Da," he said with heartfelt agreement. "The smell alone . . . I had to go through car wash to get even a little clean. So I start taking more jobs, to get enough money to remove the suit." He shook his head. "Is like low-budget horror movie. I thought that suit was an incredible asset, but it turns into horrible curse. You have no idea." He shook his head, finished the tea, and carefully put the cup back on the table. "As I say, stupid. What kind of moron gets himself stuck into costume he cannot even remove?"

My face turned red and I glanced at Mary Jane.

Her whole upper body started jerking in little hiccuplike motions from the effort of holding in her laughter, and she had to leave the room.

"I've got to ask you something," I said. "Just something I've wondered."

He nodded. "Da."

I did my best to keep my voice neutral and calm. "Why do you keep that look? The big gray rhino suit. And . . . the *hat.*"

"Bozhe moi." He sighed. "The suit and hat. I hate the suit. I hate the hat."

I tilted my head and leaned forward. "Then why do you keep them?"

He waved both hands a little, a gesture of helpless frustration. "I have no choice," he said. "They have become business asset. Trademark."

I frowned. "What do you mean?"

"When I finally get the first suit off, I swear to myself never again. Hired a public image consultant. Bought myself business suit. Armani. Dark glasses. Big trench coat. Was good look, very hip, very professional." He sighed. "First contract was in Colombia and it falls apart."

"Why?"

"Because I reach employer for meeting, and he does not believe I am the real Rhino. He says I am fake. That real Rhino has hat with horn on it and big gray body armor suit. He says everyone knows that. So I must be fake, and I must prove I am real Rhino."

This conversation was like listening to a train wreck: fascinating, novel, and more than a little confusing. "What happened?"

"I get angry and prove it," he sighed.

"How?"

"I throw his yacht into his billiard room." He shook his head. "After that, no more questions, but contract falls through. Unprofessional. Is better for business to wear stupid costume. And stupid hat."

I shook my head. Good grief. Felicia was even more right than I thought. I had also been young and ignorant when I got my powers. There but for the grace of God, Spidey.

"You ever see yourself retiring?" I asked him.

His body language shifted, from politely conversational to totally closed. He shrugged a shoulder. "Do you?"

"Tried," I said. "Couldn't really stay out of it."

"Da," he said quietly, nodding. Then he relaxed a little and did a half-credible Pacino impersonation, complete with hand gestures. "They pull me back in."

I broke out into a sudden laugh, and he joined me.

Maybe three seconds later, both of us realized we were laughing with one another and not at, and there was an abrupt and awkward silence.

"Dinner," Mary Jane said with absolutely angelic timing. She'd returned to the kitchen unnoticed, but when she spoke I got a whiff of something delicious and my stomach threatened to go on strike if I didn't fill it immediately. She came out with spaghetti and meat sauce, flavored from Aunt May's own spice rack, and both me and the Rhino started wolfing it down.

In the afterglow, the Rhino sat back on the couch and covered a quiet belch with one hand. "Excuse, please."

"Why not," I said.

"You are not what I expected," the Rhino said.

I grunted. We were both guys, so the Rhino heard, *You aren't what I expected, either.*

"I do not like you," he said, his voice thick. "That is not something that changes."

"I hear you."

He nodded, evidently satisfied at the response, and settled onto the couch a little more comfortably. Even if his face hadn't been all messed up, he would have looked exhausted. Add in the damage of Mortia's touch and he looked like death. He was asleep and snoring within seconds.

Mary Jane frowned at the Rhino for a moment. Then she set her plate aside, took one of Aunt May's quilts from the little trunk next to the couch, and spread it over him. She turned to me and reached out a hand.

I took it and regarded the sleeping Rhino for a moment. Then we gathered up dishes and went back to the kitchen together. She sipped a cup of tea while I did the dishes.

"It was good to hear you laugh," she said after a while. "I like it when you laugh."

"It's weird," I said. "It's like he's a person."

Her eyes sparkled. "Amazing."

"Heh. Yeah." I kept at the task. The hot water on my hands was soothing. Cleaning the plates and the pan was comfortable, a job at which I could achieve tangible, immediate progress. I found myself moving more and more slowly, though. If I finished the dishes, I'd have nothing but time—and not much of that.

"You should try to rest," she said. "Even if you can't sleep. Get a shower, lay down, and close your eyes. It will be good for you, and you'll need your strength."

"Maybe," I said.

"Definitely. After you kick the Ancients back to wherever they came from, you're coming with me to the driving test Monday. You'll need all the nerve you can get."

I tried to smile at her, but her flippancy didn't change the facts any more than mine did. I was alone, and I had no idea how to survive the night.

"All right," I told her. "I just need to make a call first."

She'd figured me out a long time ago. She already had her cell phone in hand, and she passed it to me. "Aunt May left me several numbers in case we needed to reach her. They're in the phone book."

I took the phone and got a little misty-eyed. "What in the world did I do to deserve you?"

She kissed my cheek. "I have no idea. But I'm fairly sure it isn't the sort of thing to happen twice."

I took the phone into the bedroom with me and opened up its list of contact numbers. The time flashed sullenly on the little display screen, the seconds ticking down with relentless patience.

19

THE SILENCE WORE ON as I stared down at the little clock on the phone. I really, really didn't want to die.

It's going to happen eventually. I know that. Death comes to all of us, sooner or later. That's just part of the deal of being born. All the same, though, I didn't want it to happen *today.*

I'd faced danger before, too, situations where I could have lost my life. Most of those situations, though, had been blazing seconds of fast-moving action, while I was high on adrenaline and the fury of a fight.

The fear I felt now was a different flavor. It was patient. It had hours and hours in which to keep me company and it was comfortable doing so with each inevitable second that went by. To make things worse, I was relatively rested, alert, and not in any particular pain, which meant that all my attention was free to feel the fear. To watch death coming.

There was some part of me, the part that had made me try to walk away from the mask, that was simply furious at my stupidity. I didn't have to be doing this. I could run, and to hell with all the people who would suffer for it. What had they ever done for me? I'd spent my life trying to protect them, and despite that I still got scorn and derision and hostility as many times as I received any gratitude. Even if a thousand people died because I ran, I figured I had saved the lives of three or four times as many as that—and that was directly, face-to-face, not counting the times where I'd shut down some maniac who would have killed tens of thousands with various gases, bombs and death rays. If I bugged out (ha, get it?) now, I'd still be ahead by the numbers.

Maybe I was just getting set in my ways, because I knew I wouldn't do it. But part of me really, really wanted to. It made me feel ashamed. Weak. Tired. Simultaneously, though, there was a sort of peace that came along with it. That's the one good thing about inevitable death. It clears the mind wonderfully. Once it's done, it's done. There would be no more agonizing questions, no more of others suffering for my mistakes, no more madmen, no more victims. I had done all that I could, and I would be able to rest with a clean conscience, more or less.

The worst part was that death would mean saying painful good-byes.

I wasn't sure how much time passed before I turned my attention to the phone, but the lighted panel had gone out, and seemed far too bright to my eyes when I turned it on.

When I finally got through the cruise ship's phone system to Aunt May, there was a lot of talking in the background and a slight lag in speech from the satellite transmission times. "Peter!" she said, her voice pleased and warm. "Hello, dear."

"Hi, Aunt May," I said. "How's the cruise?"

"Scandalous," she said happily. "You wouldn't believe how many self-styled Casanovas and Mata Haris are on this ship. It would not shock me to find a complimentary Viagra dispenser in every bar."

That made me smile. "Sounds noisy there. What's going on?"

"We're at a glacier," she told me. "Everyone's quite impressed that the water is blue and that one can see through it. They're off cutting ice from the glacier now, so that we can have hundred-thousand-year-old ice cubes in our drinks. Despite the fact that up until now we've been given perfectly good fresh ice. And there are whales."

"Whales?"

"Yes, some sort of whale, at any rate. They look like half-sunken barges to me, but everyone's at the rail taking pictures. Then there's going to be some kind of drinking game, as I understand it. Most disgraceful."

I laughed. "Just don't drive afterward."

"Oh, I won't be drinking, naturally. It's far more amusing to watch a fool drink than to be the drunken fool. The sun is still up, can you imagine? It must be, what? Nearly midnight there."

I checked the clock. "Pretty close."

"Apparently, night is only a few hours long this far north. I think it may have contributed to how juvenile everyone is acting."

"You're loving it, aren't you," I said.

"I can't remember the last time I laughed so hard," she confirmed with undisguised glee. "We're having a ball. How are you?"

"Oh, great," I said. "They put me in charge of basketball practice at the school Friday afternoon. I'm supposed to coach the team until next Thursday."

"Well, you always did have such a fondness for sports," she said, her voice dry. "How is it going?"

"I'm supposed to be teaching their star athlete to play nice with the team," I said. "He's not having anything from me, though. And everyone else is following his example. I figure by Tuesday they'll try to give me a wedgie and shut me into a locker. Gosh it's nice to be back in high school."

Aunt May laughed. "I take it your star player is talented?"

"Too much so for his own good, apparently."

"That can be difficult," she said. "Sooner or later he'll run into something he can't do alone. It's important that one learn to work with others before that happens."

"That's why the coach wanted me to teach him different." I sighed. "But I've got no idea how to get through to him."

"Think about it for a while," she suggested. "I'm sure it will come to you. And I suspect it might be good practice for when you have children of your own."

I blinked. "What?"

"Oh, I'm not lobbying for an instant baby, mind you," Aunt May said. "But I do know you, dear. You'll be a wonderful father." She paused for a moment and said, "Is that enough small talk now, Peter, or shall we make a little more before you tell me what's wrong?"

"Oh, nothing's wrong, Aunt May."

"This is a cruise ship, Peter dear. Not a turnip truck."

I didn't have another laugh in me, but I smiled. Aunt May would hear it in my voice. "There's nothing unusually wrong, then," I said.

"Ah," she said. "A business problem, then. Have I mentioned, Peter, how glad I am that you are willing to discuss your business with me now?"

"About a hundred times," I said. "I was so glad that we could . . . talk again."

"It is a very good thing," she said in warm agreement. "How is MJ?"

"Worried about me," I said.

"I can't imagine what that must be like," Aunt May said, her tone wry. "But I'm glad she's with you. She loves you to no end, you know."

"I know," I said quietly.

"And so do I," she said.

I closed my eyes, still smiling despite the quiet

ache in my throat and the wetness on my cheeks. "I know. I love you too, Aunt May."

She was silent for a moment before she said, "If I could do more, I would, but in case no one has told you, remember this: You have a good heart, Peter. You've grown into a man to be admired. I am more proud of you than I can possibly describe—as Ben would be. You have always faced the true test—the times when you are alone, and when it seems that everything is as bad as it possibly could be. That's the moment of truth, Peter. There, in the darkest hours, not in whatever comes after. Because it is there that you choose between music and silence. Between hope and despair."

I sat with my head bowed, listening to her voice. I could smell her perfume in the room around me—the scent of safety and of love and of home. I hoped the phone was waterproof.

"You have only to remember this, Peter: No matter how dark the night, you are not alone. There are those who see your heart and love you. That love is a power more potent than any number of radioactive spiders."

I couldn't say anything for a minute. Then I whispered, "I'll remember, Aunt May."

"Listen to your heart," she said, her tone firm and quiet, "and never surrender. Even if you are not victorious, Peter Parker, no force in creation can defeat a heart like yours."

What can you say, faced with a love, a faith like that, warm as sunshine, solid as bedrock?

"Thank you," I whispered.

"Of course," she said, and I heard her smiling. A bell rang somewhere in her background. "Well. It is time for me to go to supper and wait for the floor show. I'll leave you to your work."

"I love you, Aunt May."

"I love you."

We hung up together.

Neither of us said good-bye.

My peace was gone, shattered by the conversation. Hope can be painful that way, and part of me longed for the return of peace and quiet. That peace, though, is not for the living—and I was alive.

And I intended to stay that way.

So long as there was a breath left in my body, the fight was not over and the darkness was not complete. I had faced and overcome things as deadly and dangerous as Mortia and her kin, and I'd be a monkey's uncle before I accepted defeat. I was rested. I was smart. I had the kind of home and life and happiness a lot of people can only dream about.

I refused to let Mortia take that from me. I refused to allow my fear to make me lie down and die.

I rose from where I sat on the bed and felt suddenly clear, focused, and strong. Nothing had changed. I still had no idea how I was going to get myself out of this one. But I would. I would find a way. I suddenly felt as certain of that as I was that the sun would rise in the morning. I always felt that my powers came to me for a reason, and while I did not know what that reason might be, with God as my witness, it had *not* been to feed some psychotic monster-wench and her kin.

I would beat these things. I would find a way.

The phone in my hands suddenly let out a series of chiming notes, the theme from *Close Encounters of the Third Kind.* I don't know why Mary Jane used them as her ring tone. She said it just made her happy.

I flipped the phone open and said, "Hello?"

"It's me," Felicia said, her voice cool and professional. "We found Dex."

20

Mary Jane appeared at the door, eyebrows lifted in inquiry.

"Felicia," I reported, handing back the phone. "Oliver, her guy at the company, found Dex."

MJ nodded, frowning. "What are you going to do?"

"They're bringing him here," I said quietly. "I'm going to go talk to him."

Her mouth quirked at one corner. "Aren't you getting a little old to be throwing parties when Aunt May is out of town?"

"We'll party tonight and clean it up tomorrow," I responded. "What could possibly go wrong?"

She put her hand over my mouth and said, "If you don't shut up, you're going to bring on a montage."

"Is that some kind of seizure?"

"Actually," Mary Jane said after a moment of thought, "that's not a bad description." The whimsy faded out of her face. "Seriously. Up here?"

"They're bringing a car. I'm going to go talk to him."

"I see," Mary Jane said. She glanced from me to the recumbent Rhino. "And I stay here?"

"I think you'll be all right. I'll be on the street right outside the building," I said. "I put Felicia's cell number on your speed dial. If you even *think* there *might* be a problem, you hit that, and I'll be up here inside of fifteen seconds."

Mary Jane considered that for a moment, and then nodded. "I suppose I'll make some coffee, then. Stay alert."

"Keep the lights dim," I said, "and stay away from the windows."

Mary Jane's eyes glittered. "I'll keep an eye on our guest. If he gives me any trouble, I'll subvert him with cheesecake."

"There's cheesecake?" I said. "I didn't see any cheesecake. Why didn't I get cheesecake?"

"Because I haven't made it yet."

I considered that for a moment. "I suppose I'll accept that explanation."

"You're a reasonable man," MJ said. Then she stepped close to me and pressed herself against me. I held her quietly, eyes closed, until her phone beep-beep-beep-BOOP-booped. She flipped it open and checked the screen. "Felicia." Rather pointedly, she did not answer the phone.

I released her reluctantly, walked to the window, and looked down. A white van that looked like an unmarked bakery truck pulled up on the street outside. A pair of professionally unremarkable cars pulled out from spaces they'd somehow secured, making room for the van, which slid up to the curb and came to a halt.

I gave MJ a quick kiss, hit the fire escape, flipped myself across the street so that I wouldn't be approaching the van from the direction of Aunt May's place, and moseyed on down, landing on the van's roof. Then I stuck my head down in front of the driver's face and said, "I hope you guys take credit cards, 'cause I can't find my checkbook and the only cash I have is a bucket of pennies."

Felicia looked back at me without any amusement whatsoever in her expression. She shook her head, then turned and vanished into the back of the van. The side door whispered open, and I crawled on in.

The inside of the van looked like a cramped office. There were several low seats and an abbreviated desk, complete with a clamped-down computer and monitor. There were several people in there. Felicia, dressed in her bodysuit and leather jacket, sat behind the desk, her legs crossed, her eyes cool.

A small man hovered next to the desk, and he was the only one there short enough to stand up. He was a dapper little guy in a casual suit of excellent cut. He had sparse, grizzled hair, spectacles, an opaque expression, and unreadable blue eyes.

"Spidey," Felicia said. "This is Oliver."

I folded my legs, Indian style, only I sat on the ceiling. It's a rare man who can honestly say that his butt has a superpower. "'Sup, Oliver?"

His eyebrows lifted. He didn't say anything. He looked like the kind of man who was used to patiently suffering while other, more intellectually limited people tried to catch up with him.

Sitting across from the desk were three men. Two of them were bruisers—though older and more solid than most of the thugs I've tussled with. They also had suits and wedding rings. Law-abiding bruisers, then, I supposed. Security personnel.

"Mister Walowski," Felicia supplied. "Mister Gruber."

"Howdy," I said to them. Then I tilted my head toward the last man, who sat between them, his shoulders hunched defensively. He was as skinny as I remembered, almost famished-looking. His hair was a mess, his eyes sunken and lined with what almost looked like bruises rather than bags. He hadn't shaved in a few days. He was dressed plainly, in jeans, a T-shirt, and a blue apron bearing the words, "Sooper-Mart!"

His eyes, though, were dark, intent, calculating. He reminded me of a trapped rat, spiteful and stubborn, holding still in hopes that the predator might simply leave, but ready to fight with berserk desperation if pushed too far.

"Is this the guy?" Felicia asked.

"Yeah, that's him. Where'd you find him?"

"Hartford," Oliver said. He had a very calm, quiet voice. "The convenience store where he works was robbed, and another clerk was stabbed. They took prints from all the store's employees so that they could sort out which belonged to the suspect. The prints were put on file and the company found them."

"You found them, Oliver," Felicia corrected.

He favored her with a small smile.

I nodded at the bruisers. "You been sweating him?"

"Just doing a lot of looming," Felicia said. "Apparently, he doesn't scare easy."

I snorted. "No. He wouldn't. Hi, Dex."

Now that I'd spoken to him by name, Dex let out his breath in a hiss. "I did what you told me to. I stayed away from New York."

"That's good," I said.

"Then what do you want?" he asked.

"I want you to talk to me about Morlun."

"He's dead," Dex said in a monotone, and closed his eyes. "What else is there to say?"

"I'm sure there must be something," I told him. "His sister and his two brothers seem to be really upset about the whole situation."

Dex looked up at me sharply, and for a second his expression became frightened, before congealing into that ratlike calculation again. He said nothing.

"Dex? Did you hear me?"

"Yes." He took a deep breath. "What makes you think I know anything?"

"You were with Morlun for a while. You ran his errands. Handled his books. Went out for coffee. You were his Renfield."

"No," Dex said, in that same flat monotone.

"Renfield got to die; Dracula killed him. Morlun kept promising, but he never would do it."

I wasn't sure which was creepier—the words Dex had said, or the way my instincts told me that the faint shades of longing in his eyes were entirely genuine.

"Dex," I said. "I know he was a monster. But I'm looking at three more just like him up here, and I need to know whatever you can tell me."

"Or what happens?" A faint sneer colored his voice. "You tell them about me?"

"No," I said. "They're blaming me for his death. I doubt they know or care who you are. You aren't in any danger."

"I wouldn't say that," Felicia said sweetly. "Dex, Spidey is a longtime associate of mine. I'd be very upset if something happened to him."

"Oh," Dex said. He paused for a moment, then asked, "What are you going to do to them?"

"Whatever I have to," I said.

And then something in the man's demeanor changed. In that instant, his weakness and fear abruptly vanished, and his eyes widened, gleaming.

"Kill them," he said, his voice suddenly hard-edged, hot, eager. "You beat him. You *beat* him. You can do it again; you can beat them again. You can kill them. Kill them. *All* of them. Promise me you will kill them, and I'll tell you everything you want to know."

He stared at me, panting as if he'd run up a long hill, fever-bright eyes locked on my face. I'm not a therapist, but I've been around it enough to know what crazy looks like, and Dex was it. Something told me that if I pushed him or put him under any pressure or strain, he might crack.

Violently.

After all, I'd seen him do it once before.

I had to give him what he wanted. Or at least a reasonable facsimile thereof.

"Talk to me," I said, gently, "and I promise you that I will send them to the next world."

Dex choked out a breath and his eyes sagged halfway shut. He let out a low, shuddering sigh, a disquietingly intimate sound, and closed his eyes. Then he said, "What do you want to know?"

"Tell me about Morlun's feeding habits," I said.

He paused for a moment, frowning in concentration, gathering his thoughts. "Morlun was never alone when he fed. Sometimes he would dismiss me for days. But always, when he fed or hunted, I was there. Always."

"I thought they only fed every few years," I said.

"From the source, yes," Dex said. "The pure, primal life energy. Like yours. But others have the same energy, though in lesser quantity, very diluted. It wasn't very satisfying to him, but it pleased him to snack on such folk from time to time."

"Like popcorn," I said.

Dex smiled at me. His teeth had been stained by cigarettes. Too much of the whites of his eyes showed. "Like popcorn. Normal humans with some kind of personal association with a totemic source.

Something about their personality brushed on the source, gave them a minuscule amount of the same energy."

"Someone like a lion tamer," I said quietly. "Or someone who worked with and rode and loved horses. Maybe Grizzly Adams."

"Yes," Dex said. "Those, he'd take every few months. And always he made sure I was there."

"Why?"

"To watch for intrusion," Dex said. "To notify him if anyone approached. He was very specific about it. Paranoid, really, even for him. He would repeat the instructions every single time, in full, every time."

"Do you remember them?" I asked.

Dex shuddered and licked his lips. "I remember everything." He folded his arms and shook his head several times. I gave him a minute to work himself up to it. Felicia leaned forward and began to speak, but I made a small, discouraging gesture with one hand. She saw it, and for a second I thought she'd go ahead anyway—but then she settled back into her seat and waited.

Dex looked up and spoke. His voice, when it came out, hardly sounded like his own—it had gained richness and depth and had taken on a faint, vaguely British accent. It sounded a lot like Morlun. "Pay attention, Dex."

Then Dex answered in his own voice, toneless and quiet. "Yes, Morlun."

His voice changed back to that echo of the Ancient's. "The usual arrangements are in place? A private suite?"

"Yes, Morlun."

"Security has been notified that I wish privacy?"

"Yes, Morlun."

"You are armed?"

"Yes, Morlun."

"You have checked the locks?"

"Yes, Morlun."

"The windows?"

"Yes, Morlun."

"The outer cameras are in place?"

"Yes, Morlun."

"The new locks to my chamber door are installed?"

"Yes, Morlun."

"Give me the keys."

Dex held out his hand, his eyes focused on nothing, as if dropping something. "Yes, Morlun."

"You will remain on guard outside my door."

"Yes, Morlun."

"If the security measures are disturbed, by anything whatsoever, however small, you are to make me aware of it at once. If any unauthorized persons appear, you are to slay them."

"Yes, Morlun."

Silence fell. Oliver looked more than a little uncomfortable. The bruisers were creeped out. Heck, even Felicia had that narrow-eyed, casual stare she got when she put her poker face on.

Dex hadn't simply been sharing a memory. He'd

been all but reliving it. For him, it had been almost as real in replay as in real life. God, what torture, to remember every twisted detail experienced under the thumb of a thing like Morlun.

"Eidetic memory," I said quietly. "And then some."

Dex opened his flat, lifeless eyes and shrugged a shoulder. "It's why he chose me. It made me more useful to him."

"I take it he would bring victims back to a prepared location," I said.

"Yes. It wasn't difficult for him. He was charming, when he needed to be."

"Must have been the cravat," I said. "Did he always use additional security forces?"

"Yes. Sometimes hired bodyguards. Sometimes hotel or resort security. Sometimes he would use underworld muscle."

I nodded. "Sounds like he shut even you away."

"Yes. Morlun never wanted to be disturbed while he fed."

While he fed . . . Blast it, the answer was there. It was in there somewhere, so close I could taste it. I had what I needed, but for the life of me, I couldn't piece it together. Literally. It was like working out a badly tangled cord—if I could just find one end and get it out of the first stubborn knot, I was sure the rest would be workable.

"Dex," I said quietly. "Thank you."

"Will that help?" he asked, his voice again surging with smoldering rage. The sudden shift in tone made the bruisers tense up. "Will it help you kill them?"

"It might."

"Don't hesitate," he snarled. "Don't think twice. Kill them."

"Dex," I said. "You need to calm down, man. You don't want to—"

"You have no idea!" he shouted. There was spittle collecting at the corners of his mouth as his breathing became labored again. "You don't *know* the things I saw. You must kill them. Kill them. *Kill them all.*"

He snapped on the last phrase, screaming and thrashing. The bruisers piled onto him, telling him to relax. Dex fought with more strength than I would have given him credit for, howling up a storm as he did. I felt a little bit sick. Dex had been hanging on by a thread, and all my questions hadn't done anything to make his situation less precarious.

"He's getting a little worked up," Oliver noted quietly. "Do you have any further need of him?"

"Spidey?" Felicia asked.

"I'm good," I said.

She nodded while the bruisers subdued Dex. They were careful about it, not using any more force than they had to while holding him down to prevent him from harming himself or others.

"Perhaps we should step outside," Oliver suggested.

"Good idea. Spider?"

I went out first, crouching on the roof of the van as Felicia and Oliver exited and closed the door. The noise from the van cut out at once, but I knew that inside Dex was still struggling, because the van was rocking back and forth.

I bit my lip beneath the mask, looked at Felicia, and asked, "He going to be okay?"

"Relax. They won't hurt him," Felicia said quietly.

"Unless he forces them to," Oliver contradicted her. "That young man is clearly disturbed and dangerous."

"They won't hurt him," Felicia said again, louder.

Oliver glanced at her, sighed, and then drew a cell phone from a pocket and stepped a few feet away to make a call.

"I'll see to it," Felicia said quietly.

"Dex suffered," I said quietly. "Maybe a lot more than I thought he had. He needs help. Not getting dragged off to be interrogated in the middle of the night." He probably hadn't needed to be banned from New York on pain of torment and death, either. Granted, I hadn't exactly been in a state of perfect clarity after my marathon beating from Morlun, but all the same. I hadn't seen Dex as another of Morlun's victims. Maybe I should have. It made me feel bad, that I'd added to his suffering by dragging him here.

Except that I hadn't.

I frowned. "Why didn't you just make a phone call, instead of bringing him here?"

"They were fairly close," Felicia said. "We thought it would be best for you to see him in person. He wasn't exactly the soul of cooperation."

I nodded, feeling my lips purse thoughtfully. "I need to make a call," I said. Then I turned to Oliver, as he lowered the phone and turned back to us. "Can I borrow your phone?"

Most people wouldn't have seen it, but Felicia froze in place for a tiny moment, her head tilting a fraction to one side in interest.

"Hmm?" Oliver said. "Oh, certainly. How often does one get to lend a phone to a superhero?" He offered it up to me.

"Thanks," I said. I reached down from the van's roof and took the phone from him.

"I'm impressed, Oliver," Felicia was saying behind me. "This was quick work, even for you."

"I was well motivated," Oliver replied. "Whatever I can do to help one of New York's most colorful heroes."

Felicia smiled widely. "Two of them."

"Yes, two. Of course."

My, but Oliver had a neat phone. It had all kinds of things in it, a full PDA among them. People seem to take security much more lightly when it comes to PDAs, for some reason. Maybe it's because they're always kept safely tucked in a pocket. I opened Oliver's e-mail. Then I looked at his call logs.

The PDA beeped a whole lot while I did, and Oliver noticed it. "Hey," he said. "Hey, what do you think you're doing?" He came over and reached up as if to take the PDA out of my hands. Like that was going to happen. I held it maybe six inches out of his reach and kept going. "Give me that!"

The incoming calls all had neat identifying tags on them—except for one, which was quite conspicuously blank. I checked the outgoing calls. Ditto. Oliver kept everything neatly labeled—except for a single phone number. I dialed that one, and told Oliver, "You got an e-mail, by the way. Your offshore bank confirms a money transfer with a bunch of zeros, Oliver."

The phone rang once, and then Mortia's voice spoke. "Do you have the cat? The spider?"

"Tick tock, Mortia," I told her in a cheerful voice. "Don't be late for our appointment."

I hung up the phone and tilted my head at Oliver. "Thanks, bud. All done. Hey, Felicia, where'd you get your phone?"

"From the company . . . ," she said, after a moment. Then she corrected herself. "From Oliver."

"His has a GPS built into it," I said. "Betcha yours does, too. And on a completely unrelated note, do you remember how we were wondering how Mortia and company found us back at the apartment? Any thoughts on how that happened?"

Oliver stood frozen for a moment. Then the traitor bolted.

21

OLIVER WAS AWFULLY QUICK for a man his age.

Felicia let out a snarl like a furious mountain lion, startling and savage enough to make me wonder—again—about the source of her grace and agility, and she flung herself after Oliver.

His suit was an expensive one—it hid the gun Oliver was carrying to perfection. He drew the weapon and pegged a pair of shots at Felicia, slowing down enough to make sure they went more or less in her direction. She flipped into a lateral tumble—though with uncontrolled shots like that, you run almost as much risk of dodging *into* a badly aimed bullet as you do of dodging an accurate shot.

I gave them enough of a lead to make sure I wasn't going to be crowding Felicia, and then went after them.

Oliver darted down an alley between two apartment buildings, and I shook my head. The runners are always doing things like that. Maybe it's some kind of burrowing instinct left over from our ancestors, little mammals hiding from dinosaurs, right before a big rock fell on them. Whatever the reason, Oliver went down the alley, throwing glances over his shoulder.

One thing about the narrow alley, I supposed. Had Felicia simply sprinted after him, he'd have had a really hard time missing her when he opened fire again. Oliver might have been smart enough to have thought that through. Most of the time, though, it's just a side effect the thugs aren't really bright enough to appreciate. There are several means of ending a chase in a place like that, and Felicia employed my personal favorite. She outthought Oliver and got ahead of him.

He was a few feet from the other end of the alley when a patch of shadow erupted into movement, and the Black Cat fetched Oliver a kick to the belly that took him from a full sprint to a full stop as he folded around her boot. He went down, the wind knocked all the way out of him. Felicia, furious, stomped down on his gun hand until he dropped the weapon. She kicked it away. Then she picked him up by the front of his coat and slammed him against one wall of the alley.

"You greedy little *toad,*" she snarled, slamming his shoulder blades against the wall for emphasis. "What did you *do*?"

"Ms. Hardy," he gasped, hardly able to speak. "Contain yourself. This is not a professional means of—"

She threw him against the other wall of the alley, then popped him in the back of one thigh with a simple snap kick. He cried out as his leg buckled, and fell onto his side. Felicia's boot flashed out again, this time striking Oliver's head in a firm push, trapping it between her foot and the brick wall.

"Oliver," she purred. "I am not prepared to be a sensitive, reasonable, professional individual right now. I'm not feeling my normal, elegant, stylish, and ladylike self." She leaned toward him a little, making him writhe at the additional pressure, and her voice sweetened. "So I want you to believe me when I tell you this: You get one chance. If I even *think* you're trying to lie to me in any way whatsoever, I'm going to crush your skull and wipe your brains off my boots with your expensive jacket. Have I expressed myself clearly?"

He let out a pained sound and gave her as much of a nod as he could manage.

Felicia leaned back slightly, folding her arms and supporting herself against the alley's other wall as casually as if she'd been resting one foot on a crate instead of on a man's temple. "What did you do?"

"She's a big-money client, Felicia," he said. "She's hired the company before. There's an established relationship. She came to me complaining that you were stalling and feeding her false information."

"Yes. Because I suspected she was plotting murder. Doing the fieldwork for murderers is not good business, Oliver, and it never will be." She paused and then said, "How much did she offer you?"

"Enough," he said, grimacing.

"What did she want?"

"To keep tabs on you," he said. "And when she heard about this Dex person, she wanted him as well."

"The going rate on this kind of thing is, I believe, thirty pieces of silver. I hope she offered you that much, at least."

Oliver lifted one hand in a gesture of surrender. "It wasn't personal, Hardy."

Felicia went completely still and silent for a second. Then she whispered, "Not personal?"

"No."

"This creature you worked for has attempted to kill my friend twice. If it gets the chance, it will kill me, too—not to mention all the bystanders who might get hurt when the music starts. And you pointed them *right* at him." She twisted her heel, grinding it slowly into the side of Oliver's head. "In what way is that 'not personal'?"

"Wait," Oliver choked out. "Look, it doesn't have to go down like this. We can negotiate, cut you out of the deal. That was what I was trying to do from the start. Trying to look out for one of the company's assets."

"And to pick up some money on the side while you did it?"

"Don't do this," Oliver said. "You don't know these people, Hardy. They're rich, richer than rich. They've got connections, power. You *can't* survive being their enemy. But if you let me help you, I think I can work something out. Protect you."

Felicia snarled, bent down, lifted Oliver against the wall again, and suddenly flicked out the fingers of her right hand.

I tensed. She had the gloves on. The deadly, razor-sharp talons built into it deployed with a wicked little rasping sound. Very deliberately, Felicia reached out and ran her clawed fingertips lightly down the bricks beside Oliver's head. Sparks flew up. There was an awful, steely sound.

Oliver turned white. He glanced aside at the five long furrows Felicia had dug into the wall. Sweat beaded his skin.

Felicia picked up his tie with the same hand, her fingers idly toying with it—and soundlessly slicing it to slivers as they did. "Oliver," she said. "I am disinclined to let you betray me and simply walk away. So there's something I want you to think about."

His eyes were all on the claws. A cut across one cheek was bleeding a little. "I'm listening."

"First, you're going to go back to the van. You're going to get Dex somewhere safe, without telling anyone anything about him. You will never speak to Mortia or her flunkies again. Resign. The money you took to betray me is forfeit. You will find a place for it to go. A good place, where it might help someone."

"I have done nothing wrong," he said. "I have broken no laws."

"Which might matter to courts and lawyers," Felicia said pleasantly. And then her eyes blazed and she struck suddenly and savagely at the wall again, this time gouging out a six-inch-long section of brick as deep as the second joint of her fingers. "But you hurt my *friends,*" she snarled. "Do it, Oliver. Or I'll destroy you."

"You aren't a killer," he said, eyes narrowing.

"Who said anything about killing? By the time I'm finished with you, you won't have a penny. You won't have a home. You won't have a job. What you will have is nothing. And everyone you've ever crossed is going to know exactly where to look you up."

Oliver licked his lips, and his voice trembled. "You wouldn't do that."

She released him, springing the claws on the other hand, and simply leaned the tips of her fingers against the bricks on either side of his head, creating a steady trickle of sparks, a grinding, growling chorus of scrapes and tiny shrieks of protesting brick.

Her eyes turned wide and cold and angry, and leaned in close enough that he had to have felt her breath on his face. "Try me," she purred.

Oliver shivered and looked away.

"Get out," she said, her voice quiet and full of contempt. "Get out of my sight."

She stepped back from him, and Oliver tried for a dignified retreat.

She kicked him hard in the seat of the pants as he left, sending him out onto the sidewalk in an undignified sprawl. Oliver hurried away, limping.

Felicia watched him go for a minute. Then she

recovered his gun, disassembled it in a single smooth motion, and dropped the pieces into several different trash cans. She put the lids back on the cans, shook her head, sighed, and looked up to where I sat thirty feet up the building's wall in a patch of heavy shadow. "I thought you'd have come down there, at the end."

I dropped to the alley to stand with her. "You had him under control. Why would I do that?"

She did not look at me, and shrugged. "The bit with the claws. I figured you'd grab my wrist any second, all worried that I was about to kill him in cold blood."

"What?"

"If the positions had been reversed, you'd have stopped Oliver."

"Well, yes, but—"

"If it had been the Rhino, you'd have stepped in."

"Felicia," I said, a little frustrated. "Where are you going with this?"

Her eyes grew cold, and she said, "Nowhere. Never mind. You'd probably want to help Oliver if he was in trouble. Just like you're helping the Rhino. No one is too black-hearted to be worthy of the Amazing Spider-Man's protection."

Then she began walking back down the alley toward the van.

I stared after her, and in a sudden flash of insight I finally understood her recent attitude—at least a little bit.

Felicia wasn't defending the Rhino.

She was defending *herself.*

I knew that she'd tried, she'd really tried to be one of the active good guys, but . . . well, she hadn't been all that *good* at it. Her past sins had weighed against her, and she'd had a rough path to follow. She'd given up, largely, on the whole freelance-hero gig. Now she worked in private security. Like the Rhino, like Oliver, she was a mercenary—one on the side of the law and civilization, true, but a mercenary nonetheless.

Maybe my initial contempt and antipathy toward the Rhino bothered her, because she saw too many similarities in herself. Maybe it made her wonder if I harbored some degree of the same contempt for *her.* Maybe she wondered if she had just been another sad charity case on whom I'd taken pity. Maybe that was why we hadn't worked out. Maybe my opinion, which had been important enough to her to help motivate her to abandon a life of crime, was *still* important to her.

If so, then by causing her to question the nature of our relationship, maybe I was eroding the foundation of the new life she was building.

I sighed.

Maybe if I rented a crane, I could pull my foot out of my mouth.

I caught up to her, prowling along the wall at head height while I tried to talk to her. "Felicia, wait."

She never slowed her pace or glanced aside at me. "Look. I found your toady for you. And you made it clear that you don't want me involved in your problems. So has MJ. So I'm leaving."

"Don't do this," I said. "Come on, would you hold up a minute?"

She didn't slow down or answer me, and I stopped as she stepped out of the far end of the alley.

"You were right," I said quietly. "You were right about the Rhino. And I was being a pigheaded idiot about it."

She stopped in her tracks. She turned her head enough that I could see the curve of her cheek.

"Only a real friend would have tried to point out a blind spot like that," I said. "And I didn't even try to listen to you. It was stupid and arrogant of me, to disrespect you like that. You deserve better from me, and I apologize."

The lines of her body shifted almost imperceptibly. Her shoulders sagged a little. Her neck bowed her head forward a couple of degrees.

"Yes," she said after a minute. "A pigheaded idiot."

I dropped to the ground and walked over to her, crossing my arms and leaning my shoulders against the wall. "I haven't ever said this," I said. "But I admire you, Felicia. When you went legit, you picked a hard road for yourself. You knew it would be hard, but you did it anyway. That took a lot of courage."

She turned to look at me. Her eyes were misty.

I put my hands on both her shoulders. "You're beautiful and strong, and you don't let anyone tell you how to live your life. You're a good friend, and you have a good heart. When the going gets rough, you always have my back, and I trust you there."

She blinked her eyes rapidly. Her voice came out quiet and a little shaky. "Then why don't you want me to help you with this?"

"Um," I said.

Felicia suddenly tilted her head to one side and her eyes widened in understanding, then narrowed in anger. Her hands came up and slapped mine from her shoulders. "You were trying to *protect* me! Like I'm some kind of china doll!"

"No," I said. "Wait."

"You *pig,*" she said, pushing her fingers stiffly at my chest. "You arrogant, reactionary, egotistical . . . My God, I ought to pop you in the mouth right now!"

"I'd really rather you—"

"I don't need your protection," she snapped. "I'm not a child. How *dare* you make that kind of decision for me! How dare you take that choice away from me!"

I rubbed at the back of my neck. "Listen. If I just hit myself in the mouth a few hundred times, would it make this rant go away any faster?"

"You're going to be hearing about this for years, Parker."

I sighed and lifted my hands in surrender. "All right, all right."

"So no more noble-defender crap. From here out, I've got your back. Right?"

I nodded. "Right."

Her cheeks grew a little rounder as she kept a

smile off of her face. Then she nodded back and said, "Apology accepted."

"Sheesh," I said.

"So," she said. "Did it help? You figured out the silver bullet?"

"I think so," I said. "But it's right on the tip of my brain and I can't get it to come out."

She fought off another smile. "The tip of your brain?"

"You know what I mean," I said. "I've got all these facts, and once I put them together the right way it should be possible."

"Which facts?"

"Paranoid solitude during feeding," I said. "Feeding upon smaller victims for between-meal snacks. My fight with Morlun. The folklore accounts. The information you discovered. The way the Ancients shy away from crowds. The fact that Mortia was, apparently, interested in finding you, even *after* I agreed to meet her."

The Black Cat frowned. "Mmm. Maybe we should get everything written down. Brainstorm. Two heads will be better than one, right?"

And suddenly it all fell into place, like the wheels on a slot machine coming up all cherries. Suddenly I saw what had been right there in front of me the whole time. I had picked out the false note, made a positive identification of the active variable.

I could beat them.

"That's it," I heard myself whisper. "I can *beat* them."

Felicia's eyes widened. "You've got it?"

"Eu-freaking-reka," I confirmed. I ran over the solution in my head a few times. It seemed sound. "But I can't do it alone."

She arched a brow and then smiled sweetly. "So what you're saying is that you need my help."

"Um. Yes," I said.

"How *interesting.*" She folded her arms, expression amused. "Say 'Please.' "

"Please," I said.

" 'Pretty please,' " she prompted.

"Pretty please. I need your help."

She sniffed. "It wasn't nice of you to provoke me into a fight so I'd walk away, you know."

"Then why'd you fall for it?"

She rolled her eyes. "I'll think about it. But I'll walk you home first. You'd just get lost on your own."

"Very generous," I said.

She gave me a pious smile. "What are friends for?"

22

I LED FELICIA BACK TO AUNT MAY'S apartment, filling her in about the Rhino and Mortia's phone call on the way. We went in through the same bedroom window by which I'd left earlier. I shut it behind us, and we headed into the living room.

Mary Jane had turned out the lights, presumably to let the Rhino sleep. The only illumination came from several candles on the kitchen counter, where Mary Jane was sitting with a copy of the Scottish Play, a notebook, and a pencil.

She glanced up at Felicia and me as we appeared from the bedroom, and arched an eyebrow. "You know," she said, "a lot of wives would not react to this particular situation with patience and understanding."

I sighed.

MJ smiled, mostly with her eyes, and said, carefully polite, "Felicia."

Felicia nodded to her. "MJ."

"I thought you had left," my wife said.

Felicia shrugged. "I got bored. I decided not to let your husband hog all the excitement for himself."

Mary Jane considered her for a moment, and then nodded. Her voice warmed considerably. "It's good to see you again. Tea?"

"Please." Felicia smiled and then looked down, settling on a chair at the kitchen table.

"The Rhino?" I asked.

"Out like a light," she said. "He snored for about five minutes. Some plaster fell out of the ceiling. How did the interview go?"

I stripped off my mask, leaned against the kitchen counter, and smiled at her.

MJ took one look at my face, and there was a sudden fire in her eyes. "You figured it out," she said.

"I think so," I said. "It was right there in front of us, too."

MJ gave me a mock scowl and asked Felicia, "Isn't that annoying? The way he makes you ask him to explain things?"

"It's his great big brain," Felicia said, nodding. "He likes to remind everyone about it, to make up for all his other shortcomings."

"Look," I said. "The real problem with fighting the Ancients is their sheer durability. They can fight for days without slowing down, and it's all but impossible to fight them head-on. They don't get hurt and they're strong. So every little ding and bruise they inflict on you makes you tired faster, while they just shrug off whatever you do back to them. They grind you away."

Mary Jane shivered. "Go on."

"I was looking for a weakness, but I had already found it—partially, anyway. Morlun got hurt twice. The first time was when he had me down and was starting to do to me what Mortia did to the Rhino. Ezekiel jumped him and bloodied his nose for him, literally. It was the first time in maybe eighteen hours of fighting I saw him injured.

"The second time was at the reactor, when he started taking a bite of me and got a mouthful of uranium instead. See?"

Felicia tilted her head, frowning. "From what Dex said . . . that's when they're vulnerable. When they feed. Right?"

"Right," I said. "Strange told me that the Ancients' powers were a result of their will focusing all the latent energy they've devoured. Morlun wasn't super-strong and nearly invulnerable all the time. He had to be concentrating on it, *willing* himself to be that way. When he started to feed, he couldn't keep his focus, or at least it seriously reduced his defenses—and when he panicked, at the end, he couldn't use them at all."

"It explains why they get nervous at taking on more than one opponent, too," Felicia said. "More distractions."

"And why Mortia didn't stay on your trail after you saved the Rhino," Mary Jane added. "You hit her at the only moment when she was vulnerable. For all she knew, you knew exactly what you were doing when you did so. You probably scared the wits out of her."

I nodded. "Exactly. So we use that against them."

Mary Jane sat a cup of tea down in front of Felicia. "How?"

"I don't think I like where this is going," Felicia said.

"We decoy them," I said. "We tempt them into feeding."

The Black Cat sipped her tea. "I was right. This plan has a major flaw in it."

"Flaw?" Mary Jane asked. "Which part is flawed?"

"The part where they have to be feeding when we attack," she said. "To feed, you have to have, well, *food.* I don't want to be food. That's really the point of the whole exercise, isn't it."

"It's a risk," I admitted. "But if I'm right, it could work. We wait until they start, blindside them, knock them out, and use the magic rocks to get rid of them."

Felicia's eyebrows went up. "Oh, sure. And if you're wrong?"

"I didn't say it was a perfect plan," I said quietly. "That's why you're carrying the rocks and I'm going to be the decoy."

Felicia shook her head, rising with the teacup to pace restlessly. "That isn't a good idea."

"Sure it is."

"No it isn't. I'm good, but you're better, and a lot stronger. Of the two of us, you're the one most likely to be able to KO one of the Ancients, even if they are in a weakened state." She smiled, showing teeth, and took a few hip-swaying steps across the room. "And let's face it, Parker. I've forgotten more about distraction than you'll ever know."

"I hate to point this out," Mary Jane said quietly. "But once they start feeding, whoever they're attacking is essentially paralyzed. Right?"

I chewed on my lip and nodded. "Yes. Morlun barely got started on me before Ezekiel decked him, but the pain was . . ." I shivered. "Yes. You can't put up much of a fight after one of them starts on you."

"There are three of them," Mary Jane said. "No matter which of you is the decoy, there are still going to be two of them who *aren't* feeding. Do you think they'll just stand around and let you knock the third one out?"

I shook my head. "We'll have to separate them."

"Like you did last night?" Felicia asked.

"Exactly."

"Last night, when you scared Mortia to death?" Mary Jane asked. "Do you think she'll be as careless and confident this time? Do you think she'll be dumb enough to get separated from the others again?"

It was a big worry of mine, too, but I tried not to show it. "Maybe. Maybe not. Either way, this is pretty much the best plan we've got."

Felicia laughed. "That's because it's the *only* plan we've got."

"You say tomato . . . ," I said.

We stood there, looking at one another for a silent moment.

"That's the plan, then," I said quietly, taking MJ's hand.

"Right," Felicia said. She checked her watch, and her mouth twisted with distaste. "Now comes the fun part. Five hours of waiting."

I nodded. "I know what you mean. I hate waiting, too. I think Aunt May has some cards. We could play a round or two, or—"

Felicia lifted both hands. "No offense, Pete, but you could really use a shower first. Really."

"Thank you," Mary Jane told her. Thinking back later, there was a little bit of emphasis on the phrase I didn't notice at the time. "I didn't want to be the first one to say something."

Felicia grinned at MJ. "No problem. Go on, Pete. I'll keep an eye on Snoozy here." She took a sip of tea and regarded the Rhino. "Awww. He's kind of cute when he's sleeping."

"Fine, fine." I sighed, and trooped off to the bathroom for a shower.

I had barely gotten my hair wet when the shower door opened and Mary Jane joined me, pressed against me, and kissed me with abandon.

Two minutes before, I'd said that I hated waiting.

But we made time fly.

23

I ACTUALLY SLEPT. Not for long, but every minute of it was precious. I woke up in the quietest part of the night, hours after the bars had closed, hours before the heavy Sunday morning traffic would be under way.

I lay in bed for a moment, my arm around Mary Jane, and she sighed in her sleep. The night showed me only a ghostly image of her, absent of makeup or artifice of any kind. Nor was her face touched with worry or fear—only the relaxation of peaceful sleep.

My God, she was beautiful.

I'm a lucky man.

After a few minutes, I rose and went to the window, staring out at the quiet city. It was a quiet moment. A good moment. I faced the city I have always fought to protect, focused on what was before me. There was a chance I would prevail, a good chance. Victory was by no means likely, but I had that fighting chance.

That's all I've ever had, really.

And it's all I need.

After a little while, I felt Mary Jane's presence behind me. Her reflection in the window wore only the loosely wrapped sheet from the bed. She stepped up to press against my back, and wrapped her arms and the bedsheet around me. She rested her cheek upon my shoulder and stared out at the city with me, sharing my silence, her warmth and love pouring into me through her touch.

We stayed that way until the eastern sky began to lighten.

I turned to her, and nodded. She smiled a little, then brought me my colors. I started to put them on, but she gently pushed my hands back down to my sides, and dressed me herself. She stood up with the mask last, and pulled it slowly over my head—leaving my mouth uncovered. Then she leaned into me and gave me one more kiss on the lips, slow and sweet. I returned it the same way, as gently as I knew how.

She broke off the kiss after a time, and murmured, "For luck."

I smiled a little and said, "You want to go out for some dinner later?"

"Not Thai. Never again."

"Not Thai," I agreed.

"I'll think about it," she said.

"You are quite a tease, Mrs. Parker."

She lifted her hands to cup my face, green eyes bright. "I'll make it up to you."

I smiled again, and turned to the door. I opened it as quietly as I could, and when it began to open, I heard voices. MJ touched my hand, silently telling me to wait and let her listen.

"Is not so much that I am stupid," the Rhino was rumbling. "But I do not think well on my feet. I try to plan ahead, da? To be careful. But he always makes all plans fall apart."

"Believe you me," Felicia answered, "I know exactly what you mean."

"Is maddening. Someday I will beat him, my way."

"Yeah?" Felicia asked. "Even after tonight?"

The Rhino paused before saying, "He is man of honor. Maybe I have more respect for him. But I must beat him. I *will* beat him."

"You're more alike than you realize," she told him. "I've read the files on you. I know why you volunteered for the procedures for the armor, the enhanced strength."

The Rhino grunted.

"I'm just saying, I understand your motivations. He would, too."

"Maybe you are right. It changes nothing."

"Why not?" Felicia asked.

"Because of what I am," he said. "A mercenary. A criminal. An enemy to him and those like him."

"So far," Felicia argued. "What's to say that the future can't be different?"

There was a silence so long that I thought maybe the Rhino had fallen asleep. But then he said, "Is too late for me."

"Why?"

"Because of what I have done. The alliances I have made, the mistakes I have made. There is no going back."

Felicia exhaled slowly and said, "What about your family? Do they think that?"

The Rhino's voice gained a faint edge of bitterness. "When they hear I am criminal, they disown me. My brothers and sisters hang up phones when I call. My mother sends back all my mail unopened."

"It's never too late, Aleksei," Felicia said. "My past isn't exactly white as the driven snow. But I turned things around."

"Your past had less blood in it. I have made enemies, and I owe too much to some of my allies," the Rhino replied. "Money. Favors. I try to leave now, I will not survive it." The couch creaked. Maybe he had shrugged. "I am a man who pays his debts. Besides. I have nothing else to do. Nowhere else to go."

Mary Jane pushed the door silently shut, frowning.

"What?" I asked her.

"I'm not sure," she said. "There's something about his attitude . . . I feel like I should be understanding something about him, but it's eluding me."

"Ah," I said. "Yes. Nothing is so subtle as the elusive Rhino."

She stuck her tongue out at me. "I'll think of it sooner or later." She frowned. "The poor man. He made himself into a criminal to try to provide for his family and bring them to the States—and he lost them because of it."

"Yeah. Breathe in the irony." I frowned and said, "Must have been tough to live through."

"Ready?" my wife asked me.

"Yeah," I said. "Let's do it." Then I opened the door and walked out into the living room. "Morning," I said to Felicia. "Rhino."

"Spider-Man," he replied with a nod. His ravaged face was no longer swollen, though there were still heavy welts and marks, and the way the skin was flaking off was none too pretty. Still, he was visibly less damaged than only a few hours before, and it was possible that the cataracts on his eyes were not as densely white as they had been. He also looked more relaxed. He must have been in a lot of pain earlier that night; he'd endured it long enough to allow him to sleep. He took a sip from a small silver flask, and then passed it back to Felicia, who sat in Aunt May's armchair.

"Tell me you're sober," I said to Felicia.

"Sober enough to know how crazy this is," she replied, taking another hit off the flask. "Mellow enough not to mind."

"As long as you don't throw up on me. You ready?"

"Yes," Felicia said, standing.

"Da," Aleksei said, rising.

"Whoa," I said. "Who said anything about you going, Rhino?"

"I did," he said. "Just now."

I sighed. "Ladies. Could you excuse us for a minute, please?"

The Black Cat narrowed her eyes for a moment—but then glanced at MJ, waiting for her response.

Mary Jane nodded at her and said, "Sure." The two of them withdrew down the little hall to the bedroom.

"There is something you wish to say?" the Rhino rumbled.

I picked up a cork coaster, and flicked it at him. It bounced off his face. The Rhino scowled and rubbed a finger on his nose.

"You're blind," I said, my tone frank. "And even if you weren't, there's a big difference between calling a cease-fire and believing you've got my back."

"The Black Cat told me what you have learned about the Ancients, and your plan," the Rhino said. "I wish to help."

"I'll say it again: You're blind. You'd do more harm than good."

"Perhaps not," he said.

"Oh?"

"I cannot see," he rumbled. "But I do not need to see to serve as your decoy."

I lifted my eyebrows, surprised into a brief silence.

The Rhino's ugly mug slid into a grim smile.

"You'd be willing to do that?" I asked him quietly.

"Da."

"Why?"

"If the Ancients kill you," he said, "I will be their

next meal. There is better chance for survival in co-operation."

"That's not what I meant, exactly," I said. "You'd be running a huge risk. If an Ancient starts in on you, there's no guarantee we'll be able to get to you in time. Even if we do, if my hypothesis is flawed you could die anyway." I snorted. "For that matter, how do you know that I won't just let you get eaten?"

"Because you already didn't," the Rhino pointed out.

I folded my arms, frowning. "You're willing to trust me to save your life?"

"You are Spider-Man," he said, as if the phrase embodied some kind of answer.

"What's that supposed to mean?"

He let out a caustic little laugh. "Of course. You cannot see it. Or you would not be who you are."

"Um. What?" I asked.

"Give me your word," he said. "That if I do this thing for you, you will do your best to save my life. Not that you will. Just that you will try."

"I will," I told him.

"That is enough," he said. *"Tempus fugit."*

"It is," I said, thoughtful. "Be right back."

I went down the hallway to the bedroom and opened the door. Felicia and Mary Jane were sitting on the edge of the bed together, hugging. Felicia looked . . . absolutely awkward. She wasn't the sort who'd had a lot of girly friends.

"You know," I drawled. "It's not just every husband who would walk in on this and be patient and understanding instead of leaping to conclusions." I leaned on the door frame. "Carry on."

They broke the hug, gave each other a glance, then in practically a single voice said, "Men are pigs."

I beamed. "I figured putting the two of you in one room might get you to talk. Or start a fight. I'm not sure which one I was rooting for."

My spider sense warned me about the incoming pillow as Mary Jane threw it, but I let it bounce off my face.

Felicia folded her arms, too dignified to fling objects at me. "Well?"

"Well what?"

She arched a brow and then glanced pointedly past me.

"Oh. Cat . . . I've worked with you before," I said quietly. "But him . . ."

"Come on, Spidey," the Black Cat teased. "Who *haven't* you teamed up with at one time or another? You're the biggest team-up slut in New York."

"That doesn't mean I enjoy it."

"Why wouldn't you?" she asked.

I grunted and muttered under my breath.

"I'm sorry. What was that?" Felicia asked.

"I said, there's a reason it's 'the Amazing Spider-Man,' and not 'Spider-Man and His Amazing Friends.'" I shook my head. "You know that if I had a choice, I'd be doing this alone."

"But you don't have a choice," Mary Jane said quietly. "Thank God."

I sighed. "MJ . . ."

"I know." She sighed. "You're a great big he-man and you don't need anyone. Been working on your own for years. But I worry about you being alone out there, because I'm your wife and that's what I do. I'm glad Felicia is going to be there. And if our guest can help, too, more power to him. You should take all the help you can get."

Felicia's expression sobered. "Believe me, I know what you're feeling. I don't play well with others, either. But Aleksei's got a point. If we can use him as our stalking horse, it will leave the two of us to handle the two Ancients who are still focused. I can try to distract those two while you finish off whichever one is taking a bite."

"Simple, eh?"

Felicia nodded. "That's the idea. Take one down, rinse, and repeat."

I took a deep breath, and released it slowly, thinking it over. Sure, the plan sounded swell—well, sweller than doing it with just me and the Cat, anyway—but I wasn't entirely convinced that the Rhino wouldn't be nearly as dangerous to Felicia and me as he would be to the Ancients. On the other hand, I didn't think I could manage to get myself into all that much more danger even if I tried. I still would have preferred to be the only one at risk.

And I suddenly felt like an arrogant high school basketball prodigy, too young and foolish to realize that no one can do everything alone.

That realization sparked another idea—a way to

minimize the risk the Rhino's undisciplined strength presented, and to further use the Ancients' own natures, their confidence and their arrogance, against them.

"Okay," I said, feeling newly confident, and raised my voice. "You're on the team, Aleksei."

His expression grew pained. "Please," he called back. "Rhino. From you, Rhino."

I grinned, heading for the living room, beckoning MJ and Felicia to follow me. "Okay, Rhino. We're short on time, so huddle up. Here's the plan."

24

The murky light of predawn fell on the auto yard. Colors were washed out to various shades of blue, darkening to perfect black. The streetlights nearby were mostly broken, but where they were on, they added the occasional shaft of yellowish light. The low light softened edges and deepened shadows. It made the stacks of crushed cars and mounds of discarded parts look positively alien, and the mounds and mounds of deceased vehicles created an oxidized labyrinth. The place smelled like rust and rot and old motor oil. Pools of liquid rippled under a ghostly wind, and the light reflecting from them danced through too many colors for them to be puddles of water.

The whole place was on a long lot, behind a high fence. It was maybe a hundred yards in length, maybe half as wide. About the size of a football field, in fact. Maybe that was just a coincidence. But then again, maybe Mortia picked it for that exact reason—to tell me that I was simply a game to her.

If so, that was all right. I can play games, too.

Two features in the yard stood out: first, an enormous industrial machine, one of those dinosaur-sized hydraulic car-crushing gadgets. The other, not far from the entry gate, was a small and run-down building with the word "Office" painted on the door. A small and dilapidated mechanics' garage was attached to the building.

My spider sense started twitching when I was a block away from the junkyard. By the time I actually swung over the fence to land high atop the car crusher, it was screaming at maximum volume. The Ancients were there ahead of me.

I remained in place for another two minutes, just to be punctual, and then called out, "Mortia! Thanis! Malos! It's on!"

The three of them appeared from the interior of the run-down garage, their pale faces visible first, so that they gave the appearance of three skulls drifting toward me. Eventually, they came out enough for me to see that once again, they had all come in pseudo-formal attire. It made sense, I supposed. MJ and I dress up a little when we plan on a nice dinner, too.

Mortia stopped a step ahead of her brothers, smiling up at me. "Ah. I am glad that you saw reason."

"I'm a reasonable guy," I said. "Which is why I have a proposal for you."

She tilted her head to one side. "Oh?"

"A trade," I said. "I looked it up and it turns out

that Spider-Men my size only make a decent meal for two, not three, and that I'm full of carbs and bad cholesterol. I thought I might be able to arrange something healthier and more profitable."

And with that, I pulled the Rhino, once again bound limply into a cocoon of webbing, off of the papoose-style carry on my back, and began lowering him to the ground. "I figure this ought to stick to your ribs better than me. I'm all string and gristle."

Mortia touched a forefinger to her chin, a pensive gesture. "And why would you offer such a thing?" she asked.

"Because I'm not an idiot," I said. "What happened with Morlun was a fluke. I'm never going to be able to survive the three of you."

Mortia gestured at the Rhino. "Yet it is a poor gift you offer. We can take him at will."

"Think of him as a down payment," I said. "I can set you up with all kinds of totemistic super folk. I can point you to a Lizard, an Octopus, a Vulture, a Scorpion, a Sabretooth—oh, and Serpents. There's so many of them that they formed their own society."

"You would doom others of your ilk to preserve your own life? It seems uncharacteristic of your behavior."

"They're all enemies," I said. "Criminals, thugs, and good riddance to them. I can't beat you, but I *do* want to survive. It's an acceptable compromise from which both of us profit."

Mortia turned and looked at each of her brothers in silence. They returned an equally placid, inhuman gaze. Then she turned back to me and said, "Lower the brute."

My mouth felt a little bit dry. "Here we go," I whispered. "All set?"

"*Da,*" the Rhino whispered.

I lowered him slowly, steadily to the ground. Mortia and her brothers walked over and stood there in their little formation as the Rhino sank to the ground at Mortia's feet.

She regarded the Rhino with hooded eyes, then looked up at me.

"Do we have a deal?" I called.

Mortia's sharklike smile returned, and she murmured, "Arrogant worm. Kill them both."

Let the games begin.

"You're going to wish you hadn't said that," I predicted.

She regarded me with scorn. "Why?"

"Because even a blind man can find you when you yammer on like that."

The Rhino ripped out of the cocoon as if it had been made of tissue paper—and parts of it were—and seized Mortia by the ankle. Then he grunted, rolled, and threw her.

Here's a business secret not everyone knows: Super strength, after you get to a certain point, suffers from a case of diminishing returns, especially in combat. That's just physics, old Sir Isaac rearing his oversized melon. When you lift something heavy, you're pushing up at it, but it's pushing *down* at you, and through you to the earth. That downward force eventually gets to the point where it starts forcing your feet into the ground.

Sure, the Hulk can free-lift better than a hundred tons, but when that much weight is pushing down on a relatively small area—like his feet—it tends to drive them down like tent stakes. (Not to mention that there just aren't all that many hundred-ton objects that won't fall apart under the stress of their own weight when lifted.) Similarly, the Thing can throw a big punch at a brick wall, but if he uses too much of his strength, the impact of the blow will shove against him, pushing his feet across the floor or even throwing him backward. He has to brace himself if he's really going all-out.

(Which is one reason I've done pretty well in slugfests against guys a lot bigger and stronger than me, by the way—my feet *always* hold on to the ground, or wall, or whatever, allowing my punches to be delivered far more efficiently than those of most of the powerhouses.)

Anyway, once you get into the heavyweight division of super strength, the differences are kind of academic, and they only really stand out in a couple of different areas.

Ripping an object apart between your hands is one of them. It's isometric.

Throwing things is another.

The Rhino can trade punches with the Hulk. He can flip an Abrams main battle tank with one hand. And, apparently, he can throw gothed-out brunettes halfway to Jersey.

Mortia shrieked and flew out of the junkyard like a cruise missile in a red cravat. She clipped the edge of a ten-story building a block away, sending up a cloud of dust and a spray of shattered bits of masonry. The impact didn't even slow her flight down. She just kept on going, tumbling end over end, over the nearest buildings and out of sight, screaming in feral rage all the way. The scream faded into the distance.

For a second, the remaining Ancients were stone-still in surprise, and it was time enough for the Rhino to come to his feet in a fighting crouch, arms spread. He might have looked intimidating if he hadn't been facing approximately ninety degrees to the left of his foes.

Malos moved, quick and certain, his body darting for the Rhino, dropping, spinning, so that he kicked the big man's legs out from under him. The Rhino had far too much of a mass advantage on the Ancient. Malos's kick was viciously strong, but he wasn't properly braced to transfer enough of that strength into upsetting the Rhino's balance, and all he was able to do was kick the Rhino in the ankle hard enough to annoy the big guy.

The Rhino kicked him back. It was a blind kick, and didn't land with full force, but it was still strong enough to send Malos flying into a half-stripped old pickup truck, slamming him through the safety glass to a painful impact with the steering wheel and dashboard.

We had to work fast. The Rhino had taken Mortia out of the equation, at least for a little while. I had no idea how far he'd actually thrown her, but if she didn't hit something solid, wind resistance would slow her down eventually—say, within half a mile. Then she'd land and head back. Given how fast I'd seen her move, we had maybe a minute to take out at least one of the other Ancients; ninety seconds, tops.

That made me eager to mix it up as soon as I possibly could—but that wasn't the plan. We had to see if my theory was correct, and to do that I had to let them start on the Rhino. So I clenched my hands into fists and waited.

Thanis closed on the Rhino in perfect silence, and as a result slammed his first couple of hits in without opposition. Hits like that probably would have broken my neck. The Rhino just grunted at the first, and was a savvy enough brawler to roll with the second. He swiped one huge hand in an arch and got lucky, more or less. The blow landed, and Thanis staggered back a pair of steps.

Great. Of all the times to have a great opening round, the Rhino picks *now,* when he's supposed to be *losing.* At this rate, he'd probably rough them up just long enough for Mortia to return. I debated tripping him or something. It wouldn't be like I was trying to get him killed. I would just be sticking to the plan, which was everyone's best chance of survival.

As it turned out, I didn't need to do it. Malos came back into the fight with a vengeance, literally seizing the Rhino by the horn and sweeping him up and over to slam the big guy's back onto the ground with earth-shaking force. The impact stunned the Rhino. Malos stepped forward and, with brutal efficiency, stomped a heel down on the Rhino's head, a motion similar to that of a man crushing an empty can of beer. The Rhino's thick skull withstood the impact (of course) but the sheer power of it drove his skull six inches down into the gravel and mud of the junkyard's ground, and it seemed to daze him even more thoroughly.

"Take him," Malos snarled, and lifted his eyes to me.

Thanis bared his teeth in a nasty smile, lifted a hand, fingers spread, and then drove it flat against the Rhino's chest, where another burst of sickly light flared out between his fingers. The Rhino screamed again, and the sound sent a surge of adrenaline and rage through me.

I went into a swan dive, aiming for the Ancient kneeling over the Rhino. As I expected, Malos threw himself in the way, leaping up to meet me in the air. I folded into a roll and, as the Ancient met me, brought both heels into a lashing kick that tagged him squarely on the forehead and killed both his momentum and mine. We dropped the last fifteen feet or so to the ground and landed ten feet apart, facing one another over one of the chemical-spill puddles of various auto fluids.

On the way down, I hit the top tire of a stack behind me with a short webline, and used the elasticity of the line and my own strength to fastball it into Malos's chest. The blow knocked him back—

because super strength doesn't mean you suddenly have more mass. Malos might have checked in at around two hundred and fifty pounds, and the tire hit him hard enough to take him off his feet and dump him onto his butt. Best of all, the old tire had been half-full of stagnant water, and it splashed all over his fancy clothes. He looked up and directed a snarl of hatred in my direction.

"Welcome to New York, chump," I said. Then I bounded up onto the tire stack, and from there went over a twelve-foot-high wall made of crushed cars.

Malos let out an angry snarl and chased me. He came sprinting around the corner, focused entirely on my red and blue costume, intent on catching up to me and neutralizing me before I could take a swing at his brother.

Of course, if I had been *in* the costume he was chasing, it probably would have worked better.

Instead, I hopped up to a shadowy section of the wall of cars and froze, while Felicia bounded through the predawn dimness in my backup costume. In better light, or if she'd been still, there would have been no way anyone with eyes would have mistaken her for me—but wouldn't the Ancients have thought of that kind of thing before they set up the time and place for the showdown?

Malos ripped free a heavy mirror that had somehow survived its parent truck's crushing, and flung it after Felicia. The Black Cat dodged it with contemptuous grace, cleared the wall of cars, and hit the car crusher with her grappling line, then retracted it, hurtling through the air as it pulled her, just ahead of the enraged Ancient, leading him away from the Rhino.

I went back over the wall and flung myself at Thanis. Once upon a time, I probably would have said something cute to make him turn around before I hit him, but wasting time on such a thing in this kind of fight could get me killed.

That said, though, I'm freaking Spider-Man.

"Warning!" I shouted. Thanis blinked and half-turned his head, just in time for me to lay a haymaker directly across his jaw. He flew back from the Rhino and slammed into the side of a junked school bus, and I followed right on his heels. "The surgeon general has determined that attempting to eat the Rhino may result in unanticipated side effects." He bounced off the bus and ran into my fist. I heard teeth break, and felt a rush of furious satisfaction. "Including but not limited to dental problems." I gave him a double-handed sledgehammer blow to the guts. "Nausea." I sent a flurry of jabs at his head, pretending it was a speed bag, and bounced his skull off the bus maybe fifty times in seven or eight seconds. "Headache."

Thanis wobbled forward, his eyes gone glassy, his face broken, bleeding, swelling. He could barely keep his feet. "And," I said, drawing back. "Drowsiness."

It's rare for me to go all-out, but I hit the jerk with every fiber of my body and sent him clear *through* the bus's metal siding.

The bus rocked a time or two, but the Ancient did not arise. He lay sprawled and motionless inside.

Not bad. Maybe it wasn't as impressive as a Rhino-strong blow, but for a guy who weighs in at one sixty-five, it was a pretty good hit. Even better, my hypothesis had been proven. Thanis had indeed been vulnerable as he fed.

"Don't let me down, Doc," I muttered, and flicked one of the three Alhambran agates at the downed Ancient.

There was a whisper of sound, no louder or stranger than that of a door sliding closed, and Thanis—and the agate—vanished. Gone. Poof. Just like . . . well. Magic.

Hot diggity dang, it worked!

I threw myself over to the Rhino's side. He lay on the ground, his breathing labored. "Aleksei," I said. "You all right?"

"I," he wheezed, "think I do not like these Ancients. Did it work?"

"Yeah. One down. Can you move?"

He shuddered, and after a second I realized that he was trying to get in a sitting position. He gave up with a groan. "It would seem not."

"Okay," I said. "I'll get you out of here."

"No!" he wheezed. "You must finish them before they realize the danger. You may never get a second chance like this one."

"I can't just leave you here. Mortia won't be gone long, and she'll be angry."

The Rhino growled, and swiped an arm weakly

at me. It was an improvement, of sorts. "Will be fine in a moment," he said, glaring in my direction. "Now, you must fight. You are using your wits. Speed. They have only strength. And they do not know the danger they are in. This is your kind of battle, Bug Boy. Take it to them."

"Bug Boy?" I said, and felt myself grinning.

"Spidey!" called Felicia's voice from the other end of the junkyard. "I lost him! He's heading back to you!"

A vise-clamp settled on the back of my neck, and bounced my head off the nearest car. Which was twenty feet away. It hurt.

An undetermined amount of time later, I managed to sit up, only to find Malos standing over me. He leaned down and grabbed the front of my costume, hauling me to his level. "You forget that you touched me," he said in a quiet voice. "It struck me that while I seemed to be pursuing you, my sense of your presence told me that you were, in fact, behind me. A clever enough ruse, little spider. But your bag of tricks is now empty."

My spider sense's terror-reaction was nothing to that of my mind, as I scrambled to gather up my wits and try to defend myself.

I was too slow, the blow to my head too severe. Malos held me high off the ground with one hand, made a talon of the other, and his fingers suddenly dug into my abdomen.

Pain.

Pain.

Pain.

White hot. Ice cold. Nauseating. Terrifying. My senses were overloaded, the pain something that somehow gained sound and taste, color and texture and scent. The pain was as fundamental, solid, and real as I was—in fact, more so. I tried to scream, but the pain had priority on reality, and no sound came out. This was worse than what Morlun had tried to do. He'd barely touched me for a second. This went on for an eternity, and mixed itself with a horrible sensation of something being *ripped* out of me, like someone had shoved a blender into my belly and turned it to puree.

Somewhere behind the pain I could dimly sense the real world, but it was disconnected and unimportant, a shadow play being performed far away. I saw it all through a hallucinogenic haze. Saw myself running atop a wall of crushed steel. Saw myself take off my mask and become Felicia. Saw her look up at the power lines passing by on the street, saw her raise her baton, saw a thin black line extrude from it as the hook arched up and up, sailed over the power lines, and then fell—onto Malos.

The Ancient's expression was quite calm—except for the maddened frenzy of hunger dancing in his eyes—and he paid the shadow-play world no mind. But his expression turned to shock and sudden agony as the Black Cat's line touched him and electricity from the power cables surged through to him.

I felt it, too. It hurt, but not necessarily in a bad way. The burning tingle was an honest pain, a real-world pain, not the nightmare agony of the feeding Ancient. I felt my body contort along with Malos's—and then the agony was gone and I was in my body again, burned and breathless and utterly exhausted.

I lifted my head enough to see Malos stirring, attempting to rise. I had to get on him right away, knock him out before he gathered his wits and focused his power into his defenses. I managed to wobble upright. Then I staggered over to him and kicked him in the chops. The blow was weak, and it knocked me down, but it got the job done. He fell to the ground in a pile of loose limbs beside me.

I fumbled out the second agate and flicked it at his nose. It missed and struck his cheek, but once more, without a flicker of showy lights, with barely more than a whisper of sound, the Ancient simply vanished.

I heard Felicia come running toward me. "Spidey?"

"Mmm, fine," I slurred. "Jusht ducky." I started to stand up and staggered again.

Felicia had to catch me. "Is that all of them?"

"Two," I managed to say. "We got two."

"What about Mortia?" Felicia hissed, looking around.

She turned her face directly into a blindingly swift blow. The Black Cat went straight down, body gone instantly and entirely limp—unconscious or dead.

Mortia, her dark clothes and hair soaked from her landing in the river, looked coldly down at Felicia for a moment. "Don't worry, darling," she purred. "I'm sure she'll turn up."

25

I MANAGED TO KEEP MY FEET and throw a punch. It wasn't a fast punch or a strong punch, but it was the best I could do.

It wasn't good enough. Mortia slapped it aside, seized me, slammed me into the same car her brother had not two minutes before, and then threw me through the air to land near the Rhino.

"Quite the interesting morsel you are," she murmured, regarding me with amused eyes.

I counted birdies and stars. At least she'd hit the *other* side of my head. That way, my brain could be equally bruised on both sides. The agony of the Ancient's devouring touch was fading as my heart kept on beating, and I felt some of my balance returning.

Mortia flicked a bit of debris from her sleeve. "But all things in their due course, trickster. First, the tart little aperitif."

With that, she turned and walked deliberately toward Felicia.

At which point I found myself suddenly angry enough to chew barbed wire and spit nails. I'll say this for the bad guys: Just when they pound me the worst, they have this ongoing tendency to provide me with oodles of motivation.

So I motivated Mortia right through a mound of scrap metal by way of saying thanks.

She came out on the other side furious, her jacket and pants in tatters. The steel had torn the expensive clothing to rags, though it hadn't broken her pale flesh. "Do you have any idea," she snarled, "how difficult it will be to replace this outfit?"

"You're one to talk!" I shot back. "At least you can get someone *else* to make yours!"

She came at me hard and fast, leaping from the ground to propel herself off the fence around the yard and straight at me.

This time there was no dodging, no webs, no tricks. I stepped forward to meet her and swatted her out of the air with a punch that killed her momentum cold. She bounced back from it with a spinning kick imported straight from Hong Kong that nearly took my head off. I managed to get away from it with nothing worse than a chipped tooth, but was reminded that I couldn't fight stupid against Mortia. She was too fast.

I ducked a second whirling kick, knocked her ankle out from underneath her with one leg, and got in a good stomp on her stomach, but then she drove her knuckles against the side of one of my knees, forcing me to hop away before I got knocked to the ground. After that, she came in close and brought a lot of hard, vicious, swift punches with her, throwing everything from less than a foot away, and all of it aimed at my eyes and nose and neck—Wing Chun, I think it's called. She'd had formal training somewhere.

I'd done all my learning in the school of hard knocks, and even if I don't have a pretty martial arts sheepskin, I can get the job done. I did a lot of bobbing and weaving, more boxing technique than anything else, spoiling the occasional blow with a quick slap of one hand. We closed and struck and counterstruck and parted a couple of times, each exchange several seconds long.

Whether it was the formal technique or just her sheer weight of experience and untiring speed, I missed a beat and took a chop to the side of the neck, followed by a stiff blow from the heel of her hand to the tip of my jaw that snapped my head back in a sudden whiplash.

I barely blocked a haymaker of an uppercut, and in a single motion splashed a blob of webbing into Mortia's face and followed up with a hard, driving strike with the same hand. I caught her on the forehead and knocked her tail-over-teakettle into one of the toxic-looking pools of the junkyard's liquid refuse.

She rose from the pool, her pale eyes cold and angry.

"There's something on your face," I told her.

She only stared at me with that intense, alien stare, and replied, "You're getting tired. You're slowing down." She prowled around the little pool toward me. The top of her head never changed height as she walked; you could have balanced marbles on it. Her eyes, similarly, never varied in height above the ground, just floating along, wide and intent. It was extremely graceful in an insectlike way, and highly creepy.

Especially because she was right. This wasn't going to be like my fight with Morlun. With him, even after I'd gotten tired, I had still been a lot faster than he was. With Mortia, I'd barely had an advantage when I was fresh, if I'd had one at all. As fast as she moved, it would not take much fatigue to slow me down enough to be overwhelmed by her sheer speed.

"Tired, mortal," Mortia murmured. "It's almost over. You can't avoid me for very much longer."

"Maybe not," I said. "But at least *my* outfit's still clean."

I guess she expected more whimpering and pleading, because my reply clearly enraged her. She came at me like she intended to tear my head off, and it was suddenly all I could do to stay alive.

The fight got blurry after that. I had no frame of reference for time. Every move she made came at me too quickly to see, and at the same time it seemed to take forever, if not longer. I remember landing a couple of good ones, and shrugging off a lot of lighter blows—a whole lot of them. She wasn't trying to KO me. All she wanted was to continue to inflict pain through smaller, repeated blows, to grind down my endurance.

It must have worked. I saw bloody knuckles rush at my face—her knuckles, my blood—and then a flash of white light.

After that, I stared up at the slowly brightening sky, which looked like it was getting ready to turn into a pretty day, and wondered why I wasn't back home in bed with MJ.

"My brothers are gone," she said. Her voice echoed and rang oddly, as if coming to me down a long tunnel. "Which I admit is mildly disturbing, but probably inevitable." She picked me up and threw me into a heavy beam supporting the structure of the car crusher. I struck sideways across the small of my back, and heard things crackle when I hit.

"They were always incautious, you see. Impatient. Once they saw the prey, they could only pursue it, devour it." She paused over the weakly stirring Rhino and crushed her heel down upon his head in several vicious kicks as she spoke in a conversational tone. "Ultimately, of course, I would have had to kill them. The world will not bear the strain of feeding even the few of our kind who remain, in the next several thousand years. As the source drains from this world, fewer and fewer of your kind appear, spider. And subsisting on lesser beings"—here, she paused to step over the unmoving Felicia—"is simply no way to live."

I got up and hit the car crusher with a webline near the top, using my left hand, intending to jump and swing and get some distance from Mortia. I was moving too slowly, though, too weakly.

"All in all," she said, "I suppose I should be thanking you, in some ways." She seized my left arm, and with a squeeze and a twist she snapped the webline—and broke my wrist. I felt and heard my bones cracking under her viselike fingers.

Fiery pain took away whatever strength was left to me, and I fell to my knees.

"Yet," she continued in the same conversational tone, "they were family. Companions over the empty years. They would have amused me, somewhat, until I had to kill them." She threw me with both hands—she wasn't as strong as Malos had been, but was at least as strong as I. I slammed into the mechanics' garage and left a deep dent in the rusty corrugated sheet metal that passed for its walls.

It hurt. A lot.

"Your struggle has been useless, of course," she said. She kicked my ribs several times, and all I could do about it was to try to exhale when her foot impacted me. It hurt even more. I'd have been screaming about it if I'd been able to get a breath. I'd have been running away if I could have managed to stand. "That's the way of the world, spider. Predators and prey. Your fall was inevitable. But the tricksters are always the most interesting hunts. Certainly more so than the brutes."

I tried crawling away, around the office building and garage. I dimly remembered that the chain-link gates had been there.

She picked me up with one arm and slammed me into the office building. I could see the gates, see the street outside through the chain links. It wasn't thirty feet away—but I'd never reach it.

"Truth be told," Mortia purred, her voice growing deeper, huskier, "the brute will make a more than acceptable meal. But you will taste simply divine. A spirit such as yours will be most rich; most delightful." She idly ripped off the front of my costume, and pressed a kiss against my chest. Flickering sparkles appeared in my vision, and the nauseating pain of the Ancient's hunger brushed against me for a minute.

Mortia looked up, licked her lips, and shivered. "But your passing need not be agony. I can take you gently. Peacefully. It will be like falling asleep in my arms." Her eyes brightened. "All you need do is ask me to be merciful." She pinned me to the wall with one hand, looking up at me with the same horrible hunger I'd seen in the eyes of Morlun and Malos, just before they fed. "Beg, spider."

So this was it.

Huh. I hadn't really figured today would be the day.

But then, who does? Am I right? You never really wake up and think that it's your last day on this rock.

She leaned closer, almost close enough to kiss me. "Beg, spider."

I swallowed and faced her, no longer attempting to struggle or escape. I was through. No one was left to attack her when she fed. I was alone. I was going to die alone. But I'd taken down three out of four, and I hadn't abandoned anyone doing it. Not bad. Not bad.

"I have seen gods and demons at war," I told her, my voice hoarse. "I have seen worlds created and destroyed. I have fought battles on planets so far from Earth that the light from their stars has never reached us. I have seen good men die. I have seen evil men prosper, and I have seen scales balanced against all odds. I have seen the strong oppress the weak, the law protect criminals instead of citizens. I have fought with others and alone against every kind of enemy you can imagine, against every kind of injustice you can imagine." I met her eyes and said, quietly and unafraid, "And because of what you are, Mortia, you will never understand why."

She tilted my head, staring at me as though puzzled, the way someone might regard a talking lobster being held above the pot.

"In all that time," I said, my voice growing weaker, "I have never surrendered." And all the defiance I had left in me rose—too weak to stir my limbs, but giving my voice a hard, hot, edge of anger. "I will never beg you for anything. So you'd better stop flapping your stupid mouth and kill me. Or so help me God, I will destroy you just like I did your brothers."

Those cold, alien eyes grew colder. "Very well," she said, her voice low, throbbing with excitement. "Then you will feel every second. May you live long enough for the pain to drive you mad."

Her hand slammed flat to my bared chest.

My world *drowned* in pain. This time, as she began ripping at me, I wasn't even strong enough to writhe.

The shadow play of the world went on in the background.

I saw a bright white light, from far away, begin to rush closer. And closer. And closer.

A roaring sound began, and I thought to myself that heaven needed to get itself a new muffler.

The shadow play rolled on, and what I saw there sent hope pouring through me again, one last surge of defiance that I had never imagined could have survived what the Ancients had done to me. It gave me one last tired wave of awareness, one last weak and weary burst of motion. I managed to twist my body enough to get my feet onto the wall of the junkyard office, then walked them sideways and up, until they were level with my head.

Mortia let out a flushed, ecstatic laugh at this last, tiny defiance, as she ripped into me.

And then Mary Jane's rusty, lime-green Gremlin blew through the junkyard's chain-link gates at seventy or eighty miles an hour and smashed into Mortia and the office building, ripping her hands away from me as the car's hood went entirely through the wall beneath me, taking Mortia with it.

The Gremlin's engine surged. Smoke and steam were coming from under the hood, but it backed out of the hole it had pounded in the office wall, and then crunched to a stop. Mary Jane got out, wearing her jeans, a sweater, and leather driving gloves. She opened the trunk, her expression focused and smooth, though her hands were visibly trembling, and emerged with a tire iron.

Mortia staggered out of the wreckage, bloodied, one of her arms smashed beyond recognition, one of her legs obviously broken. Dust clung to her damp clothing and hair, and her expression was dazed, almost childishly confused.

Mary Jane walked to face the battered Ancient, eyes narrowed, and tapped the tire iron against her palm.

Mortia stared at her, dumbfounded. "Who . . . who are you?"

"That which hath made them drunk hath made me bold," Mary Jane quoted. And delivered a two-handed blow with the tire iron. Mortia staggered. My wife's voice, full of fury, rang out in the predawn air as she swung again. "What hath quench'd them hath given me fire."

She struck the Ancient on the head, and Mortia fell senseless to the ground.

Mary Jane snarled at the fallen Ancient and spat, "What's done is done."

"MJ," I croaked. I fumbled at my left hand with my right, where I'd stuck the last agate to my glove with a bit of webbing, and passed it to her.

She took it with a nod, knelt down, and after a second of consideration, shoved the stone hard into Mortia's ear.

The last Ancient vanished, and Mary Jane stood up. She stared at her tire iron for a moment, then at the car, and then she came to me. I more or less dropped off the wall, and she crouched down to wrap her arms around me. Compared to the last hellish minutes, her touch was pure heaven.

"Thanks," I told her, and meant it.

She shivered and cried a little. Then she pressed a fierce kiss against my head and whispered, "I love you."

I smiled at her. "You," I croaked, "are going to make one heck of a Lady Macbeth."

26

I don't know how we would have gotten Aleksei home if Wong hadn't driven up in a heavy-duty pickup.

He just pulled up without a word, lowered the tailgate, and wheeled out a hand truck. I wasn't in terribly good shape, but I was able to web up the Rhino—again—and attach him to the hand truck. Getting him into the back of the pickup was another issue with one arm out of commission, but with Wong's help I managed it. Wong isn't big, but he's wiry. Not wiry like me, but stronger than he looks. I was still kind of unsteady on my feet, though, and Wong and MJ moved Felicia themselves.

Wong drove us to Strange's place, and MJ followed in her now-wheezing car. No one seemed to take any notice of us. Granted, it was sunrise on a Sunday, but even so no one seemed to actually make eye contact with the vehicles or any of their occupants. Maybe Strange had done some of that voodoo that he do so well. Or maybe it was just because we were in New York. It would take something a lot weirder than a cocooned bruiser in a Rhino hat, a shirtless Spidey, and a bald Tibetan martial arts expert in a pickup being tailed by a stunning redhead in a crumpled, wheezing lime-green Gremlin to attract attention.

Wong had a pallet ready on the floor of the reception hall, and he put Aleksei on it. He glanced at me, and I pulled the webbing off of him. Felicia rated a cot, and Wong and MJ put her there. Wong examined the large swelling on the side of her head for a few moments, then drew out an old leather valise and opened it, filling the room with the pungent, pleasant fragrance of herbal medicine. He applied a fragrant salve of some kind to her head, another to her neck, and bound a bracelet of some kind of braided plant around her left wrist.

Within minutes, Felicia blinked her eyes open, peered around groggily, and said, "We win?"

"We won," I said.

"Go, us," Felicia mumbled. "You owe me big time, Spider." She then stripped out of my spare costume, staying only more or less covered by the blankets as she did. She sighed in contentment, dumped the clothing on the floor, rolled over, snuggled naked under the blankets, and promptly went to sleep.

Wong looked somewhat startled and uncomfortable at the sight.

I savored the moment.

I was next to get the herbal treatments. I don't know what Wong has growing in his garden, but his stuff makes Tiger Balm look positively anemic. I had so many bruises that he had to open a second jar, and MJ helped him slather it on me. Then he got to Aleksei, applying medicines to his much-abused face and head.

The pain began to fade, and it was a delicious sensation. I sat there hurting less and breathing deeply despite the twinge in my back and my broken wrist, and loved every minute of it.

Wong got to my wrist, frowned, and left.

He returned with the doc, who settled down next to the chair I was slumped in to examine my wrist.

"A clean break," he said. "I can set this for you, if you like."

"Can't you just fix it, O Sorcerer Supreme?" I said in a whimsical voice. "For you, this is just a bippity-boppity-boo-boo, isn't it?"

Strange arched an eyebrow. "Healing magic is quite complex, and its employ must take into account several and various factors which—"

I winced, though he really couldn't see it through the mask, and interrupted him. "Doc. My head."

His eyes wrinkled at the corners. "No," he said.

"Now was that so hard?" I asked him.

"You've no idea," he said.

"Wong," he said to his servant, "I was looking for my Alhambran agates, and I couldn't find them anywhere. Do you have any idea where they are?"

Wong bowed at the waist. "Abject apologies, my master. I seem to have misplaced them."

"Ah," Strange said. He glanced at me. "It's always the little things you wonder about." He bowed his head to me and said, "Congratulations on your victory. It was well done and well won."

"Thank you for your help," I said.

Strange put a hand over his sternum. " 'Help'? I can't imagine what you mean. One ought not confuse my natural concern for your current state of health as partisanship in your recent struggle with the Ancients, which would be against my obligation to maintain a strict balance of mystic forces."

"Oh, right," I said. "Sorry. Thank you for the not-help."

"It was my pleasure not to provide it," he said, his voice warmer. "Let me check on your allies." He circled to Felicia and Aleksei. He lingered longer over the Rhino, murmuring something to Wong, and then returned to me, his expression grave.

"Bad news, Doc?" I asked.

He spread his hands in a noncommittal gesture. "He has taken a terrible beating, and in more than a merely physical sense, but he should recover within the next few days."

"His eyes?" I asked.

"Those too. He seems to be most resilient."

"Yeah," I said. "Annoyingly so."

"You sound as if you do not care for him," Strange said.

"I don't," I said. "Well. I do. I mean, I didn't want him to get killed or anything, but . . ." I shook my head. "I guess it might have been simpler if he had. He's dangerous."

"Dangerous?" Strange asked.

"You've seen him," I said. "What he's capable of."

"True," Strange said. "And I have seen what you are capable of, as well, I might add. You yourself can be most dangerous, Spider-Man. As can I. And Wong. And, apparently, even Mary Jane."

"You aren't going to rampage anyone into the ground, though," I said. "Neither is Wong or Mary Jane. But the Rhino, I'm not so sure about. He's habitual."

"Ah," Strange said.

"I'm the one who saved his life," I said quietly. "Whatever he does with that life in the future, I'm going to share some of the responsibility for it. If he hurts someone. Or kills someone . . ." I shook my head. "How would I live with that? I feel . . . really stupid."

"Do not think the less of yourself for your ignorance. It is a weighty question," Strange said. "Many wise men have struggled to answer it. I am aware of none who have done so."

"Maybe I should do something, then," I said.

"Maybe I have a responsibility to try to limit the harm he could do."

"Or the good," Strange said.

I grimaced. "Do you really think he's going to do anything good, Doc?"

"It seems to me that he aided you and the Black Cat only this morning."

I sighed. "Yeah, he did. It's making it hard to figure out what to do."

Strange nodded. "If you like, I shall summon the authorities."

I thought about it for a minute more. Then I shook my head. "No. We had a deal, and he more than lived up to his end. In fact, without him, we would never have been able to pull it off. He's got twenty-four hours before I make any moves."

Strange got an odd little smile and nodded once. "I am glad to see that you are still a man of your word—as he is. Good never came of treachery. It wounds betrayer and betrayed alike."

The conversation—and his offer—had been a test, then. A lesson. Freaking wizards. Strange really needed to get out among the nonmystical crowd more often. Maybe go bowling. Put back a cold one or two. Watch a movie. But he's the Doc. He's pretty much all about the weird wizardly wise man shtick. And he was probably right.

"We just do what seems right," I said.

He nodded. "We're only human."

"Maybe you could do me a favor," I said. "Besides the wrist, I mean. The Rhino, ah . . . maybe it would be better if he woke up here, and you could call him a cab."

"Certainly," Strange said. "I am pleased to be able to offer you more conventional help."

I frowned at the unconscious Rhino for a moment. "How are you at fortune-telling, Doc?"

Strange followed the direction of my stare. "The future of beings like the Ancients is easily seen. They have no true sense of self-determination, you see. They are driven by their needs. Ruled by their impulses and fears." He shook his head. "The future of mortal beings, though, is generally imponderable."

"Stop dancing," I said. "Do you think he can straighten out?"

"He *can*, certainly. Though I sense there would be a very heavy price to be paid—perhaps one which would be too high." Strange shook his head. "The question is will he choose to do so. In the end, his future will depend upon his choices. Just as yours does."

I frowned and nodded. "I suppose I shouldn't expect much."

Strange smiled faintly. "Even should he dare to change his path to run along near your own, I think it would little change his attitude toward you."

"Gee. Why doesn't that shock me," I said.

Strange actually chuckled. "Let's get that wrist straightened out, hmmm?"

Mary Jane leaned into me and murmured, "He *is*

a real doctor, right? Not like a doctor of magicology or philosophy or something? He's qualified to do"—Mary Jane glanced at Strange and gave him a very mild, elegantly reproachful look—"something? This time around, anyway?"

Strange blinked at her, then at me, and let out a very brief, very quiet sigh.

I savored the moment.

"There," he said, a few uncomfortable minutes later. He had my wrist set, held stiff by layers of wrapped tape. "It's a simple fracture. Leave it for a day or so, and you should be fine, given your own exceptional recuperative capacity."

I sighed. "Thanks, Doc."

He put a hand on my shoulder and squeezed. "Of course. Is there anything else I can do?"

I blinked at him. "You know," I said, "there is. There are two things, actually."

His eyebrows went up.

"Doc," I said. "I assume your doctoring credentials are still good. You know, like, legal?"

"As far as I know," Strange said, his tone cautious. "Why?"

"And do you know if Wong plays basketball?"

"Excuse me?"

"Simple question," I said. "I mean, it's not brain surgery, is it? Does he shoot hoops?"

"I'm . . . actually, I'm not sure," Strange mused.

Somewhere in the background, Wong started whistling "Sweet Georgia Brown."

"Peter," Mary Jane said, smiling at Strange. "I'm

sure you shouldn't press the good doctor. After all, he's done so *much* to help you already."

Strange looked helplessly at her and then lifted both hands. "Mercy, lady, I beg you. By all means, Spider-Man, just tell me what I may do."

27

The gang wasn't loitering around outside of Samuel's apartment at eight o'clock on Monday morning. I guess it isn't exactly gang-hanging prime time. The doc and I took the subway and walked the last couple of blocks. He was wearing fairly normal clothes again, and had added an old bomber jacket to his ensemble, as well as an archetypal doctor's bag. Even in the "civvies," though, he didn't exactly fit in on the street. Strange . . . is. It goes deeper than just mystical mumbo jumbo and Shakespearean wardrobe. It's no one thing I can put my finger on, but Strange never seems to fit in much of anywhere, unless maybe it's in the middle of serious trouble.

It's probably one reason we get along so well.

I cruised up to the Larkins' apartment and knocked. Sounds murmured through the gap beneath the door—children running, talking, laughing, the tinny sound of a television playing one of those seizure-inducing cartoons, and the occasional sound of a strident, confident woman's voice. I heard rushing footsteps and then Samuel's little sister, the one I'd seen wheezing on my first visit, opened the door. She stared up at us for a minute, then slammed it shut. Her footsteps retreated.

A minute or two later, Samuel opened the door. The big young man glanced from Strange to me, then frowned like a thundercloud. "What."

I made a show of checking my watch. I didn't have one, since my wrist was still all bandaged up, but I didn't let that stand in the way of good drama. "You're late for school, Mister Larkin."

"That's real funny," Samuel said, his glower deepening. "You know the score. Office lady already got me suspended. I ain't there no more."

"Samuel," said the woman's voice. "Who are you being rude to?"

"Nobody good, Mama," Samuel said.

"Look, if you're more than two hours tardy, you aren't going to be eligible to practice tonight. We'd better get a move on."

"You deaf?" Samuel growled.

"Samuel Dewayne!" snapped the woman, and she came to the doorway. She was nearly as tall as her son, her hair was threaded with gray, and she wore a waitress's apron over a gray dress and comfortable shoes. She regarded me and Strange with a wary eye, then asked, "Something I can help you gentlemen with?"

"Hi, Ms. Larkin," I said. "My name is Peter

Parker. I teach science at Samuel's school, and I'm temporary coach of the basketball team."

"What do you want with Samuel?"

"Just to get him to school, ma'am," I said. "We're already several minutes late."

She shook her head. "I thought he got suspended."

"Only if he doesn't get his vaccinations up to date," I said. "This is Doctor Stephen Strange. He's agreed to help with that."

Ms. Larkin pressed her lips together. "I don't have the money to pay you for this. You might as well go on."

"There's no charge," I said.

Samuel scowled and lifted his chin—maybe in unconscious mimicry of his mother, who did the same thing. "We don't need charity," she said.

"This isn't charity," I told her. "The doc here is part of a new neighborhood health program some of the action groups have kicked off. He'd have been here in a few more days, anyway, to get your kids looked after—he just started here, as a favor to me."

Strange arched an eyebrow at me, but nodded. "Indeed."

"Mmm-hmm," Ms. Larkin said. She was clearly skeptical, but she didn't push it. Instead, she just glanced at Samuel, as if waiting for him to speak.

Samuel looked from his mother to me and back, biting one lip and clearly uncertain. It made him look like the boy he still was.

"Well?" I told him in my exasperated-coach voice. "What are you waiting for, Larkin? Me to carry you on my back? Let the doc look at you and then let's get to school."

Samuel looked as if he didn't know whether to sneer at me or hug me, but he finally sighed and said, "Yeah, all right."

"If there's time," Strange said, "I can take a look at any of your other children, ma'am, and make sure they're all caught up on their shots."

Ms. Larkin almost smiled. "Well," she said, "if you hurry. I have to drive the rest to school in ten minutes."

"Don't worry," I assured her. "He's the fastest mouse in all Mexico."

"Come in, then," she said. "Come in."

Strange was good to his word, if not precisely popular with the little ones. He diagnosed a burgeoning ear infection and left a bottle of children's antibiotics for it, as well as providing the wheezy little sister with an inhaler after she described what sounded like a fairly heavy asthma attack.

"Samuel," Ms. Larkin said. "Help me get them all in the car, and then you can walk to school with Coach Parker."

"Yes, ma'am," Samuel murmured, and set about doing just that while Strange and I exchanged farewells with Ms. Larkin and left to wait outside.

"A new neighborhood help program?" Strange asked me, once we were alone.

"Brand-new," I said. "You up for it? It isn't glamorous or exciting, and there aren't any demons or super magical powers involved—but you know how hard it is to get good health care these days. Especially for folks like the Larkins. People in this area can use the help you could give them. It's not brain surgery, but it's a *good* cause, Doc."

Strange looked from me, to his medical bag, and then up toward the Larkins' apartment. He let out a long and rather satisfied sigh, the kind of sound I make after I hear a favorite song that hasn't been on the radio in a while, and his eyes wrinkled at the corners. "Why not."

"Yeah," I said, folding my arms in satisfaction. "Why not."

Wong met me outside the gymnasium after school.

He wore simple gray shorts, a loose gray top, and a gray sweatband around his shaved head. He had worn, simple high-topped basketball shoes on his feet, and held under one arm a standard Wilson basketball so well used that barely any of the pebbling remained on it.

"You any good?" I asked him.

Wong gave me his Wong face and a little bow. "I saw the Globetrotters once when I was young."

"You shouldn't brag so much, Wong," I said.

When we walked in, it was the same as Friday. The team was all over the place, shooting and jawing and goofing off to no end, with Samuel driving himself hard, working out against several teammates.

I blew the whistle. No one even looked at me.

I blew the whistle again, louder. A couple of the kids drifted a few grudging steps toward me.

I sighed. Then I stripped out of my button-down shirt and my pants. I wore a tank top and shorts underneath. I walked over to Samuel and took the ball away.

Maybe I cheated and used my super-duper spider reflexes, just for the hand speed. But it was for the boy's good. I slapped the ball aside when he was in mid-dribble, and bounced it over to Wong.

That got his attention. The gym got quiet, fast.

Samuel turned to loom over me. "Ain't like I don't appreciate your help," he said. "That don't make you Coach Kyle. Give me the ball and get out of the way."

"I decided to take you up on your offer, kid," I said.

His mouth twisted into a white-toothed smile. "Shoot. Half court. We go to ten. You playing with one hand, so I'll spot you six. Then when you lose you can go sit down."

"No," I said. "We play two-on-two. No points spotted."

"What?" he asked.

"Two-on-two," I said, and jerked my head at Wong. "Me and him. You and whoever you like. And when you lose, I run practice the way I'm supposed to, and you go along."

"Don't need whoever I like. Take you both by myself. Don't need anyone else."

"Sure, if you say so," I said. "But I don't want you saying it wasn't fair when you lose."

"Whatever, man," Samuel said after a moment's hesitation. "A-Dog, you up for this?"

"Sure," said the second-tallest kid on the team.

I bounce-passed the ball to Samuel. "You want it first?"

He bounced it back. "Age before beauty, Mister Science."

I nodded to Wong, who came over and nodded pleasantly to the two boys. Everyone else went to the sidelines to watch. I went to the top of the key, passed the ball to Wong, and the game started.

Let me tell you something.

Wong got game.

He blew past A-Dog while he was still flat-footed, faked to one side on Samuel, then rolled around him for an easy basket.

Samuel frowned at Wong and narrowed his eyes.

After that, he got serious. He nearly blocked my next pass to Wong, and was all over him on defense. Wong had more quickness, but not much more, and Samuel's long arms and prodigious talent made up for it. Wong missed his next shot, and Samuel recovered it, took it out, and then drove back in for his own point.

Wong gave Samuel a smile and a little bow and then said, "School's in, Grasshopper."

Wong and I had talked it out earlier. Samuel pressed him again, but Wong passed off to me and I mimed a shot, forcing Samuel to turn to me. Instead,

I shot it back to Wong, who went through A-Dog and scored again.

The game went like that, with Samuel getting more and more frustrated, trying harder and harder, his efforts growing almost violent. Every time he pressed one of us, the other was there for an outlet. Neither A-Dog nor Samuel seemed to have a real solid grip on the idea of coordinated effort, and their defense was never quite quick enough to make up the difference. I took a few shots, and made one. Wong did the rest, and I was happy to set him up. I played the harder defense for us. Samuel was too much for Wong to handle, but he rarely passed, and the kid was nowhere near fast enough to get by me. I tried to keep my effort down to just footwork and hand speed, taking the ball from his control whenever he came by.

And somewhere between Wong's seventh basket and his ninth, Samuel got what was happening. He started looking for his partner, passing more, actually working with A-Dog, or at least trying to. It was too little, too late. Final score: Team Spidey 10, Samuel and A-Dog 6.

Samuel was angry about it for maybe a minute. Then he shook his head and snorted, regarding me thoughtfully. "You ain't never played before, huh."

"Not really," I said.

"Where'd you find Little China?"

"Little Tibet," Wong corrected with a small bow.

"Friend of mine," I said.

Samuel grunted. "Guess I lost the bet."

"Guess you did," I said.

He passed me the ball, jerked his head at A-Dog, and then started off, running laps around the gym. The rest of the team followed him. I watched them for a moment. My wrist ached a bit, but I didn't mind. Wong started whistling "Sweet Georgia Brown" again.

"Thanks, Curly," I said quietly.

"You are welcome," Wong replied.

I went back home, grabbed a shower, and took the wrapping off my wrist. My hand opened and closed without the same sharp pain I'd felt yesterday, though it was still tender. I didn't want to do any web-swinging or wall-crawling for another day or two, but it could have been a lot worse.

The injuries I'd received weren't life-threatening, but recovering from them always left me hungry. My stomach started growling loudly enough that I half-expected a neighbor to pound on the ceiling or a wall, and I stuffed my face on anything I could find in the kitchen that didn't take too much effort to prepare. Then I crashed on the living room couch.

I woke up when a square of light fabric landed on my chest. I opened my eyes to see Felicia, in jeans and a T-shirt, her hair held back in a ponytail, standing over me. She smelled like strawberry shampoo and a delicate floral perfume. The red and blue outfit she'd borrowed now lay on my chest, laundered and folded.

I gave her a smile. "Hey."

"Hey," she replied. "I brought your suit back."

"Thanks."

"Don't mention it. Red and blue aren't a good combination on me anyway."

I shook my head and met her eyes. "No, Felicia. *Thanks.* For coming here. For staying by me."

She frowned and shook her head. "I was stupid, Pete. I led the bad guys right to your home. To MJ."

"Not your fault," I told her. "You didn't think Oliver would stick a knife in your back."

"But I should have thought of it," she said.

"Maybe next time. Did you find out how he was tracking you?"

She rolled her eyes. "How *wasn't* he? GPS in the phone, the visor, the power unit on the suit—and tracking chips woven into the fabric of the suit itself. I had to ditch it."

"Back to the old outfit?"

"It's not old," she said. "It's classic. Or at the worst, retro."

I snorted out a little laugh. "As long as it isn't the one with the shoulder pads and the headband. How's our buddy Oliver?"

She gave me a smile filled with very white teeth. "He's out of the company already. He's probably out there trying to plot a way to keep his money without me ruining his life."

"Seems to me if he could subtract you from the equation, he could do that."

Felicia shrugged. "He wouldn't be the first to try it."

"Just so long as he's not the last."

She gave me a coy little look and shifted her hips. "I'm a big girl, Petey. I can take care of myself."

"Just be careful," I said.

"Maybe I'll get a bodyguard," she said. "If I could find one who would guard my body instead of ogling it."

"You and MJ worked things out, I guess?"

" 'Worked out' is a rather strong term. We called a cease-fire," she replied. "News flash, honey: It's a rare thing for wives and ex-girlfriends to get along. I don't think she's ever really gotten past that portrait I had taken for you." She smiled. "Watson's got guts, though. I'll give her that."

I remembered said portrait of Felicia, and hoped my blush didn't show. "And how," I said. "Thank you for helping me protect her."

Her expression grew serious for a moment. "I know you think the world of her. Maybe we aren't together anymore, but I care about you. A lot. So even if she tried to claw my eyes out every time I came in the room, I'd do the same thing next time. It'd kill you if something happened to her. I don't want that. And she loves you, too, Pete. She makes you happy."

"Yeah. She does." I smiled for a moment and reached up to take her hand for a moment, squeezing. She squeezed back, then leaned down and kissed me on the forehead. "Don't be a stranger," I said.

"Of course not," she replied. "And don't wait for it to get as bad as this before you call me for help, either. No one does it all alone."

"I'll remember," I said.

"Tell MJ I said good-bye?"

"Will do."

She winked at me on her way out. "Take care of yourself, Pete."

"Don't do anything I wouldn't do," I replied.

"You're no fun at all," she said, and closed the door behind her.

Mary Jane got in late—after eleven o'clock. But she came through the door smiling and humming to herself. I was dozing in front of the TV. My metabolism gets me back on my feet faster than the average bear, but mending broken bones really takes it out of me.

"Hey there," I mumbled, and smiled at her. She came to the couch and kissed me thoroughly and then just sort of draped herself over me. "Someone had a good day," I observed. "The car ran? The driver's test went okay?"

"The car," she said, smiling, "is fixed. You'd never know I crashed it into anything at all."

I blinked. "How . . ."

She wriggled pleasantly, and drew an old business card from her pocket. The front said, "Stephen Strange, MD." She flipped it over. The back read, in Strange's scrawling script, "Bippity-Boppity-Body Shop."

I laughed and hugged her. "And the test?"

"Somehow, it seemed a whole lot less dramatic on Monday than it had been on Saturday," she replied, her tone smug.

"There's a shocker," I said. "How was your first rehearsal?"

"Wonderful," she said, and kissed me again. "The lead was all surprised that I had a mind. He thought he was just getting to hang around with a bit of mobile scenery."

"So long as he looks with his eyes and not with his hands," I drawled. "You need me to beat anybody up, you let me know."

"I think I'll manage that on my own, should it become necessary. Which it won't, of course." She kissed me again, then drew back, eyes bright. "How was practice?"

"Wong got game," I said. "Apparently he saw the Globetrotters when he was a kid. I guess when he wasn't learning mystic kung fu and herbal remedies, he was teaching himself whatever he could about basketball."

"The plan worked?"

"And how," I said.

"Broken wrist and all?"

"Yep," I said. I grinned. "I cheated. Just a little. Not enough to look weird."

Mary Jane grinned back. "I thought you said cheating would defeat the purpose."

"One-on-one, sure," I said. "But the kid needed to learn that sometimes you run into something you can't handle on your own. So I made sure he couldn't." I put on a pious face. "It was for his own good."

She laughed again. "Did Felicia get out of town all right?"

"Yes," I said. "She said to tell you good-bye."

"Good."

"Good that she said that, or good that she's gone?"

"Yes," Mary Jane said in a cheerful tone. "You're never going to believe who came by the rehearsal."

The phone rang. I sighed and fumbled around for it. Mary Jane sort of wormed her way up my stomach so that she could reach the phone. Which was quite nice, really.

She picked up the phone and held it up to my ear for me.

"Hello?" I said.

Wong's voice came over the phone. "The Rhino asked to speak to you before he left. I took the liberty of contacting you so that he would not know the number I called."

"Right," I said. "Put him on."

"Spider-Man?" the Rhino asked, the strong Russian accent thick and rolling.

"Da?" I said.

He snorted. "You kept your word to me."

"Yes," I said. "It's been more than twenty-four hours."

"I know. Called to tell you am keeping to our deal in any case. Am on the way out of town in a moment. No trouble for you or anyone."

"Good," I said. "Don't suppose I could talk you into extending the deal."

The Rhino grunted. "You going to pay my debts? Give me job?"

"No."

"Then is no deal." His voice turned thoughtful. "Maybe one day, things are different. But for now, is no help for it."

"Too bad," I said. "Someone like you could do a lot of good. It wasn't bad working *with* you for once."

"Maybe. But things between us do not change," he said. "One day, I will beat you. My way. One day, I will show you."

"Well," I said. "We'll just see about that."

I swear, I could hear the big guy's smile. "Da. We will."

And we both hung up. Well, technically Mary Jane did. My hands were . . . elsewhere.

"You know," she said thoughtfully, "I think I've worked out what was bothering me about him. Our friend Aleksei is not stupid."

I frowned. "He's not Gump or anything, maybe, but I promise you he's not the crispiest chip in the bag."

"I'm not so sure," she said, voice intent. "You think that because you've always thought it, and so now you expect him to be a big dope. But stop and think for a minute. *Everyone* in your circle expects it, don't they?"

"Well. Yes. I mean, everyone knows that the Rhino isn't all that bright."

"What if he's bright enough to be hiding it from everyone?" Mary Jane asked. "When people expect you to be an idiot, assume you haven't got a brain in your head, letting them continue to think so can be very advantageous." She gave me a wry smile. "Believe me. When it comes to people's assuming abject stupidity based on expectation and appearance, I know what I'm talking about."

I blinked and thought about that one for a minute. "Then how come when he fights me, he keeps falling for the same routine, over and over?"

"Exactly," Mary Jane said. "Even a moron would have changed their tactics by now. I think it's become a matter of principle for him. He wants to beat you his way, and he won't be satisfied until he does." She mused. "You know, I'll bet you anything that he wasn't unconscious as long as you thought he was, when you brought him in here. If he was as stupid as everyone thinks, do you really think he would have been so calm and rational when he woke up blinded and bound?"

"Admittedly," I said, "I was sort of surprised that he let me talk to him. I knew the webbing would hold him long enough to let me throw him out a window if he got rowdy, but all the same, he did take it awfully calmly."

"Right. I think that was because he'd been listening and he already knew you had no intention of hurting him."

The Rhino with a brain. That notion was at least as disturbing as the occasions when the Hulk had managed to hold on to Banner's intellect. "I don't know . . ."

"I'm not saying he's going to be a *Jeopardy* champion or anything. But think about how many mad geniuses he works with. The Goblins, Doc Ock, Mysterio. I think he knows that they're a lot smarter than he is. So he hides the brains he does have, so that if it ever comes to a fight, he'll have a card up his sleeve."

I hated to admit it, but I knew MJ might have a point. "If that's true," I said, "then he might have heard my name. Or yours."

She nodded. "If he did?"

"If he did . . ." I shook my head. "He's just got first names. And I don't think he'd do anything with them, anyway."

"Why not?"

"Because you're right about one thing: He wants to beat me his way. Man to man."

Mary Jane smiled. "Then you've got nothing to worry about. You're more of a man than anyone I know, Mr. Parker. Russian Rhinos included."

"You sound awfully certain about that, Mrs. Parker," I murmured, and kissed her.

"I am," she said, gorgeous eyes half-lidded. "Let me show you why."

And she did.

About the Author

Author Jim Butcher picked up his first Marvel comic during the Mutant Massacre story line in *Uncanny X-Men,* went back and bought everything from the Secret Wars on, and spent the next four or five years buried in every original Marvel comic printed, with a particular focus on every issue of *Amazing Spider-Man* he could get his hands on. The vision and skill of Stan Lee and dozens of talented writers and artists fed a young man's imagination all too well, and when he grew up he wound up writing stories of his own, albeit wholly in print.

For him, when *Spider-Man* hit the big screen it was like seeing a geeky old high school friend made good, and when offered an opportunity to actually write Spidey, he jumped at the chance with the proportionate strength of a long-term fan. The author of the best-selling *Dresden Files* series and the critically-acclaimed *Codex Alera,* he lives in Independence, Missouri, with his wife, son, and a vicious guard dog.